# BOOKS BY

Cartier Cartel: Part 1
Return of the Cartier Cartel: Part 2
Cartier Cartel - South Beach Slaughter: Part 3
Bad Apple: The Baddest Chick Part 1
Coca Kola: The Baddest Chick Part 2
Checkmate: The Baddest Chick Part 3
Face Off: The Baddest Chick Part 4
South Beach Cartel
Guard the Throne
Dirty Money Honey
Killer Dolls Part 1
Killer Dolls Part 2
Killer Dolls Part 3

# SOUTH BEACH
# CARTEL

NISA
SANTIAGO

This is a work of fiction. All of the characters, organizations, and events portrayed in this novel are either products of the author's imagination or are used fictitiously.

www.melodramapublishing.com

Library of Congress Control Number:  2013946110
ISBN-13: 978-1620780268
ISBN-10: 1620780267
First Edition: February 2014
10 9 8 7 6 5 4 3 2 1

Interior Design: Candace K. Cottrell
Cover Design:  Marion Designs
Cover Models: Latecia, Vanessa, Kameron

# SOUTH BEACH
# CARTEL

**Buy**

♡

**for Melodrama**

# PROLOGUE

### FEBRUARY 1, 2014

It was a bitter-cold day in New York City. The sun was gradually fading behind the horizon, and the temperature had dropped to a menacing ten degrees. The wind nipped at Kola's face like sharp needles as she stood in the Trinity Church Cemetery and Mausoleum. Kola, wrapped in a long, blue iris mink coat, stood near the graves of three of the most thorough and realest women she had ever known. It was hard to believe that they were all dead, including her sister, Apple. Their lives had been snatched away from them—they died the way they lived: fast and violent. If Kola had known then what she knew now, she reasoned, things would have turned out differently. Your past is always a part of you, like a shadow. And just because you don't see it all the time doesn't mean it isn't there.

Kola stared at the shiny granite stone as she clutched the small toddler in her arms. The child was maybe the only good thing left in her life. The toddler was her niece. She was a beautiful little girl, more precious than a bag of uncut diamonds and equally sought after. She was also wrapped in a beautiful mink coat, costly diamonds in her small ears. Even though the little girl was too young to appreciate the quality of clothing and jewelry she had on, Kola had to have the only family in her life looking like wealth.

Her niece was about two years old. She didn't know the girl's actual birth date, but Kola thought fondly of future extravagant birthday parties and expensive gifts she'd shower on her niece. The child would be protected by top security teams and would attend the finest private schools. Kola wasn't settling for less.

The adorable girl clung to Kola tightly in the frigid cold, unaware that her mother was dead and put to rest not too long ago in the scenic plot just a few feet from her. It was a sad moment. Kola looked at the wall of tombs with her sister Apple's name etched into the granite. Even though they'd feuded some time ago, Kola deeply missed her sister. She was her twin; now there was yet another void in Kola's heart.

"Now what am I supposed to do?" Kola muttered sadly. "I told you not to come back. I told you to stay away."

Apple refused to listen to Kola's advice. She couldn't accept they had a good thing going on in Colombia.

Kola held the little girl closely and thought about avenging her sister's death. She was too young, and her death, along with those of the other two women, was so violent. Tears continued to fall from Kola's eyes, and her mind was spinning with, *What now? What next? How will the story continue?* Would she give this story—her niece's story—a better ending than she and Apple ever had? Kola asked herself, *When does it end?*

Kola looked over her shoulders and saw Eduardo sitting patiently in his chauffeur-driven Maybach. The curtains were open so Eduardo could keep an eye out for the woman he loved.

Parked behind the sleek, black Maybach were two Range Rovers and one Yukon Denali. They were Eduardo's security—heavily armed trained killers. They were riding deep, considering the circumstances. With power and wealth came jealousy and hate, and Eduardo wasn't taking any chances that a hit could be out on Kola as well.

The cemetery was still. The wind continued to blow hard, but the armed men standing around seemed resistant to the cold. They were clad in dark suits and long black coats. Kola remained still, grieving silently.

Apple's daughter had been recovered just forty-eight hours earlier. Apple had given her life for her daughter, and Kola knew the little girl had been through a lot. It was a giant task, but with Eduardo's resources and influence, they'd found her and brought her back to her family. The girl didn't speak one word of English. She spoke Spanish and was given the name Marisol. Kola knew better. She remembered her sister saying that her baby girl's name was Peaches. Now came the daunting task of communicating with Peaches and getting her used to her new surroundings.

Kola took one last look at the graves and inscriptions written across them: *Apple Evans, gone but not forgotten. Cartier Timmons, you will be missed. Cynthia "Citi" Byrne, a shining star forever.* She wondered how three women so street smart could have all been taken out in one night.

Kola stepped away from the burial site and walked toward the Maybach. Before she got close, the door was opened for her by one of the goons. She climbed inside and looked at Eduardo.

"You ready?" Eduardo asked.

Kola nodded.

"Back to Colombia. That is your home now, Kola. Forget about this place; forget about the trouble it brings. Your sister will be missed, but you will live on, and live on with this precious angel," Eduardo declared.

Kola didn't respond. She closed her eyes. In less than twenty-four hours, she would be back in Colombia. She knew Eduardo was right: There was nothing left for her in the States. This country, America, New York—took away everything.

She watched as the cemetery headstones of unfamiliar people whisked by her passenger window and hoped that this wouldn't be her fate any time soon. She wanted to reach her twenty-fifth birthday, but knew that the life she was living made it a long shot.

Kola knew it was time for a change.

# CHAPTER 1

*Apple*

### REWIND

The beauty of the Colombian countryside belied the dangers that lurked on its land. It seemed like paradise with overflowing greenery, rolling hills, and warm weather—one could easily let their guard down.

It was another beautiful day with clear blue skies and the smell of freshly cut grass in the air. But no matter the beauty and luxuries the country had to offer Apple, from the magnificent mansion she was staying in to the elite staff of dozens to serve her at any time of the day, she was still miserable. It didn't feel like home and would never feel like home. She missed Harlem. She missed the streets, the stench of that urban life—the bodegas and street niggas that cluttered the corners.

Apple stood butt-naked on the wide terrace that connected to her bedroom and overlooked the picturesque countryside. She gave the non-English-speaking male workers below tending to the lawn and hedges a peep show of her womanly curves and shaved pussy. She stood near the railing and sighed heavily. Eduardo's home was some baller shit. It had the obligatory luscious landscape, 15-car garage that housed some of the most expensive cars in the world, lavish indoor spa, 80-foot-long bowling alley, tennis courts, and two Olympic-sized pools. It was a place fit for a king—and Eduardo, in Colombia, was the king of all kings.

It had been six months since she'd arrived with Kola at his supposed haven. They had escaped prosecution in the States, and now Colombia was supposed to be a new start. But Apple was becoming restless. She didn't feel like the queen-bee bitch—she felt, once again, second-rate to Kola. Kola had it all. She had Eduardo, power, and respect. Apple spoke little Spanish and was given menial tasks, but nothing to get her hands really dirty.

Apple stared down at one particular worker who was trimming the hedges with shears. He was short with dark curly hair and physically built. He was clad in dirty overalls and would occasionally glance up at Apple and smile—fixated on her nakedness. She was making it hard for them to work. She was teasing them.

She lingered out on the terrace for a moment with the sun beaming against her tanned skin. The hot Colombian weather caused perspiration to drip from the workers' brows. South America was hot and muggy. It made her throat dry and her skin sticky. Apple stood above the men and then saw Kola and Eduardo strolling into the yard below. Apple suddenly frowned. Her sister seemed so content because she was Eduardo's main chick. Kola was flourishing. Her skin glowed and her eyes lit up whenever she was around Eduardo.

Eduardo spoke to one of the workers and the man nodded. When Eduardo spoke to you, you listened and did what you were told. He seemed cool and in control of everything on his sprawling estate. He was never in a rush, because he didn't have to rush for anyone. Men and women yearned to have his undivided attention, and they prayed having his attention didn't lead to their murder.

Apple stared at her sister with contempt.

"Look at this bitch, thinking she's Cinderella all of a sudden," Apple said to herself. "I feel like punching her in her fucking neck."

The couple walked around the expansive, vibrant garden like they were Adam and Eve. Apple continued to frown. Eduardo was walking hand-in-hand with Kola. The smile on Kola's face was sickening to Apple. It seemed her twin kept herself entertained day and night and couldn't care one bit about Apple's needs. No one spoke any English, and the ones who did—the men—they were part of Eduardo's camp, and they were always out doing something for their boss, either killing someone or making more money for Eduardo. Apple wasn't in charge of anything. She felt like some pet straggling around in the mansion, being ignored. She didn't need anyone to take care of her; she was able to take care of herself.

The one thing Apple was most disappointed about was not having her daughter. Six months had passed, and Eduardo had yet to fulfill his promises to find Peaches. With his powerful connections, Peaches should have been in her arms by now. Kola was his priority, and it was making Apple jealous.

Kola looked up and noticed Apple standing on the terrace butt-naked. Kola's smile dissipated. She looked up at her sister showing off her naked body to the workers and was mortified. The sisters locked eyes, but Apple wasn't intimidated. Eduardo soon noticed what caught Kola's attention, and when he saw Apple's nakedness above him, his expression was blank. It was hard to tell what he was thinking.

"Excuse me," Kola said, removing herself from Eduardo's side quickly.

Apple smirked, knowing Kola was coming her way. She hurried into the mansion.

"Here it comes," she uttered.

Apple turned around and faced the doorway. She walked into the bedroom and refused to cover up. She could feel her sister's presence looming; an argument was inevitable.

Kola didn't bother to knock; she came barging into Apple's room like a gust of wind and shouted, "You're a dumbass fuckin' skank bitch! How dare you embarrass me like this?"

"I do what the fuck I want!"

"Don't nobody wanna see ya stink-ass pussy! You need to put some damn clothes on!"

"Why? It's my room, right? I'm home, supposedly. I was told to be comfortable and whatnot…so this is comfortable for me," Apple snapped.

Kola cut her eyes at her twin sister and was ready to snatch hair out her head. She approached Apple with a scowl and exclaimed, "Why you gotta be so fuckin' insecure?"

"Insecure—"

"Yes. You need attention. Is that what it is? You jealous of me again?"

"Fuck you, Kola, you can't see me!" Apple barked.

"Fuck me? No fuck you, cuz if it wasn't for me, then you would have been dead or locked up. I saved you."

"You truly believe that?" Apple laughed in Kola's face. "I know how to handle myself."

"Yeah, you handled yourself really well when you were shot up and lying in the hospital. Or when you were a sex slave in Mexico, suckin' and fuckin' tricks. Yeah, you a gangster bitch, right…done turned Harlem upside down fighting with Chico," Kola said. "If you knew how to handle yourself, then Nichols would still be alive."

Apple was ready to tear her sister apart. Bringing up Nichols's death was always a sensitive subject for her. She glared at her sister with a heart filled with hate. The peaceful bond between them was gradually fading. Sibling rivalry was about to come into full swing again—and world war three was about to ensue.

"Like fuckin' always, you gotta bring up Nichols's murder," Apple shouted.

"We can't change the past, can we? But I'll be damned if I allow you to fuck up this future for me. We got it good here, Apple. And you, you're a childish, fuckin' little immature bitch!"

"Bitch! Fuck you, Kola. I don't like it here."

Kola shook her head in disgust. She continued to glare at Apple, her eyes saying, *You can't ever be happy.*

"What do you want, Apple? What do you want from me, huh? I forgave you. I brought you to safety and have you living in a fuckin' palace where you're waited on hand and foot. I tried lovin' you and letting bygones be bygones...but once again, you are a bitter, miserable bitch!"

The room became tense as the twins glared at each other, their words becoming nasty and harsh. Apple remained naked in front of Kola, defying her sister's wishes. Kola didn't run her, nor did Eduardo. She was her own woman.

"If it wasn't for certain circumstances last year, I would have—"

"You would have what?" Kola chimed.

"I brought it to your trifling ass in the streets," Apple retorted.

"You what?!"

"You heard me, Kola. I was the baddest bitch in Harlem. I was running shit. I was that bitch makin' shit happen. I never asked fo' your fuckin' help!"

"That's always the problem wit' you, Apple...it's always about yourself, right?"

"I'm the selfish one? Are you fuckin' serious? Where's Peaches, Kola? Where's my daughter? Huh? Eduardo supposedly has all this power and connections, but my daughter remains missing."

Kola sighed.

"You have nothing to say now, right?"

"You're a trip, Apple. I told you, things take time. We will find her."

"I don't have fuckin' time. Every hour, every day that goes by, Peaches could be hurting or closer to dying. You know what—just get the fuck out my room, Kola. I don't need you or ya fuckin' man. I'll find Peaches myself."

Apple turned her back toward her sister and walked back onto the terrace. It was a disrespectful statement to Kola. It was silently yelling out, *Kiss my phat, black ass.* Her succulent ass cheeks swayed back out onto the terrace into the gleaming sunlight. She was still butt-naked and didn't give a fuck what anyone thought about her.

Kola narrowed her eyes and had the urge to shove her sister over the railing. She wanted to break Apple against the concrete, but she kept her composure. Something had to be done with Apple. She was getting out of line.

Apple stared at the workers doing their jobs below. Internally she was still hurting from Kola's remark.

Once again, she started to cause some distraction with the men below. She could still feel Kola standing behind her. Without turning around to address her sister, Apple said, "Can you please leave my fuckin' room so I can continue getting my tan on?"

Kola scowled. "Fuckin' whore!"

"Just like my momma…"

Kola spun around on her heels and marched out of Apple's room. Apple continued to flirt with the dudes in the yard. Then suddenly Eduardo came into her view. He stood below her with his white linen shirt unbuttoned, revealing his sexy abs. The two locked eyes for a moment. Eduardo was a very handsome man—powerful. And power was sexy. However, he belonged to Kola. The way Eduardo was staring at Apple with his dark, onyx eyes spoke an unspoken feeling. Her eyes lingered on Eduardo for a moment and then she turned and walked back into her bedroom. She had stirred up enough controversy for one day.

# CHAPTER 2

*Citi*

Kanye West lyrics blared throughout the Miami nightclub, many partygoers spotting their favorite celebrities in the crowd. It was packed in the sexy nightclub B.E.D. on Washington Avenue. It was a trendy, sexy spot to lounge, dance, and enjoy dinner and cocktails with your friends on one of the seventeen king-size mattresses.

The ladies were clad in some of their sexist and skimpiest attire, and the fellows were popping bottles in VIP, wearing heavy jewels and carrying wads of cash. South Beach was the place to be when the sun went down. Ballers flaunted their riches all through the club, and the ladies were beautiful and flirtatious.

The dance floor was crowded as the DJ put on hit record after hit record. He played Rihanna, 2 Chainz, Kendrick Lamar, and Rick Ross. A few Miami Gotti Boys were in attendance. They had their own private VIP section near the crammed dance floor. The half-dozen gang members in the place were thugs that had made it to the big time. These were the shot-callers of the moment. They eyed the pretty women and were ready to invite a few to join them in VIP. One particular female whom the men watched intently was Citi. She was on the dance floor moving seductively in her expensive stilettos and body-hugging dress. She was alone. She seemed to be in her own world, moving in time to the DJ's catchy mixes.

When the DJ threw on Rihanna's "Pour it Up," that's when Citi stepped her dance game up and seemed to have the floor all to herself.

Bones, one of the most notorious gangsters to be bred from the Miami Gotti Boys, eyed Citi intensely. He loved what he saw. His attention was fixed on a pair of long, gleaming legs standing vertical in stilettos, and her curvy body wrapped in a tight dress. She was beautiful. She seemed classy and young. Bones tapped his right-hand man, Shotta, and asked, "Yo, who's ma on the dance floor?"

Shotta focused his attention on Citi. "Don't know."

"I need that in my life," Bones joked.

"I know you do," Shotta replied.

Both men were in relaxed jeans and white Air Force Ones, and were bejeweled in platinum and diamonds. They flaunted their money by popping bottles and partying in the VIP section.

Bones took a sip from the Moët bottle clutched in his hand and moved gingerly to the beat.

"You gonna holla, my nigga?" Shotta asked.

"Yeah, definitely…"


Citi continued to dance. She loved clubbing. Miami's vibe was so much different from New York's. Coming down to be with her mother, Ashanti, was the best decision in her life. The two had reconciled, and their strained relationship was gradually mending. With her older brother, Cane, in Miami with her, Citi had a small piece of happiness. The only one missing was her brother Chris. He was doing hard time up north, and some days her heart felt heavy when she thought about him and her father, Curtis. She would have many nostalgic moments. Even though Cane had avenged their father's death by killing Maino, she still didn't feel any closure.

With her mother being married to Marcus, who was known throughout Miami as the Black Mamba, Citi was treated like royalty. She felt comfortable in the vibrant and multihued city. She went on lavish shopping sprees, drove around in the best cars, and partied in the top-notch clubs on a regular basis. Miami was now her home, and she was determined to take advantage of everything that the city had to offer. Living under her stepfather's roof, she observed his actions. Citi watched everything like a hawk. She envied Ashanti for having such an iconic man in her life. Marcus ran everything from drugs and extortion to murder—it all fell under his empire, which had an estimated net worth of two hundred million. The Black Mamba had connections throughout the world, from war tyrants in Africa and drug cartels in Mexico to the shot-callers down on Wall Street.

Citi had so much admiration for him that when he entered a room, her breath would hitch, her heart would flutter, and she would linger on his every word. In her eyes, he was her father Curtis all over again—but a different version.

L watched Citi from the bar with a keen eye. He nursed his drink and became antisocial in the place. His caramel skin and slender frame had caught eyes from a few beautiful women in the club, but his only agenda for the night was to watch Citi and make sure she was okay. He didn't give a fuck about the other whores. He only loved Citi. He had followed her to Miami to be with her. He took up work under Marcus's organization and did the dirty work in the streets of Miami because she asked him to. He was a gun for hire, and with his Harlem swag down in Miami, the sun-drenched streets would soon become blood-drenched streets if anyone ever fucked with Citi or the organization she and he were now a part of.

L admired Citi from where he stood. He took a sip from his drink and remained straight-faced. Citi was a dancer; he just wanted to chill.

He noticed the attention she was getting, and understood it wasn't going to take long before some knucklehead stepped toward her with disrespect. Niggas were watching the woman L loved like hawks. They were thirsty to get with her and wanted her undivided attention. But the one group he was focused on was the Miami Gotti Boys. Jealousy started to stir up inside of L. Ever since he'd arrived in Miami, Citi had been acting like a whole different woman toward him—detached. He constantly showed her love and respect, but it seemed her attention was elsewhere. It bothered him deeply. In Harlem, he was moving weight, becoming the man up north, and he had to admit, it was because of Citi's help and connections that he got the weight needed to make moves. But now, he felt demoted.

L finished off his drink and made his way toward Citi. But at the same time, another man was headed her way.

Bones moved through the crowd with authority. Everyone knew his status and quickly moved out his way. He stepped toward Citi, and his black eyes met hers.

"You know you sexy as hell in that dress, ma. Let me have a talk wit' you in VIP." He gently took her by her wrist and pulled her closer.

Citi looked up at the man towering over her. She already knew his type, felt his swag, but instantly she wasn't interested. She resisted. "Nigga, do I know you?"

"You can get to know me," Bones replied. He wasn't taking no for an answer.

Citi rolled her eyes and sucked her teeth at the flashy goon. Compared to the men she'd dealt with in her past, Bones was too country-looking.

"Beat it," she replied, dismissively, annoyed that he was wasting her time.

Bones wasn't used to rejection. He didn't like it. He grabbed her wrist again, this time more aggressively. "Yo, shorty, you cute but you ain't that

21

cute. Bitches like you—"

Citi interjected. "Fuck off, nigga! You think I wanna fuck wit' a nigga like you? You know who the fuck I am, what I'm about?" She looked at Bones like he was yesterday's trash.

"Bitch, who the fuck you talkin' to like that!" Bones retorted.

"Get the fuck out my face! Who the fuck is you wit' ya little bling and wack crew!" Citi's words were cutting deep. She was embarrassing Bones in a public place, and that was a death sentence for anyone.

Before Bones could react, L stepped in and chimed, "Do we have a problem here?" He glared at Bones.

"Nigga, back the fuck up!" Bones shouted.

"She ain't the one to fuck wit', partner. I'm giving you fair warning," L said coolly.

"What? Nigga, you 'n' that bitch better respect a nigga."

L could only feel sorry for Bones. Unbeknownst to him, his mouth was biting off more than he could chew. He had no idea that she was the stepdaughter of Black Mamba.

"I'm tellin' you, son, step the fuck back before it gets ugly," L warned.

"So what you from New York, nigga? What's poppin', nigga? Huh?" Bones mocked. He picked up on L's accent and swag. He continued to taunt and clown L. "Yeah, son! We lay New York niggas down out here, son!"

Bones was a hothead and he felt slighted. Eyes were watching the confrontation, and the crowd around were on high alert. When the Miami Gotti Boys were in the house, anything could pop off, even gunfire. They were reckless hoods with no compassion for life or innocent bystanders. They were deep in the clubs .

The men continued to exchange harsh words, and then, suddenly, Bones took the first swing at L, and L went falling back into the crowd. The right side of his face was on fire. Bones continued to come at him, and a fight ensued. It didn't take long for the rest of Bones's crew to clear out of VIP and aid their comrade. There was no such thing as a fair fight when it came to the MGB. They were ready to fuck L up. He was alone—his only ally was Citi, and she wasn't any help. L got a few licks in. He wasn't going down without a fight. The two men tussled—L had Bones by his shirt collar, swinging, striking Bones repeatedly in the face until he felt a barrage of fists pounding against him. He was suddenly inundated with punches coming from every direction.

"Get the fuck off him! Get the fuck off him!" Citi shouted.

The revelers stood aghast at the fight happening. They didn't know what to expect; at any moment, they felt gunfire would erupt. But the fight didn't last long. Security rushed over and pulled everyone away from each other. L was still standing, but the damage had been done. He had a bloody lip and a bruised face. He was unarmed, and furious. His pride had been hurt. He had never been jumped before.

"L, c'mon, let's go," Citi screamed out. She pulled L by his arm, but he was resistant.

"Fuck that…niggas disrespect me up in here, fuck that! I'm gonna body these niggas," he shouted frantically.

"Let's just go," Citi shouted back.

L glared at her. He didn't want to be comforted or to leave without having his payback. He touched his bloody lip and bruised face. It angered him that they got the best of him on the dance floor. L rushed outside and hurried toward his ride, a black 750 BMW parked a block away. Citi hurried right behind him in her heels. L hit the alarm and quickly reached under the driver's seat. He removed a .9mm handgun and cocked it back. Citi saw the fire in his eyes. There was no calming him down. He had already made up his mind—somebody was going to die tonight.

Chaos continued inside club B.E.D., with security trying to maintain order. The Miami Gotti Boys were riled up and ready to start a war inside.

They started to fight with security and anyone else who wasn't affiliated with them. Bones was in the middle of it all. He went blow for blow with a bouncer near the bar. But the personal squabble didn't last too long before Bones's goons jumped in, smashing a bottle over the bouncer's head. They pounded him into the floor, leaving the man a bloody mess. Partygoers started to flee from the club. It was becoming a jungle inside with chairs and fists being thrown and glass smashing everywhere.

Bones and Shotta exited the club, hyped. They weren't too badly injured. Both men were satisfied with their reckless actions—being the goons that they were, they got the club shut down for the night and were able to knock niggas out. It was what they did best—act the fool. They wanted their gang's name and reputation to continually ring out. The men hurried toward the parked Escalade in the shadows, thinking that the five-0 were on their way.

"Fuck that club, yo...Miami Gotti Boys in the house, real talk. We run this shit out here! Who fuckin' wit' us...nobody! We get money out here 'n' we fuckin' niggas up," Bones shouted with energy. He was hyped and ready to continue with fucking somebody up.

Shotta laughed. "Say that shit again, my nigga!"

They found the night amusing. The men weren't armed, but once they entered the SUV, Bones was ready to grip his Glock 17 and Shotta was ready to grab the .45 stashed in the console. The men continued toward the truck, calling out to their goons who weren't too far behind. "Y'all niggas meet us at club Mansion."

The night was still young and there was still plenty of shit to get into.

Bones went to reach for the passenger side door handle, but before he could open the door, a shadowy figure caught his attention. He saw the threat creeping close. His eyes narrowed in on the darkness and he felt something wasn't right. Shotta caught on too.

"What you seein', Bones?" Shotta asked.

"Somethin' ain't right…"

Before both men had any time to react, L sprung out of nowhere and shouted, "Yeah, what now, niggas!" his eyes burned with hatred.

He opened fire like a maniac.

*Bam! Bam! Bam! Bam! Bam!*

The hot shells ate Bones's chest up, dropping him to the concrete. He was still alive. But the sixth shot exploded into his skull while he lay by the side of the truck.

Shotta reacted. He shouted, "Oh shit!" as he snatched open the driver's door trying to retrieve his pistol. But L was already on him. He fired a few hot shells into Shotta's back. Shotta collapsed on the floor between the seat and stirring wheel, feeling the searing rounds swimming inside of him. It felt like acid was in his bloodstream.

L didn't linger around. He took off running to his Beamer. Citi was behind the wheel of the car. She saw what L had done, which wasn't anything new to her. It had been her world since her father was murdered in Jamaica, Queens.

L jumped inside the car and Citi pulled off. Police sirens could be heard blaring in the distance. Citi slowed the car down, not wanting to get pulled over, and the two young hearts in the BMW were beating tremendously.

"Fuck them niggas!" L said. "I warned that muthafucka."

He concealed the gun underneath the passenger seat and sat back, allowing Citi to drive. He was aware that he'd just murdered two high-ranking and notorious gang members in Miami. But they had it coming. He would worry about the aftereffects later.

"Yo, if shit hit the fan, I'm on my way back to Harlem," said L.

"Don't worry 'bout it, L. I'ma talk to my stepfather and have him fix this shit. They were disrespectful, and you did what you had to do," Citi replied.

L nodded. "Yeah, do that for me, baby. I fuckin' love you."

Citi didn't reply. L always had her back, and he proved that he would murder for her. But did she really love him?

Citi arrived at the gated mansion on Indian Creek Island. It was Dade County's most prestigious private island. Citi drove the BMW toward a 21,746-square-foot estate with seven bedrooms and eleven baths on two acres of picturesque land. She parked in the circular driveway and got out. L did the same.

They stepped into the grand home that was designed with unsurpassed quality and craftsmanship. The house had a home theater, library, formal living and dining rooms, French country-inspired kitchen, an infinity pool with a cabana house, along with a seven-car garage and elevator.

The first thing on Citi's mind was Marcus. She wondered if he was home. "You can leave me and I'll speak with Marcus."

"You don't want me to go with you?" L asked, the gravity of the situation eating him up inside.

"Nah, I can handle it."

L leaned forward to give her a kiss, but she took a step back. Lately, Citi had put up boundaries, and right now L didn't want to challenge them.

Citi ran to Marcus's den to see if he was there working. He wasn't. Then she went upstairs to find him. She knew if Marcus found out about her being involved in a shootout and subsequent murder at a South Beach club via the streets, he was going to be furious.

Citi walked toward the master bedroom. It was late, a few hours before dawn. When she got closer to the master bedroom she heard sounds of passion. Citi stopped near the bedroom door and listened. She heard her mother cry out, "Ooooh, fuck me…"

Citi's heart was in her stomach. The door was ajar so she peeped inside. She was quiet while gazing into the dimmed room. She saw her mother, naked, positioned doggy style over the king-sized canopy bed. Marcus was behind her, gripping her curvy hips and pushing himself inside her womanhood. The muscles in his back, arms, and legs were being put to work. Citi watched his ass from the back pump against her mother. She couldn't explain why she hated what she was seeing, other than pure jealousy. However, Citi couldn't turn away. She continued to watch Marcus fuck her moms vigorously. Marcus's big dick had her completely filled. He pushed her face into the bed with her ass arched and her legs spread.

Ashanti cooed. "Baby, I love you! Fuck me! Fuck me!" she cried out.

Marcus squeezed Ashanti's round ass and uttered, "Ooooh, baby, your pussy is so good. It's so good."

"Damn baby, I'm gonna cum…"

Ashanti threw her ass back into him. She clutched the bed and continued to push his dick inside her while Citi watched. Ashanti let lose a wailing scream of ecstasy while Marcus came inside her.

The couple looked spent. Ashanti exhaled as Marcus pulled out his dripping dick. It was still hard. Marcus was impressive. His abs were cut up, his dark skin glistened, and he was in good shape.

"I needed that, baby," Marcus said, breathing rapidly.

"Me too."

Citi hesitated in their doorway a second too long, because before she could leave, she and Ashanti made eye contact.

# CHAPTER 3

## Apple

Apple couldn't stop thinking about Harlem. She was constantly feeling nostalgic. The feel and smell of New York were on her mind all the time. There was so much to miss. To linger in the project stairway on St. Nicks and smoke weed with niggas in the pissy building stairway was something Colombia couldn't offer her. She missed niggas speaking English and the swag of a black man. The sounds of sirens screaming by, or eating a sandwich from the corner bodega and seeing niggas roll dice on the block would have been a special treat right now.

The thing Apple missed the most about home was being in charge. She'd become addicted to the bloodshed and the gunplay. Apple was holding down blocks and corners; giving out orders to hardcore gangsters; snatching lives like it was taking candy from a baby.

It was time to get from under her sister's shadow and do her own thing again. She needed her own crew, and her own purpose. And no matter how nice the country of Colombia was and how lavish the mansion she was residing in was, it wasn't her own. The menial tasks she was doing for Eduardo were for the birds.

She also had only one friend in Colombia—Terri. He was now a lieutenant and worked for Eduardo. Things were different. He no longer took orders from Apple, and that annoyed her. She knew she should be happy for him, his new ranking position, but she wasn't that classy. She hated it. All of it. She despised the fact that he didn't even want to give her some dick and eat her pussy to help keep her sanity.

Apple stood by the French doors in the kitchen, brooding. It was late, and she was restless. She took a few pulls from the cigarette between her lips and exhaled. She was becoming like a restless three-year old. She was itching to get into something.

Apple noticed a black Escalade coming up the dirt road, leaving behind a trail of dust. It was Eduardo. She fixed her attention on the truck, watching it stop near the entryway to the home. All the doors swung open and men began exiting the vehicle. Eduardo along with Terri and two other henchmen were in her view from where she stood, unseen.

"*Eliminarlos de la carretilla ahora!*" Eduardo exclaimed in Spanish.

Apple understood some of what Eduardo had said. It was "Remove from truck."

Eduardo had a displeased look on his face as he puffed on his cigar and stood statuesque among his men. Terri and the others opened the back latch to the SUV and, with brute force, removed three unknown men. They were bound and had hoods covering their faces. They were treated roughly, beaten, and pushed toward the home. One squirmed, somewhat resistant, and that act caused him to receive a hard blow to the back of his head from the butt of an assault rifle. He stumbled and cried out. Apple already knew the fate of these three men.

"*Creen que esto es un puto juego conmigo!*" exclaimed Eduardo. He glared at all three of his captives and continued to smoke.

They disappeared around back to a separate entrance. Apple had a strong idea where they were being taken. She hurried from the kitchen, searching for Terri and the others.

Apple moved through the large home with a sense of nosiness. She needed to catch up to the men before they locked themselves away in the dungeon. She wanted to see something gruesome. If she allowed herself to go within the deep recesses of her psyche, she had to admit that she wasn't in the best frame of mind. She was becoming angrier and bitter. Her mental health was still shaky. She still had reoccurring nightmares, where she woke up drenched in sweat, panting heavily. The rapes and abuse she suffered in Mexico had long-lasting consequences. It changed her in so many ways.

Apple came to a stop at a door she had seen so many times while staying in the home. It was a jet-black, modern steel entry door located in the lower level of the home. It was isolated and odd looking. It was always locked and did not blend in with the rest of the decor. Apple instantly knew what went on behind there. She wasn't naïve to the world she'd stepped into. One of Eduardo's thugs stood by the door. He was clad in black army fatigues and holding an M-16. He scowled when Apple approached. But she wasn't intimidated by him.

The man only spoke Spanish, so conversation was limited. Apple approached him with caution.

"Hey, I need to see Terri or Eduardo…" she said.

He just shrugged.

She stepped closer to the guard. He strengthened his grip around the M-16 and glared at Apple. "I need to see Eduardo or Terri," she repeated, sternly.

"*Volver a la cama.*"

"I'm not fuckin' tired, fuckin' asshole!" Apple cursed. "Just let me speak to either man."

The goon kept his cool, but he wasn't budging. He had a job to do and he was going to do it without being harassed or bossed around by some girl—an American at that. He had a vast distaste for Americans, who thought they were better than anyone else. Since Apple was Eduardo's guest, he had to respect her.

Apple frowned at the man. She was ready to push and fight her way past him and go charging inside, but it would be a fight she would lose. He towered over her by at least a foot and outweighed her by over a hundred pounds.

"You're a fuckin' asshole, you know that, right?!" she shouted. "I fuckin' hate this fuckin' place! All y'all non-English-speaking muthafuckas get on my damn nerves."

The goon didn't respond.

"Fuck you! Fuck you!" Apple continued to shout.

"Fuckin' *perra*…" he replied.

"What the fuck you say to me?" Apple retorted.

Before the situation could get heated and out of control, the steel door opened up and Eduardo stepped out.

"Eduardo, *esta perra está loco*," his henchman said.

"I'm crazy…" Apple shouted. "I'll show you crazy, muthafucka!"

"*Amigo, relajate, voy a hablar con ella.*" Eduardo replied coolly.

The man nodded and stepped away from the door, giving Eduardo some privacy with Apple. He stared at Apple, ambivalent toward her rude behavior. He asked, "What is it that you want, Apple?"

"I'm fuckin' bored out my mind, Eduardo," she said.

"We have plenty of amenities and things in my home to keep you entertained."

"I don't care for none of that shit."

"Then what is it that you do care for?" he asked.

"I want to be a part of what you have goin' on behind that door."

Eduardo chuckled. "You what?"

"Don't bullshit me, Eduardo. I know somethin' is going down. I just want to see it up close and personal."

"First off, you watch your mouth around me and in my home," he warned harshly. "And second, you think because you have a murder or two under your belt that you are qualified to see the butchery that my men do?"

Eduardo had been busy with war for the past six months. His cartel was fighting with the Gonzalez cartel for control of the Mexican borders. Whoever controlled the borders going into Texas controlled tons of drugs being shipped into America every day—and that was millions, even billions of dollars in profits yearly. It was a deadly and gruesome battle where there were regular beheadings, torture, and men and women being slaughtered by the dozens. With the cartels, there was no value for life.

"Y'all don't scare me. I've been through more hell than you can imagine, Eduardo."

"Yes, I understand, with you being captive—abused—in Mexico, and being shot in Harlem. But this isn't Mexico or Harlem, Apple. This is my country, and I've seen horrors that you can't even imagine since I was six years old," Eduardo stated.

Apple had witnessed so much in her young life. Her sister, Nichols, being murdered and left in a Dumpster; warring with Kola herself for years; her mother, Denise, being tortured and murdered; Apple herself being raped and psychologically tormented. She'd had friends and lovers killed, and had bounties put on her head by men she'd thought loved her. What could possibly be going on in that basement that she hadn't seen already?

"Me too," Apple replied. "I feel we are the same."

"You think? I bring you and your sister to paradise and forgive you for the sins you've committed against me, and look at you, you still want to get your hands dirty. Why can't you be more like your sister?"

Apple was ready to scream out, *Fuck my sister*, but she kept her composure. "My sister and I share the same face, but we are two different women."

"Yes, I'm now starting to see that."

"And please don't ever compare me to Kola."

"Why not?" Eduardo asked calmly.

"Cuz she ain't me!"

"Same face, different hearts, I see."

"I'm many things, Eduardo, and right now, I'm curious. The three hooded men you just brought inside, what did they do to you?"

"It's none of your business."

"I wanna see."

He stared at Apple's face. The numerous plastic surgeries she'd had in the past did her justice. Apple's eyes remained cold and callous, though, which differentiated her from Kola. Eduardo admired her fire and her virility. She was definitely one of a kind.

He said to her, "A woman who was given a second chance at life with renewed looks and a new beginning would usually turn away from such horrors and carnage."

"Like I told you before, I'm a different type of bitch."

Eduardo knew she was a wildcat. Her mind was fucked up on so many levels that there was no coming back from that dark pit she'd fallen into.

Apple remained defiant. She was becoming more crazy than sane. The strutting around butt-naked on the balcony in front of his male workers and the need to see blood was disturbing.

"I'm going to grant you your wish," said Eduardo.

Apple smiled.

"But under one condition," he added. "You do what I ask of you when I ask."

It didn't make sense to Apple, but she was willing to do whatever. She nodded. Eduardo gazed at her for a moment. He studied her. He felt maybe she could be somewhat useful to him in more ways than one. But it was still too early to tell.

Apple followed behind Eduardo into the concealed room. The door was shut behind them and in front of them were narrow concrete stairs leading down into the dark. Eduardo proceeded forward. There was a chill and fetid smell in the air. The flight of stairs was short and led into a barren concrete room. It was conducive only to torture and/or murder.

Apple stepped onto the plastic covering on the concrete ground. She quickly fixed her eyes on the horrific scene. One man had already expired. His headless and beaten body lay on top of the plastic covering. One of Eduardo's goons stood over the body with a bloody machete. The other two men were on their knees. Their identity was still a mystery because their faces were still covered, but their fate was inevitable, like that of their friend.

There were plenty of ominous tools displayed, some still tainted with the last victim's blood. The men committing the torture and murder were heartless. The concrete room housed many of Eduardo's foes' final moments of life before their brutal ends. Apple looked over at Terri and he stood silent. He was the only black male face amongst the deadly Colombians. His long dreadlocks, towering height, strapping physique, and southern fashion definitely stood out. In the past several months he had gained trust and respect from Eduardo and his men. His Spanish was getting better. His reputation was spreading throughout the country, and he was becoming known as Black Kong. It was a somewhat bigoted name, but Terri loved it. The name meant power to him.

Apple stood silently in the room and allowed Eduardo to conduct his business. He went up to the two men still alive for the moment. He lit up the cigar clutched between his fingers and glared at them. The men were on their knees and helpless like mice caught in a cat's teeth. The terror they felt was manifested in the room. One had already peed on himself, and the second man couldn't stop whimpering and shaking. Eduardo picked his next victim and said to his men in Spanish, "This one. String him up and let's see if he'll talk."

The henchmen snatched the man up from his knees roughly and dragged him toward the back wall. They clamped iron bracelets around his wrists and strung him up by his arms. Then they removed the hood from around his head and stripped him naked. The victim was left exposed and vulnerable. He squirmed and whimpered in his restraints, locking eyes with Eduardo, and began pleading for his life. He shouted in Spanish, "Eduardo, please…! I haven't wronged you in any way. It wasn't me!"

Eduardo didn't respond to the man's cries. He stood next to his victim and looked at him for a moment. He remained stoic as he took a few more pulls from the cigar. While Eduardo was taunting his victim, Apple glanced down at his genitals and wasn't impressed. He was really small and bushy. Colombian men weren't the most well-endowed men. She was waiting to see what Eduardo had up his sleeve.

Eduardo spoke to the man calmly. "You stole from me, Jacob. Where is my million?"

"No, no…I didn't, Eduardo. I wouldn't dare take anything from you. I would never disrespect you. I fear you," the man exclaimed in Spanish.

"Just tell me where is my money and we can work something out, Jacob," Eduardo replied.

"I don't know where your money is. I never took anything from you, Eduardo. I swear! I swear!"

"You tell me now, and I promise I will only kill you and not touch your family. But if you play games with me, Jacob, then when I'm done with you, I'll go after your kids first. Little Maria, she's ten, correct? I will sell her off into prostitution. And then your sons, Marco and Juan—I will have them butchered and killed in front of their mother and personally place their still-beating hearts into your wife's hands. And then when I'm done with your sons, I'll save the best for last and do such unthinkable things to your beautiful wife that she's gonna wish she was dead. And I'll give her that wish, but I will make her suffer long and hard. You want that, Jacob? Do you want those horrible things to happen to your family?" Eduardo asked.

"No, no…please, don't touch them. I didn't do anything to you, Eduardo. I'm innocent! Leave my family alone! I swear I didn't take from you. If I knew where the money was, I would already have told you," the man shouted in Spanish.

Apple barely could make out what the man was saying. He was saying it fast and by his tone and cries, he was pleading for his life. She watched Eduardo. He didn't seem upset but remained casual. Then suddenly, Eduardo grabbed the man by his neck, yanked him forward and started to choke him. The calm in Eduardo abruptly disappeared and rage surfaced.

"Don't fuck with me, Jacob! I want the million dollars stolen from me!" he screamed.

"I…don't…know!" Jacob sputtered out.

"Fuck it; we'll get the truth from you one way or the other. And now that you pissed me the fuck off, when I'm done pulling you apart piece by piece, fingernail by fingernail, hair by hair, your family will suffer the same fate."

The man screamed out in agony. He could only imagine what these goons were going to do to his poor family. The tears started to pour heavily from his eyes. Eduardo had a sadistic way of torturing his victims. Eduardo grabbed a pair of iron tongs to pick up a scorching hot metal plate. He was going to blind Jacob by doing an abacination.

Eduardo pressed the hot metal against his eyes. The screaming and crying that followed was loud and piercing. It echoed from the room. No one cringed outwardly, but inside, Apple was a little queasy. Jacob's eyes were swollen and blistering. He could barely stand; he was slumped, but the restraints held him on his feet.

"Talk to me, Jacob," said Eduardo.

"I know nothing," he cried out.

"Phase two then," replied Eduardo. "You might not see now, but you will sure feel every bit of the pain."

Apple was impressed by Eduardo's innovative way of torturing. Her sick mind couldn't turn away. She looked over at Terri; he still remained distant to the fact that she was even in the room with him.

Eduardo continued to try and extract information from his victim. A few sharp cutting knives, razors, and other ominous-looking apparatus were displayed in front of him. He was done playing games. If they didn't talk, then these men would be made an example of. Eduardo picked up a long, sharp scalpel and placed it against Jacob's chest and sliced him open from top to bottom. Jacob's flesh split open like a banana being peeled back. Jacob's scream was bloodcurdling. Eduardo continued to cut away at his nipples, his fingers, and his ears, and then he snipped his genitals, causing Jacob to scream out in agony and tremble violently from the pain he underwent before he passed out. Apple wondered if Jacob had actually taken part in stealing the million dollars. Surely, he would have given it up by now so that he could go out quickly with a bullet in his dome.

Blood and body pieces were everywhere. Literally, Jacob was being torn apart bit by bit until there was nothing left of him to cut away. He turned toward Apple and asked, "Is this what you like to see?"

Apple smirked. "Are you gonna finish him off?"

Eduardo chuckled. "Soon."

Unexpectedly, Eduardo thrust the scalpel against Jacob's throat and began slowly cutting open his jugular. He could feel his victim dying in his grasp as the blood poured from his open wound like a fountain. The body lay slumped.

"Who's next?"

Eduardo's men lifted the last victim off his knees and removed the hood. Eduardo grabbed the man by his head and shouted near his ear in

Spanish, "Look at your friends, you see them? I did that! Where is my money?"

"Eduardo, I…"

Before the man could complete his sentence and beg for his life, Eduardo chimed back in Spanish, saying, "Do not tell me you don't fuckin' know! One of you knows where my fuckin' money is!"

"No…"

Eduardo wasn't going to waste his breath. Originally he had a special treat for the last man standing, but decided to shorten the moment. Eduardo nodded toward Terri who pulled out his .45 and put three bullets into the back of his head.

"Maurice," Eduardo called out, "dispose of the bodies to their families in the town. This is a strong message to everyone not to steal from me."

Maurice nodded.

Eduardo looked at Apple. "Come, take a walk with me. We talk."

Before she exited the room with Eduardo, Apple looked at Terri. They locked eyes for a moment. Apple had much admiration for her former lieutenant when they were in the States causing havoc, but she had no words to say to him at the moment. She followed behind Eduardo and they headed toward the outside.

They walked into the garden, where there was a full moon overhead. Exquisite flowers, fruits growing on trees, and shrubs were displayed everywhere. It was a quiet night. Eduardo had washed the blood from his hands and acted like everything was normal.

"I can see in your eyes that you aren't happy here," said Eduardo.

"I'm not. This isn't my home and it will never be my home," Apple bluntly replied.

"Straightforward, I like that. You seek change, power?"

"You know what I seek, Eduardo. I want my daughter in my life. It was something you promised to do for me a while ago."

"I have men on the job."

"But how long?"

"I promise that you will be reunited with your little girl."

Apple didn't want to hear any more promises. She wanted to see results. She wanted to go back to the States with her daughter and build up her empire again. Eduardo stood near Apple. He stared at her amiably.

"Do you find me attractive?" Eduardo asked.

"You belong to my sister," Apple replied.

"I belong to no one. Your sister, she belongs to me," Eduardo stated.

"And me?"

"You are more defiant in your eyes. I see…"

"You haven't experienced my kind of hell."

"And if I say I wanted to be with you, would you resist me?" Eduardo asked smoothly.

"Like I said before, you belong to my sister, and even though we ain't on the best of terms right now, she's still my sister. I can't disrespect her like that," Apple stated strongly.

Eduardo chuckled. "But you're ready to disrespect me in my country, and in my own home, huh?"

"I haven't disrespected you at all, Eduardo."

"Yes, you have. You entice my workers with your salacious behavior. You curse out my men, you dare barge into my business in the basement, and now by turning down my advances," he stated. He looked into Apple's eyes. He focused his attention on her. "You don't fear me, I see."

"I don't. I don't fear anyone," she answered honestly.

"Which makes you dangerous and a threat…everyone must fear me. I am a god in Colombia."

Apple didn't avert her eyes from him. "I'm not Colombian."

Eduardo chuckled lightly. "What must I do with you then? We will clash sooner rather than later."

"Let me leave. I can find my daughter on my own," Apple suggested.

"Leave huh? After you owe me a favor."

"Favor? What favor I owe you?"

"Oh, how we forget so soon. Remember I said to you earlier, you do what I ask of you when I ask," he reminded her.

"And what are you asking from me?"

Eduardo didn't answer right away. He continued to look at Apple.

"I can give you my blessings to leave my country, but there are stipulations," Eduardo said. "First, I wanna fuck you tonight, right here. I've desired you for too long now."

"And what about my sister?"

"She's mine for a lifetime, because she shows me gratitude and respect. But you are disrespectful and never showed any gratitude for all I have done for you. Therefore, once you leave here, you are never allowed back. You are cut off from your Kola forever. And if you ever try to contact her or come back into our lives, then I will kill you," Eduardo said sharply.

Apple swallowed hard. Was she ready to depart from Kola forever? Yeah, they once hated each other and were at odds, but she was still family, and the only family Apple had left. It was a hard decision to make. Eduardo cut his eyes into Apple. He was waiting for her immediate answer.

"So, what will it be?"

Apple released a heavy sigh. She quickly thought about it. She fixed her eyes on Eduardo and began unbuttoning her jeans, saying to him, "I hope you make it quick."

Eduardo smiled. He started to drop his pants and yearned to penetrate Apple. She stepped out of her jeans. He positioned her in the doggy-style stance, grasping his erection while Apple grabbed a small tree for support. She took a deep breath and felt the hard, aggressive thrust inside of her. He was well-endowed and started to fuck Apple like the whore he felt she was. Apple closed her eyes and took the big dick without wincing or yelping out in pain. It was nothing new to her. The way Eduardo fucked her suddenly reminded her of the hell she endured back in Mexico.

When he was done, Eduardo pulled up his jeans, and nonchalantly said to her, "I'll start making preparations for your journey back to the States."

# CHAPTER 4

## Cartier

Cartier stood by the floor-to-ceiling windows that overlooked picturesque South Beach, Miami. At twenty-five floors up in her penthouse suite, she was on top of the world. Clad in a beige silk robe with lace trim, her eyes were fixed on the deep, blue sea. The ocean was hypnotizing, and South Beach was so exquisite looking from her point of view.

Cartier sighed heavily, thinking about her deceased daughter. Cartier thought about Christian every single day. Several months had passed since the Gonzales cartel had butchered her family. Her blood still boiled from the lingering pain inside her soul. She hated every last one of those muthafuckas. They had taken everything from her, and now with Hector's help, she was ready to take everything from them. But that would take time and tedious planning. In the meantime, Cartier was ready to indulge herself with the finer things life had to offer. Hector provided her with money, cars, jewelry, homes and a place in his organization. She was grateful, sometimes. Most times she was unsatisfied and longing for the past.

Cartier slid back the door leading onto the terrace that wrapped around her bedroom and walked out. She embraced the heat. She clutched the railing and gazed over. It was a long drop. She remembered the time when she wanted to commit suicide, but those thoughts had since faded.

The plasma TV was on in the bedroom, but Cartier didn't pay it any mind until she heard the anchorwoman reporting, "Two notorious gangsters were gunned down last night at a popular Miami club."

Cartier turned to face the TV, feeling her heart skipping a few beats. That breaking news caught her attention. She walked back into the room, picked up the remote and turned the volume up on the television. She stared at the news report, praying it wasn't Hector. The news broadcast went on to say that two alleged Miami Gotti Boys, Kendrick "Bones" James and Lamar "Shotta" Jenkins, were gunned down near club B.E.D. in the early morning after a dispute inside the club. Pictures of the crime scene flashed across the screen, showing the shot-up SUV, along with two bodies being carried away in body bags. There were also images of uniformed officers and homicide detectives scouring the area. Both men were dead at the scene.

"Muthafuckas!" Cartier uttered.

It felt like a gift and a curse for Cartier. She remembered killing Bones's cousin while robbing one of his stash houses back when Li'l Mama and Quinn had her back. Because of that incident, the Ghost Ridas and the Miami Gotti Boys were at war with each other. Now the two main people were gunned down. Was it karma? How many people had they murdered in their short lifetime?

Bones and Shotta were connected, and the streets were about to be on fire. It was about to be World War Three in Miami. The Miami Gotti Boys were going to be looking for revenge. It was inevitable. It was the hood. It was the life they all had chosen.

Cartier went to get her cell phone. She removed it from her purse and quickly dialed Hector's number. She couldn't help but worry about him. The phone rang and rang, and then it went to voice mail. This troubled Cartier.

"Damn, H, pick up your fuckin' phone," she said.

She dialed again, but received the same results.

"Fuck it!" she cursed.

She turned off the TV and swung open her closet door, looking for something to put on. As she got dressed, she repeatedly dialed Hector, but he wasn't picking up. She decided to call the person who was always with Hector and had his back at all times. Cartier called Swagger M. He picked up.

"Yo."

"Swagger M, where's Hector? I need to talk to him," said Cartier.

"He's busy right now, Cartier. Call the man back later." He hung up. Cartier couldn't help but notice that Swagger M was always short with her when Hector wasn't around. It wasn't what he said, but how he said it. And his eyes were always staring contemptuously at her, like he caught her hand in the cookie jar. She couldn't put her finger on it—and had exasperated herself with speculation as to why he disliked her so much.

She called back.

"Yo, did you just fuckin' hang up on me?"

"What?" he replied, instantly bitching up.

"You heard what the fuck I said. Did you just hang up the muthafuckin' phone in my ear?"

"Nah, calm down." All the bass was now removed from his tone.

"You calm the fuck down!" Cartier barked, refusing to be disrespected. "Where the fuck is Hector?"

"He ain't here—damn, Cartier."

Cartier was fuming because she knew she was being blocked. "Bitch, tell Hector that I'm looking for him. You hear me?"

"You done?" Swagger M replied. He wanted to take his pistol and break all the teeth in her slick-ass, Brooklyn mouth.

"No, I'm not done. Did I ever tell you that you're a fuckin' faggot?

Huh, bitch? You run 'round every day up my man's ass, licking his balls. If Hector asked you to swallow his cum you would, wouldn't you!"

"Yo, Hector," Swagger M called out. "Ya girl is being real disrespectful on the phone and I ain't gonna keep listening to this fuckin' bullshit."

Cartier was in a real foul mood. She began screaming like a crazy woman in his ear until she heard Hector's voice.

"Yo, homes, what you say?" Hector asked Swagger M.

Cartier could hear some muffled sounds and then Swagger M began apologizing profusely to Hector for disrespecting Cartier.

Finally, Hector snatched the cell phone and said, "Cartier, baby, I'm busy, mama. Things are going down. I promise I'll tell you later."

"You okay, baby?"

"I'm okay...please...let me handle this business. I'll see you home later."

Cartier got dressed in a pair of skinny jeans and a low-cut tank. With a .380 concealed in her purse, she was ready to handle her business. Stepping into the elevator, she pushed for the garage floor. She stepped out of the elevator and into the dimmed parking garage with her car keys in her hand. Being the only one walking to her car, she kept her hand near the pistol in her purse. She had enemies everywhere. So many people wanted to see her dead, from members of Hector's crew to the Miami Gotti Boys, the cartels and old beef she had back in New York. Cartier knew she was a marked woman, and every move she made was done with caution.

She hit the alarm on her gleaming black Escalade sitting on 23-inch chrome rims and jumped inside. The dark tinted windows kept her a mystery behind the wheel, and the armored plating, bulletproof windows, and run flats gave Cartier security and extra comfort when she was on the road. She dropped her purse in the passenger seat and started the ignition. Her truck roared like a lion.

A K. Michelle CD was placed into the CD drive, and the Memphis-bred star's voice came to life via the ample speakers. Cartier navigated the SUV out of the parking garage and onto the streets of South Beach. Hector was heavy on her mind as she drove down Washington Avenue. Still, she had things to do.

She was on her way to a meeting with her attorney and business planner, Maxwell Stocks. Cartier had big plans for herself and Hector. She was ready to invest a small fortune into something solid. They needed to think about things on a larger scale. Back in Brooklyn, Cartier had invested in real estate with her cartel members. The market had since dipped as America went into crisis mode. Those properties weren't worth half of what they paid for them. The upside to this was that she, as the remaining member, didn't have to split any profit. The downside was that there wasn't any profit.

Now that the housing market was in the toilet, Cartier spoke with Hector and expressed that now was the time to strike. She wanted them to snatch up as much real estate as possible in all the underprivileged neighborhoods. Cartier wanted to buy real dumps, because if they thought long-term—and by long-term she meant thirty-plus years—they would make a killing.

Her dream was to also purchase land. She wanted acreage out of town, in southern states like Texas and Georgia. She knew that one thing was true: People could always make newer homes to compete with an older one, but you could never, ever make new land.

Cartier was ready. She wanted to own land, have dozens of properties—acres of real estate to build on. But that took money, resources, permits, and time. Cartier had to network with the right people in town. It was going to take gaining trust with Miami's elite—having brunches and lunches with the politicians, the judges, congressmen, senators, high-end attorneys, and business tycoons. Money respected money. And even though she had money, she wasn't respected in their world. She wasn't connected to the right individuals. Cartier was ready to live in their world and relinquish her ties to the streets. The streets had taken her daughter, mother, sisters, friends, and husband away.

She needed Hector to want the same thing.

Cartier pulled up in front of the sidewalk café on Washington Avenue. The area was bustling with pedestrians. She checked her hair and makeup in the sun visor and then stepped out of her SUV. She felt excited about her meeting with Maxwell. There was so much to talk about. She strutted toward the café, tucked away inside a neatly manicured public park, set alongside a glamorous waterfront walkway where massive cruise ships slowly passed by on their way out to sea. The outdoor tables faced the enormous boats moored at the Miami Beach Marina. In the afternoon, the restaurant's live band played by the swimming pool so guests could sip and dip. The scenery was picture perfect. Cartier spotted Maxwell seated at one of the outdoor tables underneath a red canvas umbrella. She walked over and greeted him with a gentle kiss to his cheek.

"Hey, Maxwell, sorry I'm late," said Cartier.

"It's okay. I already ordered, though," he replied with a warm smile.

Maxwell stood, allowing her to sit first. He was tall, and very handsome, with a thick goatee. He was a black Cuban.

Maxwell Stocks was a knowledgeable real-estate businessman with connections in Miami. He was a man willing to do whatever it took to get the job done for his clients.

"Are you ordering something?" he asked Cartier.

Cartier picked up the menu from the table, and said, "Yeah, I'll have a salad, some flatbreads, and a cappuccino."

Maxwell lifted his hand in the air to call over the waitress. The slim, blue-eyed waitress hurried over. She jotted down Cartier's order and was very affable. When the waitress moved herself away from the table,

Maxwell went into business mode. He hooked his sharp, brown eyes on Cartier and said to her, "There was a problem with attaining the building permits."

"What kind of problem?"

"The city denied your applications."

"Why…?"

"For right now, it could be for many reasons…maybe because of the new zoning laws in this city and error in the application, or someone had a bad day. But I'm on it, Cartier. I'll try contacting the county commissioner or the city councilman and put in a good word for you. And then I can probably contact the zoning board to see if you can get a waiver," Maxwell stated.

Cartier let out an irritated sigh. The city was always denying her something. How could she go legit if the city kept putting obstacles in her way? Unbeknownst to Hector, Cartier had purchased a sizable piece of land in North Miami a few weeks ago. It was about six acres of land and she was ready to turn it into a profit. Cartier had her plans to build some lavish condos, along with a strip mall. Cartier looked at her lawyer and asked, "And if that doesn't work, contacting the zoning board, or whoever…then what?"

"First, we can appeal the decision, but that's a lengthy process," replied Maxwell.

"How lengthy?"

"Anywhere from a few months to a year."

Cartier sucked her teeth in frustration. "I can't wait a year, Maxwell. Are they fuckin' crazy?! This is racist!"

He chuckled. "This isn't racist, Cartier. Things can move kind of peculiar in this city."

"Shit, who do we have to fuck, threaten, or bribe in this fuckin' town to get shit done? I thought you had influence in this city, Maxwell. It's the primary reason why I hired you. You're supposed to help me push this development through," Cartier said pointedly.

Maxwell perched up in his seat and fixed his look on Cartier. It was now time to get real with her. "Your permits being denied is not your only problem."

He removed the day's paper from his leather briefcase and placed it on the table for Cartier to see. The headline read: Gangland murder at popular nightclub, two dead. Underneath the headline was a picture of a bullet-riddled SUV.

Maxwell's steely glare caused Cartier to shift around in her seat a little bit.

"Is Hector responsible for this?" he asked.

She became somewhat dumbfounded by his question. She didn't know what to say.

"I don't know," she replied.

"You don't know, or you just refuse to tell me the truth?"

"I don't know," she retorted. "Are you gonna blame every gangland murder on my man? Because if so, this ain't gonna fuckin' work."

Maxwell softened his approach. "Listen Cartier, I'm gonna be frank with you. You wanna become a businesswoman in this city, then you're going to have to separate yourself from this kind of media nightmare. That means Hector, too. The people you're trying to get into bed with read and watch the news too, and if they see that you're connected to shit like this, then they'll back away from you in heartbeat and have you blacklisted in this city. That means no funding coming from anywhere, no friends in high places, scrutiny coming from every direction and so on. And if that happens, you won't be able to get a permit to throw a block party."

"So, what do we need to do?"

"You have to dress it up and slow it down. Talk to Hector and put it into his head that gangster shit ain't worth it. I'm here to help y'all, but when it comes to shit like this," Maxwell stated, pointing to the headline, "then it leaves a bad stain on us and a bad taste in everyone's mouths. You can't scare the white men that you're trying to do business with. These people, they don't want any problems."

"I understand," she meekly replied.

"Now with the building permits, I may have a guy who I can talk to. But he's gonna want a little something extra for his troubles."

"How much of a little something is this gonna cost me?"

"Twenty-five grand," Maxwell informed her. "Just to start."

"It takes money to make money, right?" she replied, sarcastically. "Okay."

"And another thing; just keep a low profile," Maxwell said. "People are watching in this city, Cartier. You're still unknown. And this problem with this rival gang, it needs to end, or it might come back to bite you. I can't afford to have my top clients locked up."

Cartier nodded.

The waitress finally came with their orders. She placed the platter in front of Cartier and Maxwell. "Will that be all?" she asked properly.

"Yes, that will be all," replied Maxwell.

She walked off, leaving the two to enjoy their meals. Before Maxwell and Cartier went digging into their entrées, there was sudden noise—*Bang!*

Cartier nearly dove underneath the table until she realized it was a nearby car backfiring. Maxwell looked at her with a raised eyebrow. She felt embarrassed. Her nerves were still on edge. She realized her transition from the streets wasn't going to be so easy.

Clad in a lace top and thong, Cartier lingered outside on the terrace with her eyes fixed on the twinkling lights of South Beach. She took a few sips of Sauvignon Blanc and exhaled. Her mind was everywhere. She thought about her meeting with her attorney and wondered if he was the right man for the job. All this talk about Hector, gangsters, murders, and permits was exhausting. Now she had to cough up twenty-five grand. Was this a shakedown? Was Maxwell trying to play her like she was an airhead? She wasn't sure if he was authentic but decided to chill and not to react until she had something tangible. Cartier was the first to admit that her rushing to judgment had cost one of her best friends her life.

Hector wasn't home yet, and it was getting late. His phone was now continuously going straight to voice mail. The worries inside her were steadily building. She was ready to jump into her truck and go looking for her man. But that would have been pointless; Hector could have been anywhere.

She continued to sip her wine until she heard the front door open. Cartier spun on her heels and rushed inside the penthouse. She could hear Hector's voice from the foyer. He wasn't alone. Cartier quickly donned a robe over her scantily clad body and hurried to greet her man. She was ready to spit fire at him.

"Ay, shit is tense out there, Hector. Since Bones 'n' Shotta got toe-tagged, the Miami Gotti Boys have been riding our peoples hard. Fuck that, ay, we ready to put like a hundred guns on the streets 'n' exterminate every last one of them spooks! I'm ready to put in some serious work on these muthafuckas!" Cartier heard someone say brashly.

"Fuck them niggas, ay? Them *putas* can burn in hell fo' all I care," another voice chimed.

"They already got one of us earlier," said another voice.

"Who got hit, Sanchez?" Hector asked him, aggressively.

"They came at Tony 'n' his family in the parking lot of Burger King.

Shot him down in front of his sixteen-year-old daughter. Tony lying up in the hospital fuckin' twisted."

Hector sighed. He looked at Sanchez despondently; the pain in his eyes was evident. Tony was good peoples and a good soldier. It was war. The bloodshed was heavy. Since Bones and Shotta had been murdered, the Miami Gotti Boys had stepped up their arsenal and were headhunting.

Hector stood stoic in his penthouse suite in his street clothes. He sported a Presidential Rolex and a diamond pinky ring. In his presence were Swagger M, Sanchez, and Miguel. It had been a busy day for them all. Soldiers were falling in his camp, and trying to handle war and business at the same time was stressful. The crown he wore was heavy, and Hector felt the crimp in his neck.

The men continued to discuss warfare and payback. Hector poured himself a drink and walked toward the window.

"Hector ay, you and me like old times, right? Drop these spooks down where they stand for all our homies they killed," Swagger M said.

Hector continued to stare out the window, ignoring Swagger M's remark. He soon saw Cartier's reflection in the window. He turned around. She stood there in the center of the room and caught everyone's attention. The men looked at her, some displeased that she was in the room with them while they were handling urgent business.

"Hector, can we talk?" Cartier said to him civilly.

Swagger M glared at Cartier like she was a rival gang member and exclaimed, "Ay, yo, you need to leave, Cartier, this is some grown-man shit we talkin' right now."

Cartier cut her eyes at Swagger M, but before she could even get a word out, Hector intervened. "Swagger M, don't ever fuckin' disrespect Cartier like that or I'll cut you down where you stand!" Hector shouted.

"I was just tryin' to—"

"I don't give a fuck what you were tryin' to say. Don't you ever fuckin' talk to her like that. I don't give a fuck how far we go back, I'll kill you myself. You understand me?"

"No disrespect to you, Hector. We cool," Swagger M apologized.

Hector glared at him. "In fact, from now on don't you even give her direct eye contact. When you speak to her say 'Yes, Cartier' and 'No, Cartier,' 'What else can I do for you Cartier?' 'Do you need anything, Cartier?' You fuckin' feel me?!"

Swagger M's jaw was tight. He was being clowned in front of his crew. He felt Hector was pussy-whipped by some hood rat.

"Yes, Hector."

Hector barked, "Not to me, muthafucka!"

Swagger M lowered his eyes. "Yes, Cartier. Do you need me to do anything for you?"

"Eat a big, fat, black dick."

Everyone except Swagger M burst out into laughter. Hector was grateful that Cartier lightened the mood with her brash humor. He could tell that she couldn't stand Swagger M and vice versa.

Hector then turned his attention to Cartier. She looked radiant in her short robe. He knew he needed to spend some alone time with her. It had been a stressful day. He had been ignoring her calls since this afternoon.

"Y'all muthafuckas leave. I need some time alone wit' my wifey," he said.

Everyone started to disperse. Hector called out, "Let me have one word wit' you, Sanchez."

Sanchez stopped at the doorway. Hector walked toward him, saying to Cartier before passing her, "This will only take a minute." She nodded.

Sanchez and Hector were alike. He resembled the singer Mark Anthony in so many ways. They both came up together in Miami, joining the gang when they were young, and became partners in crime. They also loved to dress in trendy suits and expensive clothing, and were about their business. Sanchez had gotten out of prison a few months earlier and jumped into the swing of things again like he'd never left. Hector loved him like a brother. He was smart and had a beautiful family that he adored. Sanchez was one of the few men Hector respected.

The men stepped out into the hallway. Hector looked at Sanchez and said, "You be careful out there, Sanchez. This isn't back in the day. Miami is a different place."

Sanchez nodded. "I know. But I'm always watching my back, Hector. Don't forget how we used to be…you, me and your brother. We ain't nobody to fuck with, and sometimes we gotta remind these fuckin' knuckleheads why."

Hector smiled. "*Te quiero, me hermano.*"

Sanchez smiled and the two men hugged each other. "*Te quiero también,*" Sanchez returned.

"We'll talk tomorrow and handle this business. Don't worry, Hector, I'm home now. Things gonna change," Sanchez said with conviction.

Hector went into the penthouse to have a talk with Cartier, who was still standing in the center of the room with her arms folded across her chest. She frowned.

"Bones and Shotta…was that you?" she asked.

"And if it was, so what?" Hector spat back.

Cartier sighed heavily. If she wanted to keep it one hundred, the heat upon Hector's crew came mostly from her actions. Cartier, Li'l Mama, and Quinn were out robbing and killing drug dealers in order to come up with the ransom money to get her daughter back, which had subsequently reignited a war.

Cartier unfolded her arms from around her chest. She stopped scowling at her man and said to him, "I went to have a talk with our attorney today."

"And how did that work out?"

"Not so good," she replied.

"How much money is that leech trying to suck from us now?" Hector asked with distaste. He walked toward the bar again and poured himself another drink.

"He's tryin' to help us invest in a few legitimate things, Hector."

"I'm already invested," he spat back.

"In what? Your prison fights, the streets, meth labs, gambling, a few legal businesses here and there? Or are you investing in this continuing bloodshed going on wit' the Miami Gotti Boys? I want us to invest in something major, baby, like real estate. And Maxwell is willing to help us out wit' that."

Hector took a sip from his glass and coolly looked at Cartier. He was truly in love with her. He didn't say a word to her at first. He just watched her. He listened to her rant about changing things in their lives. He heard her cry out about the Ghost Ridas bringing them down. She had a few proposals for change.

Hector stepped away from the bar and moved closer to her. Cartier continued her rant. "And why have you been ignoring my phone calls all day? What the fuck is wrong wit' you, Hector? I worry about you—"

Before she could finish her sentence, she was struck with an open-hand slap to the side of her face that toppled her to the floor. She was shocked. Hector stood over her still clutching his drink and exclaimed, "I fuckin' love you, baby, but don't you question where I've been when one of my homies is laid up in the hospital shot the fuck up, and I got muthafuckas looking to murder me."

Cartier was on her side holding her face. It stung. She was caught off guard. Just like that, Hector had changed up. "I got a lot of things goin' on right now and I don't need to hear your mouth ranting about my fuckin' business." He added, "Don't forget who the fuck I am, baby."

"I haven't forgotten," Cartier replied with contempt. "Baby!"

"As long as we have that understanding," he responded matter-of-factly.

Hector downed the rest of his drink and walked away. Cartier slowly picked herself up from the floor and took a deep breath. Hector went into the bedroom to be alone. She waited for a moment and then followed him into their lavishly decorated bedroom. He was already shirtless and seated at the edge of the bed. His pistol was on the nightstand. He was quiet; something was on his mind. He seemed troubled and didn't acknowledge her when she entered the bedroom.

"I'm sorry," he mumbled.

"Excuse me?"

"I'm sorry, Cartier. I shouldn't have hit you."

Instinctively her hand went to the side of her face. They made eye contact and his eyes seemed so heavy, sad. There was a new sadness to Hector that Cartier was only beginning to see. She wondered if it had anything to do with Quinn. Did he miss her? Neither one of them ever spoke her name. Hector pretended as if she were never born. No gravesite visits, no flowers sent to her plot, no stories reminiscing about her short life.

Cartier disrobed. She approached Hector and straddled him. "Let me help take away some of your stress," she whispered in his ear.

She pushed Hector onto his back and continued to dominate him. Her kisses were gentle and wet against his lips and in other pleasing areas. She unfastened his leather belt and unbuttoned his pants. As she teased him, she felt his growing erection between her legs. Her lips tasted like strawberries against his. Cartier could feel Hector's male instincts take over. He reached around and cupped her ass, intoxicated with her full lips and soft tongue. His hands roamed freely over her curves, tenderly caressing her small waist and sexy bottom.

They continued to kiss passionately, the fever rising higher. Hector hurried out of his pants and underwear, and Cartier did the same. Their naked bodies were pressed against each other. Cartier kissed him again and again, this time more animalistic than before. She stroked him softly, feeling his pre-cum leak onto her fingertips, and whispered in his ear, "I want you so bad, baby."

Cartier lowered her attention toward his chest, leaving a trail of wet, tender kisses down to his abs, and soon her full lips enveloped him.

"Oh shit, that feels so good, baby. Ooooh shit," Hector groaned. He cradled the back of her head and held her mouth against his genitals. The magic her lips created was spellbinding. Cartier's mouth was an erotic vacuum, coaxing Hector's cum out of his balls. He closed his eyes and fucked her mouth like it was her pussy. Her head bobbed up and down on her man, giving him pleasure. Hearing Hector moan made Cartier suck his dick harder and faster. She could taste the pre-cum in her mouth. Hector's hand became entangled in her long hair and he raised his hips off the bed, loving the blow job he was receiving.

Before he could explode into her mouth, Cartier rapidly straddled him. They both let out moans as she used the muscles of her pussy to squeeze and stroke Hector's erection inside of her. She now had control of him, her tight walls massaging his dick. He reached up and grabbed her tits. Her fingernails scraped against his chest as he pushed into her. He fucked; she fucked him back, until their bodies coiled jointly into one heated orgasm. She felt his hot semen spill inside of her, ending their passionate sex session.

Cartier laid her head against Hector's chest. She was spent. Hector remained quiet. He stared up at the ceiling feeling her soft skin. The two shared an intimate moment. But Cartier knew this was his most vulnerable moment, and while Hector lay next to her looking comatose, she said into his ear, "The world is ours, baby."

# CHAPTER 5

*Citi*

It was a beautiful and balmy afternoon in South Beach, Miami. The Palms Hotel & Spa was swamped with smiling, cheerful guests and tourists enjoying the luxuries and amenities the hotel had to offer.

It was a family affair at the resort. Children were playing and laughing by the pool, while parents and guests mingled and enjoying mixed drinks, casual conversation, and poolside massages among beautiful bikini-clad women.

No one noticed the two tatted gangsters walking in with menacing scowls at first, because everyone was absorbed in happiness. The gangsters quickly surveyed the area by the pool and spotted their target: a slim Mexican pretty boy seated in a pool chaise longue chair with his wife and kids. He was oblivious to the nearby threat. The murderous- looking men marched forward, Uzi pistols gripped in their hands . As they marched ahead, guests rapidly became alarmed. Knowing something bad was about to happen, folks started to flee the area, fearing the worst. Parents snatched up their kids and ran. The Mexican pretty boy the men came for was Sanchez, a lieutenant in Hector's camp, and this was going to be a revenge killing for Bones and Shotta.

Screams were heard. Sanchez suddenly became aware of the threat looming, but he was too late to react. As he sat next to his wife with his two kids in the pool, he stared at the men like a deer caught in blinding headlights.

"Please, not here…not in front of my family," he pleaded.

His wife's eyes popped open wide. She wanted to scream from sheer panic but didn't want to alarm the kids. She knew the life they were in and didn't want their children to be casualties of the drug war.

The two henchmen weren't going to show him any respect. Not when Bones and Shotta had been gunned down in such a savage way. They aimed at the couple and opened fire. Machine-gunfire exploded like firecrackers going off.

*Pop! Pop! Pop! Pop! Pop! Pop!*

Bullets viciously tore into Sanchez and his wife as they sat. Panic ensued. Screaming was heard and guests trampled over each other trying to get to safety from the chaos. The tranquil afternoon by the pool suddenly turned into a bloody nightmare.

Sanchez's kids remained in the pool, crying loudly. They helplessly watched as their parents were viciously gunned down in broad daylight. They were the only kids who remained in the pool. The men walked away leaving behind dozens of dumbfounded and terrified witnesses.

Citi watched her stepfather, Marcus, take strong pulls from his cigar and exhale the smoke as he stood in the great room of his home, conducting business with his associates. He was surrounded by eight of his best men. He had their full attention—as well as Citi's, from a small distance. She kept herself hidden from the men's view. She was nosy, remaining in the shadows and listening attentively to what Marcus had to say.

Marcus was the only one standing in the room, moving back and forth in the area while speaking with authority. His demeanor was momentous.

Clad in a black button-down shirt and stylish slacks, his voice boomed throughout the room.

Citi loved the way he had control, fear, and respect all at once. She wanted to feel that power between her thighs. She wanted to feel it vigorously thrust inside of her. She wanted to taste Marcus in so many ways. She yearned to be in her mother's position—to have that kind of man and that kind of power beside her.

Citi's gaze shifted toward L. He was also present in the meeting with her stepfather. He sat watching Marcus talk, showing apathy toward his actions of the other night. Citi had not yet revealed to Marcus that L was behind the killing of Bones and Shotta. Even though he did it for her, to protect her honor, to prove a point, there was this paralyzing fear inside of her. Her stepfather was an unpredictable man. She didn't know what his reaction would be. Citi wanted to be seen as a woman in Marcus's eyes, not some spoiled little brat partying in the clubs and starting trouble. It was the last thing she wanted him to think about her. So she'd had second thoughts about everything.

"I want y'all to find out anything about this shooting that went down at the club the other night. Y'all fuckin' hear me?" Marcus exclaimed. "And if this shit comes back to any of my peoples being behind this, then y'all better let me know, because that's gonna be hell for them."

L kept calm while hearing his boss throw out threatening statements. He slyly eyed all the gangsters present in the room. He was the odd one out, being from Harlem. Everyone else in the room was Miami-bred. L was also upset that Citi hadn't talked to her stepfather about the incident. She had promised L that she would smooth things out and tell Marcus why the shooting went down.

"I want this shit wrapped up quickly," Marcus demanded.

"Boss, them two assholes were livewires with a list of enemies. Why we worryin' 'bout them niggas or the Miami Gotti Boys? I mean, no disrespect, boss, but they got what was coming to them. So why not let the Ghost Ridas and Miami Gotti Boys shoot it out and we just take over what's left?" T.K. said, bluntly.

Marcus walked toward the youngster, who was in his mid-twenties, and placed his hand on the man's shoulder. T.K. was ambitious, riotous, irrepressible, and deadly all in one, but he was a loyal soldier in Marcus's organization. Marcus had love for him like a son.

"Because, T.K., this is my city, and a high-profile killing like that will only stir up the hornets' nest even more until eventually everybody ends up getting stung. And it's bad for business. I'm a businessman first, y'all understand that?"

The men nodded.

Marcus continued his lecture. "I own miles of real estate, dozens of nightclubs and cafés; I have investments in hotels and other profitable retail businesses. And guess what? If Miami becomes a city no one wants to move to or come to and they no longer feel safe in this city because of long-lasting gang violence…then I lose fuckin' money! And I hate losing fuckin' money! Therefore, I need to know who is responsible for this shit.

"Now don't get me wrong, murders and violence will always be around in our fuckin' city, it's inevitable, especially in our line of work. But when it comes to this, revenge killings around the white people at a fuckin' lavish resort in broad daylight with mothers and kids around, it's fuckin' asinine! And I want it to fuckin' slow down and be contained."

Everyone nodded.

His men listened attentively. Marcus directed his attention on L. The two locked eyes. L remained nonchalant. Since his arrival, Marcus had been impressed by the Harlem-farmed gangster. Like T.K., he was a good and loyal soldier. His reputation in Miami was growing. Marcus was also very much aware of the youngster's feelings toward Citi. He was in love with the young girl and wanted to marry her.

"L, you like it here in Miami?" Marcus asked amiably.

"I love it here," L replied, composedly.

Marcus shook his head and sized up the new recruit in his camp. He took another pull from the burning cigar and looked at him for a moment. The room was quiet—a little tense. L wanted to know where this conversation was going.

"You're a good soldier, L. I respect loyalty."

"I understand."

"L, you were out with Citi the night of the shooting, right?" Marcus asked.

L swallowed hard and replied, "Yeah, I was."

"From my understanding, you were also at club B.E.D. with her," Marcus added.

"Yeah," he replied nervously.

"Did you see anything go on that night with Bones and Shotta?"

L hated to lie to his boss, but now wasn't the time to die. He looked Marcus in his eyes as the boss stood over him still puffing on his cigar. "We left before it all happened."

"Okay. But I want your ears in these clubs. You find out what you need for me. You understand?" said Marcus.

"Yes, I understand," L replied, exhaling inside.

Everyone quickly stood up and departed from the room. Marcus was left alone to ponder a few things. He walked over to his bar and fixed himself a quick drink. He downed his scotch and poured himself another one. He was about to throw it back down his throat when he suddenly noticed Citi was in his presence. He sat the drink down on the granite countertop, locked eyes with his young stepdaughter, and brashly asked, "What do you want, Citi? You know I'm a very busy man."

Citi walked into the room wearing a woven nightshirt. Her breasts and buttery brown nipples were perky underneath the fabric. She didn't have on any panties. Her pussy was yearning for some hardcore penetration. She needed her sexual itch scratched by the right man. She stared at Marcus and felt butterflies swimming around in her stomach. She wanted his undivided attention like his men had had earlier.

"Where is my mother?" Citi asked.

"She's out somewhere. Why?" Marcus replied indifferently.

"I was just asking."

Citi approached him closer. Her eyes were fixed on him. The closer she was to him, the more her pussy came alive. Marcus remained behind the bar shuffling around a few bottles.

"Can you fix me a drink, too?" she asked with a teasing smile.

Marcus looked at her with his dark eyes and replied, "And how old are you again?"

"I'm old enough to do plenty of big-girl things."

"I'm sure you are."

"So, can I get that drink? Or do I have to continue to beg some more?" she dared to ask.

Marcus didn't respond right away. He looked at her, taking in her youthfulness. "One drink and then you leave," he said sternly.

"Okay. One drink." She smiled.

"What do you prefer?"

"How about a Screaming Orgasm? Or a Blow Job?"

Marcus remained straight-faced at her inappropriate remark. Citi decided to have some fun with the dangerous crime boss and see where it would lead to—hopefully to her having a real screaming orgasm.

"You know how to make one of those? Don't you, Marcus?" she added.

"What games are you trying to play with me, Citi?" asked Marcus sternly.

"No games, it's a drink I like to have," she said. "Look, I can show you how to make one if you like."

Citi positioned herself behind the bar with Marcus and started to pick up liquor bottles and other items like she was a regular bartender. Marcus allowed her to continue her game amused at her childish art of seduction.

"Now, with a Screaming Orgasm, you need one ounce of vodka, one-and-a-half ounces of some Baileys Irish Cream, and a half ounce of Kahlua coffee liqueur," she said.

Citi began mixing her drink while Marcus stood behind her and eyed her perky breasts, curvy backside, and well-toned legs as she stood behind the bar making the outrageously named drink.

When Citi was done mixing the "Screaming Orgasm," she turned to Marcus and said, "Here, try it and see if you like it. Which I know you will."

Marcus took the glass from Citi's hand and stared at the drink suspiciously. "You're not trying to poison me, right?" he half-joked.

Citi chuckled. "No…"

Marcus smiled lightly. He then downed the drink while Citi watched.

"You like it?" she asked.

He savored the taste in his mouth and nodded. "It's pretty good."

"See, you can never go wrong with a Screaming Orgasm. So how about the Blow Job next? You care to try that?"

The sexual innuendos were blatant and raw. Citi was trying to get a rise out of him. Her stepfather was hard to read. His nonchalant attitude puzzled Citi deeply, but she wasn't going to give up on seducing him.

Marcus gazed at his stepdaughter once again, taking in her beautiful features and childish antics. "You know, you look so much like your mother," he stated.

"You're just now noticing me?" she said with a lecherous grin. "I'd like to think I was hard to miss."

"Your mother is truly a beautiful woman," he stated. "I guess I've been preoccupied."

"I guess we resemble…only I'm so much younger and so much tighter in so many areas."

The crime boss smirked.

"You want that blow job now?" she dared ask.

It was the first Marcus ever found himself dumbfounded by a spicy remark. Citi neared her body to his and added, "And I'm not talking about a drink."

Citi focused her attention on Marcus. She wasn't playing any more games with him. She'd put it out there that she could be his however he wanted her. The desire to fuck him was building. Her pussy had not stopped throbbing with anticipation since she'd stepped into the room with him.

She turned her back to Marcus, looking forward to feeling his strong touch against her. Citi closed her eyes and said seductively, "Imagine the pleasures of having the daughter, too."

She waited. Her wait wasn't long. Marcus readied himself behind his stepdaughter and roughly pulled her into his arms, causing a smile to appear on Citi's face. She had him. He began kissing her. His kisses traveled down her neck, causing Citi to throw her head back and revel in the sensation. She cooed as his hands found her breasts and cupped and massaged them through the material of her shirt. He slowly undid the buttons that held her shirt closed and exposed her bare skin. His kisses continued to her neck as he began rubbing down her nipples. He stroked and gently pulled at them. Citi's body was on fire. Marcus peeled away the woven nightshirt from her skin and tossed it to the floor. He then slowly and methodically undid the buttons on his shirt and let his pants fall to the ground and stepped out of them.

Citi's hard nipples were like magnets to his mouth. They were sweet, hard, and dark, like Hershey's chocolate. He lapped up her sweet nectar with his tongue. The taste of her was driving Marcus insane. He leisurely slid his hand between her firm thighs and felt gold. Her slippery, sticky, sweet juices were intoxicating. Every part of her body was so enticing. He was ready to devour her delicious, wet, and inviting pussy.

Citi stared into his dark eyes. She was ready to take him in her mouth. She dropped to her knees. Settling down comfortably, she took his hardness and used her mouth, tongue and lips to sensually drive him up the wall with her intense blow job. Her full, sensual lips slid back and forth around his shaft. Her hands never stopped exploring his body. She caressed his dark frame and felt his pre-cum leaking onto her tongue.

"Ah shit," he groaned with his hands cradled behind her head.

Marcus watched this pretty young thang suck him off like a porn star. Her gentle strokes with her mouth, with the softness of her lips, highlighted great pleasures on his hard dick like he'd never seen before.

"Ooooh, suck that dick....oooh," he moaned.

Citi continued going to work on the dick being shoved down her throat. She was ready to show him tricks that her mother couldn't do. She was ready to expose her young body like it was the eighth wonder of the world. Citi continued to send this dangerous crime lord into bliss until he couldn't take the strong suction coming from her lips. He pulled his dick out her mouth and said sternly, "Get up!"

He turned her around, positioning the soft, round curve of her chocolate ass in the air like it was the perfect pillow to lay his head on, and he arranged himself between her legs and decided to have his big dick make a feast out of her punani. He placed his dick at her core and penetrated slowly. Citi gripped the counter tightly and moaned with delight when she felt the walls between her legs spreading. He grabbed her hips, and their bodies collided together with erotic purpose.

Citi's moans became louder and louder. She wanted to make him cum and cum hard. She wanted to make this sex session unforgettable to him. She reached around and pulled him closer as he drove in deeper, harder.

His mushroom head started to swell more inside her and his shaft was hardening, indicating he was about to cum inside her. He continued to drive deeper with his hand wrapped around her slim neck. "I'm coming!" he exclaimed.

"Fuck me! Fuck me!" she cried out.

Marcus continued to pound into her, causing Citi's knees to wobble, loosening her grip around the granite countertop. She was ready to surrender all of herself to him, feeling the ecstasy and pleasure at the same time. Their breath became one. It was such a good fuck.

Marcus pulled his dick out of the dripping pussy and hurried to get dressed. Citi didn't want to rush. She wanted to linger in the moment. She slowly picked her shirt from off the floor and threw it back on. As Marcus was buttoning his pants, he looked at Citi and said, "This is between you and me…don't you dare tell your mother about this shit."

"I won't," Citi assured him.

"As long as we have that understanding," he added.

"We do. But was it good to you?"

Marcus ignored her.

Citi collected herself and left the great room. Unbeknownst to her, she was being watched. And the person who witnessed the intense sexual rendezvous was angered and hurt.

# CHAPTER 6

*Apple*

Apple smiled when she observed the New York City skyline from a distance. She was moments away from landing at JFK International Airport in Queens. She couldn't wait to touch down and place both feet on American soil again.

"Ladies and gentlemen, we will be landing at JFK in approximately ten minutes," the flight captain announced via loudspeakers in the cabin.

Apple could feel the plane descending toward the runway. She was beaming on the inside. The flight was crowded and the majority of the plane only spoke Spanish. She was sick of hearing the language and couldn't wait to get around English-speaking folks again.

"Sick of this shit," she muttered under her breath.

Seated next to her was a slim male. He spoke English, but kept quiet and to himself during the duration of the flight, which Apple was grateful for. She wasn't in the mood to socialize with anyone. Her mind was only set on two things: getting back into business and finding her daughter. She had to make serious moves. So much had changed.

Apple's first-class flight was a pleasurable one. She dined on lobster and drank champagne while flying three thousand miles in the air. She wasn't going to miss Colombia at all, but Kola was another feeling. Even though they had an strained relationship, knowing she probably would never see her twin sister again was heartbreaking. Before her departure from Colombia, Apple had to go back to her sister with less bravado and ask for her blessing to go back to the States. She told Kola that she needed to find her daughter on her own. It was hurtful to be absent from someone she'd given birth to. Kola was understanding and somewhat forgiving. She had changed drastically in the past months. She had an upgraded life away from the United States.

Her one disappointment, though, was Terri. When she asked him to come with her back to the States, he had denied her. Terri was comfortable in Colombia. Although he loved and respected Apple a great deal, his position in Eduardo's organization was too profitable. Back in the States he was a wanted man by the feds with countless indictments lingering over his head, from felony murder and extortion to criminal conspiracy.

"I can't go back there, Apple, and you shouldn't either," Terri had warned her.

"I need to go back, Terri. Unlike you, I'm not happy here. I need to find my daughter and I have unfinished business to take care of back home," Apple had replied.

"Unfinished business wit' who?" he'd asked. "Mostly everyone's dead or locked up—doing football numbers. I have a bad feeling about this, Apple. Too much trouble back that way. You can build something here."

"What, I should become one of Eduardo's concubines? Share things wit' my sister? You know that ain't never been me. I want my own and I'm gonna get it," she proclaimed.

"You're chasing something empty, Apple."

"Well, let me fuckin' chase it then."

Terri knew there was no talking Apple out of leaving. She was determined to go back to America where the feds had warrants out for their arrests, and where there was a shit list of enemies who wanted them dead. Terri felt it was suicidal. But Apple was one crazy bitch, and rational thinking didn't agree with her. The two hugged each other, knowing it was going to be the last time they probably saw one another.

Apple's last goodbye to her sister was an awkward one. It was a love and hate feeling. Both girls knew it was probably for the best to separate from one another. They rarely got along, and there were bitter memories for them both. But Kola's last blessing to her sister was having Eduardo wire $100,000 into an account for her, along with a new identity and a new passport. It was a new life—a new start.

The long flight finally touched down at JFK. Apple exhaled. She was finally home. The plane taxied toward the terminal, and the minute it touched the terminal gate, U.S. customs officers were everywhere, ready to screen passengers and check luggage for any drugs or other illegal contraband being smuggled into the country via drug mules or hidden compartments in luggage. Apple instantly started to feel very uneasy. It was inevitable that she would have to go through customs, and she hoped she didn't get profiled for a random search and interrogation. The name on the passport was "Lisa Johnson." Eduardo had paid top dollar for the best specialist to forge an American passport. Everything seemed legitimate. It was risky, but Apple was ready to take the risk to get back into her country.

Passengers started to exit the plane in an orderly fashion. Apple gathered her things and followed behind everyone else. People were pouring into the terminal like a human flood, mixing in with other arriving passengers in one of America's busiest airports. Going through customs was going to be a long, tedious headache, even if Apple was an American citizen. Her biggest worry was being flagged in the computer as a dangerous fugitive and quickly being detained.

She took a deep breath and acted normal. The last thing she wanted to do was bring any suspicion on herself. The line to get through customs was long, like teenagers waiting for tickets at a Justin Bieber concert. She was hoping that reentering the country would be a speedy process, as quick as a Jiffy Lube oil change. But one mistake and she was going straight to jail without passing "Go."

Clutching her carry-on, Apple stood behind a chunky Latina woman with two small kids and tons of items to claim before the customs agent. Apple made sure she was correct before stepping into the primary screening area. As she moved closer toward the customs agent, she started to put her game face on. Two hundred and fifty federal workers were everywhere in the airport; they interviewed passengers, inspected their luggage, confiscated goods, and eventually opened the door to the good ol' USA.

It was a woman at the front checking passports and making passengers open up their luggage, then methodically sifting through their belongings. Two agents clutching German shepherds by their leashes were posted by the exit. It must be a scary thing to be a drug mule. Security was tight and technology made smuggling anything into the country more difficult.

*Okay, keep it together, Apple. Just smile, show your passport, and stay calm. You're only a few yards from your old life,* she said to herself. The closer she got to the female customs agent, the faster her heart started to beat. It was now or never. The woman was doing her job quickly and efficiently. Apple was next. The Latina woman with the two small kids started to fumble with everything in her hands, from passports to her luggage. She was slowing everything up. Apple started to become frustrated. *Why did I have to get behind this slow bitch?* she thought.

It took a moment for the woman to get everything in order. One of her kids started to cry and whine, and it seemed like the woman was bringing everything she owned into the country. The agent carefully went through her things and checked all of her documents. Five minutes later, she was declared okay to enter the United States.

"About time," Apple muttered under her breath.

The agent waved her over, "Next."

This was it. Would her past finally catch up to her? Was she on their computers as a dangerous felon? She had been gone for six months. It wasn't a long time, but it was long enough, in her eyes. She locked eyes with the custom agent, a thin black woman with a steely glare and dyed, raven-colored hair.

"Hey," Apple greeted with a smile.

The woman wasn't too friendly back. She was stoic and quickly said, "Your passport please."

Apple handed the woman her passport. She opened it, scanned it, and looked at it for a moment. She started to type into her computer. "And what was your reason for your trip to Colombia, Ms. Johnson?"

"Pleasure," she replied affably.

"Anything to claim?" the agent asked.

"No. All I have is my carry-on. Don't trust the airports too much—they lost my luggage twice," she stated.

The agent indicated for Apple to place her carry-on on the table and step back. She did so. Her bag was opened and the woman began sorting through her personal things. It was a scrupulous search. Apple could only be patient. She was just minutes away from entering home.

"Okay, Ms. Johnson, you're good to enter. Welcome home."

Apple picked up her carry-on and smiled. She was ready to do cartwheels, but maintained her composure. She couldn't wait to step foot on American soil again. She wanted to scream and shout. *Thank you, Eduardo!* His peoples had come through with everything. Apple walked by the agents with the dogs and hurriedly exited the terminal. Once she was outside, she exhaled so strongly that she felt like a balloon deflating.

"Home," she said to herself.

JFK was bustling with traffic and exiting passengers outside the terminal. Taxicabs and cars were everywhere. The noise was deafening. The people seemed too busy to care about anything but themselves.

There was no place like New York. She was back in the city without a plan, a crew, a foundation, a mother, a sister, or a daughter. She was alone with only money, and the drive of a mother looking for her daughter.

Apple lingered outside the airport terminal for a moment, taking everything in. It was going to be difficult to readjust. She watched people jump into the yellow cabs and head off to their destinations. Clad in tight-fitting jeans, a pair of white Nikes, and a Ralph Lauren polo, she wanted to stay low-key for the moment. Her last time in New York, the body count had gone up significantly.

She waited on line for a cab and hopped into the backseat.

"Where to?" the Dominican driver asked.

"Harlem," she said.

"It'll be fifty-two dollars flat fee."

Apple handed him a hundred-dollar bill and said, "Keep the change."

"Hey, thanks."

He started to navigate his cab toward the airport exit. Apple remained relaxed in the backseat and stared out the window like she was a tourist. There was so much to do, but how to do it? When the cab merged onto the Van Wyck Expressway, the driver looked at Apple through his rearview mirror and asked, "First time in New York?"

Apple sharply replied, "I'm not paying you for conversation, am I?"

"No, you're not," he replied.

"Then leave me the fuck alone!"

"I'm sorry. I was just making small talk."

"Don't."

The cabbie shrugged and turned his attention back on the road. The traffic toward Manhattan was a parking lot. Break lights seemed to go on for miles. Apple sighed out of frustration. It felt like it was going to take forever to get to her final destination. The cab slowly crept behind car after car. The driver remained silent, but he frequently kept eyeing his fare via the rearview mirror.

It took almost an hour for them to arrive in Harlem. By then, the sun was fading and the temperature was dropping. When they crossed the Triboro Bridge, Apple trained her eyes on the streets of Harlem. Six months was too long a time to be away from her place of birth.

"Where exactly are we going to in Harlem, ma'am?" asked the driver as he made his way down 125th Street.

Apple wasn't sure. She couldn't go back to her old projects. She didn't have any more reliable friends to turn to. Apple had burned down all of her bridges. And with her mother dead and Kola in Colombia, she was the last one left in the concrete jungle.

"Just drive around for a moment," she told him.

To shut him up, she passed him another fifty. "Okay, fine with me."

For the next half hour, the cabbie chauffeured her through Harlem while she vigilantly took in everything—the thugs and hustlers lingering on the corners; the bodegas on the blocks; the residents moving about, minding their business; the kids playing; the loud music blaring from cars; NYPD, making their presence known; and the smell of urban life moving through her nostrils. It was the same. Apple wondered who the man or men in charge of the streets and drugs were now. She knew that her returning was going to be looked at as a threat to rival dealers.

Needing someplace to lay her head for a few nights and come up with a game plan, she told the driver to take her to a hotel on the West Side. He took her to Aloft Harlem Hotel on Eighth Avenue/Frederick Douglass Boulevard. Apple stepped out with her head low and her bag over her shoulder and entered the posh hotel. She didn't want to be seen or recognized by anyone in the area. This was only going to be temporary until she found someplace else that was safe and low-key. She quickly checked into a room on the tenth floor, which featured a comfortable queen-size bed, a walk-in shower, extra-large windows, and a nine-foot ceiling along with a few amenities.

It was late in the evening and Apple had settled into her room. She had showered and changed into something comfortable. In her overnight bag she had packed a honey-blonde wig. She wasn't sure she'd wear it—felt slightly uncomfortable at the thought. Everything about Apple was one hundred percent real. No fake boobs, hair, or ass injections. However, she needed to be unrecognizable. It looked natural, and she resembled her mother in so many ways. Apple eyed her new look for a long moment.

"The new me," she uttered.

She stood by the window gazing down at the streets of Harlem. With her eyes fixed on the Magic Johnson Theater across the street, she remembered a time when her life was so simple. She had to be extremely careful. Her haters and enemies would easily turn her in to receive the reward money the feds were offering for her capture. Apple was sure there were many who wanted to see her fall.

Apple took a deep breath and removed herself away from the window. She had done enough thinking. It was not time to take action. The bitch was back in Harlem, and her first priority was to do some research to find her missing daughter, and her next was to hook up with a new man. She needed to connect with someone who had muscle and power—someone with a killing squad at their fingertips. Apple figured whoever Chico and Shaun had given her baby to wasn't going to give her up so easily.

Tonight she would rest; tomorrow the hunt would begin.

First thing the next morning, Apple went to a used-car dealership. She needed to buy something affordable and reliable. She knew that she could blow through her money in a few weeks hopping in and out of New York taxis.

Apple bought a Chevy—ordinary, nondescript—and headed to the Manhattan Library to begin her research. She was positive that no one would recognize her with her wig. She was able to blend into the scenery wearing a pair of wire-rim glasses and a hat. The library wasn't crowded. She went over to a kiosk of computers and typed in "illegal baby-selling rings." The information that came up was overwhelming. There were pages and pages of information about it. There was a syndicate out there profiting greatly from selling stolen children to adults who wanted a family.

Apple began to read about several scenarios when it came to baby selling and baby buying.

Apple found out that children one year old or under were sold to wealthy families in the States. If the child looked African-American, they were sold mostly in the southern regions: Alabama, Georgia, Tennessee, and New Orleans. White babies—that market was worldwide, and the child would be harder to locate. Hispanic and Latin babies were usually sold in Florida and New Mexico.

Reading about Florida made her think about Kola and Cartier. She had some reservations about heading down to Florida. Her woman's intuition told her that was the place to start her search. She knew Miami could be a beast—a very dangerous place. Kola went down there and almost lost her life, and her friend Cartier's whole family had been murdered—they chewed her up and spit her life back out in shambles. The thing Apple needed to do was get her weight back up in New York. She needed to get herself a strong crew and then have them travel down to Florida with her. It was the only way to do it. She couldn't go down to Miami looking weak.

Apple sat at the library for hours doing her research. When she walked outside, she couldn't help but shed a few tears. The way she'd gotten pregnant, through rape, and then having Peaches snatched away from her—it was an aching pain deep within her soul. It was a vulnerable moment for her. Being a mother with a missing child made her feel sick. She needed to get her mind away from the situation.

Apple lingered outside the library for a moment and smoked a cigarette. With a hundred thousand dollars to work with, she needed to get back into the drug game. It was her only way to build.

Her stay at the Aloft was short. She quickly found a studio apartment in Midtown. It was away from Harlem, but at the same time close to Harlem. Next, she needed to link back up with someone she could trust from her past.

Apple's next priority was a gun. She needed to protect herself. Living in the shadows, she purchased a few pistols from a reliable gun runner in the back streets of Harlem. She dropped a thousand dollars cash on a .9mm, a Ruger and twin .45s. Now that she was armed, she felt some power.

The west side was bustling with activity on the corners. Sitting parked in an old green Chevy on 145th Street, Apple watched the young hustlers linger on the block in front of the bodega, gambling, hustling, or just hugging the block. Her .9mm was in the passenger seat. It was fully loaded and cocked back. She wasn't taking any chances.

The warm summer day brought all of Harlem out in full force. Apple didn't recognize any of the faces on the block. It was a new team of youngsters outside slinging drugs or becoming a nuisance to their community, with their sagging jeans, fitted Yankees caps, and urban attire, along with their red beads or blue bandanas indicating their gang affiliation. The block wasn't the same.

She roamed the Harlem streets for a few hours, lurking around from block to block, searching for something familiar from her past. She went back to her old projects on 135th Street and then traveled to her old stomping grounds on the West Side. Keeping a low profile—wig, huge goggle glasses and floppy Tory Burch hat, she moved stealthily. Apple was careful that no one recognized her as she went into the stores, gambling spots, beauty shops, and project buildings. She tried keeping her ears to the streets. She was looking for information and a friend.

It was on the streets where she spotted him, posted up on a burgundy 650i Gran Coupe with chrome rims and tinted windows. He was talking on his cell phone, looking like he was conducting business. Apple watched him like a hawk. It appeared he had come up from the last time she saw him—one of Kola's ex-soldiers. His name was Row, and she'd known him most of her life. He was alone. She watched him for a moment. Row was in his late twenties, a quiet killer—but a fuckin' monster on the block. He would be the perfect goon to connect with.

Row finished his conversation and his slim, six-foot-one frame jumped into his beamer. Apple knew she couldn't lose him. She hurried toward her Chevy and followed. She jumped behind the steering wheel and when Row pulled away from the curb, she was two cars behind him. Row came to a stop in front of a barbershop and stepped out. Apple parked too and continued to watch his activity. It seemed Row was making a pickup. He was in the barbershop for no less than ten minutes when he came back out. He got back into his ride and drove away.

Apple followed behind Kola's former soldier for an hour. She was subtle. With the sun and traffic fading, Row finally came to his last stop at a brownstone on 121st Street on the west side near Morningside. She assumed this was his residence. Row got out of his ride, observed his surroundings, and then trekked up the stairway into the building.

It was getting late, and Apple was becoming impatient. She stepped out of her vehicle and walked toward his 650i. It was gleaming and sitting pretty on dubs. Scouring the block, Apple searched for a hard object. She found a lead pipe in one of the trash cans. Apple didn't give it a second thought when she tossed it through the driver's side window instantly setting of the alarm. The noise echoed through the night and lights rapidly flicked on at the brownstone she was watching. She hid in the shadows and waited. The front door flew opened and Row came rushing out his place in a pair of jeans and shirtless. He gripped a metal baseball bat.

"What the fuck!" he hollered when he noticed his window smashed in. He ran over to inspect the damage.

"Yo, who fucked wit' my ride? Somebody gonna pay fo' my shit!" Before he could make another move, Row felt the cold and unpleasant tip of a .45 being pressed to the back of his head. He froze, knowing his life was about to come to an end.

"Shit!" He frowned.

"You always this sloppy, Row?" asked Apple.

He instantly knew the voice behind him. He still felt his life was in danger. Row cringed, feeling helpless.

"I never disrespected you at all, Apple. I always had love for you."

"I know you did. That's why your brains aren't leaking on the sidewalk right now," she replied.

"Then what's this about? Why you got a gun to the back of my head?"

"I just needed to get your attention."

"Well, you definitely have it."

"I know I do."

Apple made him drop the baseball bat and then she lowered the pistol. Row was able to breathe again. Apple's reputation made him uneasy. She was deadly and unpredictable—a far cry from the meek twin she used to be back in the day. Things done changed. Row turned to face her and was taken aback by her new look. The light hair color and cut seemed to age her in his eyes. Or perhaps it was all she'd been through.

"Damn, Apple, did you have to go at my ride?"

"It's only a window. You'll get over it. C'mon, let's talk inside. Too much attention out here," she said.

Row led the way into the brownstone. Apple still had the gun in her hand, not taking any chances. She didn't care if he used to be a loyal soldier or not. People can change, and just because he'd been loyal to Kola, didn't mean he'd be loyal to Apple. The drug game wasn't built on nepotism.

When they entered the apartment, Row asked, "Where you been? People started to think that you were dead."

"I've been away."

"Yeah, I see that. New look, huh…"

"You like?" she replied facetiously, not really caring about his opinion.

"You were always pretty," Row returned. "What made you come back?"

"I came back to handle some things."

She had Row's undivided attention. His home décor was simple—the common bachelor's pad. Sixty-inch flat-screen TV, Xbox with games littered about, leather furniture, and framed pictures of notorious gangsters from Scarface to Al Capone displayed on his walls. Remnants of smoked blunts, cigarettes, and other drugs were lying around, along with snacks and empty liquor bottles scattered everywhere.

Apple refused to take a seat. She wasn't staying long. This wasn't a social meeting. She looked at Row and said, "I see you made a serious come-up. You no longer a gun for hire, Row?"

"I still bust my gun, if a nigga wanna be stupid and fuck wit' me. But I had to come up. Kola disappeared on a nigga and it was gettin' hard out here. You and Kola created hell out here for the real niggas still left, Apple. And then there were rumors and speculations in the streets right after y'all disappeared. Niggas sayin' you got murdered by the Colombians or that you and your sister's bodies were at the bottom of the Hudson River. I mean, you did stir up some shit in Harlem. You and Kola were wildin'," Row said.

"Well, we ain't dead," she replied, smirking at the thought.

"You tryin' to get back into the game?"

Apple nodded. "I need to get a crew up again."

"A crew?" Row was befuddled. "Man, most of your crew is either dead, missing, or locked the fuck up. I'm the last one left since your reign out here. And these new niggas, these teenagers and young niggas out here, you can't trust like that. Shit, once word get around that you're back in town, ain't no telling what shitstorm that's gonna bring. You left a lot of unhappy and pissed-off people behind, Apple, and they ain't forget."

"And you think I give a fuck!" she spat.

"I know you don't. You was always crazy."

"Who's the new players in the game right now, Row?" she asked.

"Shit, the game's in shambles right now. The niggas that try to take over are either too stupid, too immature, or they get murked before they can get it on and poppin'. Me, I try to keep a low profile, move a few ounces of raw here and there, take a trip O.T. once in a while and keep my clientele real tight."

"And I see you doing a'ight." Apple observed. "Then we need to expand your provincial operation."

"We?" replied Row with a raised eyebrow.

"I'm back home now, Row. Maybe it's temporary…but now is the time to rebuild and make it stronger."

"You hot, Apple…wit' the feds, and enemies out here…"

"Have I ever been a stupid bitch, Row?"

"Nah."

"Then don't worry 'bout all that and trust me on this. I have a plan, and if things work out, then I won't be in town for too long. I have other priorities elsewhere that I need to attend to," she assured him.

Row looked worried. Women were emotional, and Apple and Kola were no different. A lot of the beef they incurred could have been avoided. However, they knew how to get money, and linking up with a get-money bitch was better than holding down a broke nigga any day.

# CHAPTER 7

*Cartier*

The City cemetery in Miami—the oldest cemetery in the area, a few blocks north of downtown—was flooded with dozens of Ghost Ridas giving their respect and love to a true and notorious O.G., Sanchez. The goons were crowded around the flower-covered casket and flashing their colors and gang signs. It was a tear-jerking moment for everyone. Sanchez was going to be truly missed. He had been home from prison for just a few months, and he was already a victim to the ongoing war between the rival gangs.

There wasn't a dry eye around. Everyone was shocked at how the hit went down, with his wife killed beside him, in front of his young kids. The look in each man's eyes was strained. The monsters that snatched away their Miami O.G. were going to be hunted down and brutally taken care of.

Cartier stood next to Hector in her black dress and sad eyes, images of her daughter and family disturbing her. Death was everywhere. She lowered her head and closed her eyes, and was haunted by images of Hector and herself lying in the caskets. The murders were too close to home, and the bloodshed was catching media attention. Cartier knew that when the time was right she needed to have another talk with her man.

Hector remained quiet, not speaking much since his friend was murdered. He was distant from everyone. He stood there like a zombie. Clad in a sharp, black Armani suit with his pistol close, he couldn't believe his friend was dead. As a precaution, he was surrounded by his goons. They stood around him and Cartier like the secret service protecting the United States President and the First Lady. The Ghost Ridas had already lost one high-ranking member; they weren't trying to lose another.

"*Montamos! Montamos!*" a few Ridas shouted out, meaning, "We ride! We ride!"

The young hoods in the gang were looking at Hector for direction. They were itching to do something. They knew he was ready to avenge Sanchez's death. He had to; it was their way, and they were like brothers. It was the third homie gunned down by the Miami Gotti Boys in two weeks. Hector seemed out of it, in a senseless daze—lost in emotion. Cartier saw he wasn't looking right. She tried to talk to him, but he wasn't responding to her.

"Ashes to ashes, and dust to dust, we lay a good man to rest. A good man is down, but we still multiply. We fuckin' love you, Sanchez," one of the older gang members proclaimed, pouring liquor onto the burial site.

"We gonna ride on these muthafuckas, fo' real!" another hood shouted.

The hot sun blazing above and the blue painted across the sky were a contrast to the gloomy feeling in the cemetery that had spread everywhere. Cartier lifted her head and wiped away the few tears that fell from her eyes. Sanchez had been one of few members in the gang that showed her love and respect. She'd really liked him. He was cool and his swag was off the radar. Surrounded by so many Ghost Ridas, young and old—it was an uncomfortable place to be in. The majority didn't have any love for her. They blamed Cartier for why Hector was slipping in the game. The word circulating in the streets was that Hector wasn't himself anymore. He wasn't on point. His crew was being slaughtered while he was living lavishly in a South Beach penthouse with his new bitch and playing away games with other businesses. And with Quinn missing in action, it added more fuel to the fire—with speculations that Hector had had his own flesh-and-blood killed over Cartier.

"You okay, baby?" Cartier asked.

He ignored her. His cold, black eyes were fixed on the casket. She went to reach for his hand to give him some coziness, but he pulled away from her suddenly. Hector was in no mood to feel any comfort.

Cartier looked around and saw the glares aimed at her. Their hatred for an outsider being with their leader Hector was clear. The one Ghost Rida with the continuous scowl at her was Swagger M. He stood opposite of Cartier on the other side of the casket looking like he was sucking on a dirty lemon. Cartier refused to be intimidated by him. She shot back her own lethal look and mouthed to him, "Bitch-ass nigga."

Swagger M frowned harder. He was ready to tear that bitch apart and then hit the streets and go on a killing spree—shoot down every Miami Gotti Boy he came across. His blood boiled with rage.

"Ay, that bitch got a problem wit' her fuckin' eyes at me, I'll cut them the fuck out...and look at Hector, ay, what the fuck he lookin' lost like that for?" Swagger M said in a low tone to his comrade next to him. "He let Sanchez die, cuz he's slippin'. He ain't leading like he used to."

"Let it go, Swagger M," his friend replied.

"Nah, fuck that! We need to do somethin'," he growled faintly.

"Not here, Swagger M. Not at Sanchez's funeral."

Swagger M took his homie's advice and decided to shut up. But he was ready to stir up some shit and put into his people's ears that there needed to be a changing of the guard. He was ready to step up in the leadership position himself. He felt it was his time.

Sanchez's funeral was huge, but there was also unwanted company watching things from a distance with high-powered camera lenses, snapping pictures of everything and everyone present. Their main target was Hector and his lieutenants. For weeks Miami had been plagued with brutal, public murders. The mayor waged war on the gangs and criminals tearing his city apart. Miami was dripping in blood. Surveillance was on Hector around the clock. They had him under investigation and were ready to bring down a major crime figure. Cut off the head and the body will fall.

As Cartier, Hector, and almost a hundred Ghost Ridas watched Sanchez's casket being lowered into the ground, they started to chant, "Ride or die, *que*, the Ghost Ridas! Ride or die, *que*, the Ghost Ridas!! Ride or die, *que*, the Ghost Ridas!!"

The chant echoed throughout the cemetery. It was pride and love being shown. Every last gang member started to throw up their flags, colors, and signs for pride and honor—some stacking with their fingers. The tears started to fall from a few hardcore faces while watching the body of Sanchez was being put into the ground. Frustration and anger could be felt with so many of them.

"We love you, Sanchez…" a few of them shouted.

"*Te queremos!*"

The preacher began saying a few words, and when he was done speaking, roses and other sentimental items were tossed into the ground with the casket. Some even poured more liquor into the grave and tossed a few bullets, too. It indicated that his death wasn't going to be in vain; they were going to avenge him.

Hector continued to be detached from everyone during the burial ceremony. He had a lost a brother. When dirt started to be thrown onto the casket, the members started to disperse and go their own way. Cartier and Hector walked toward the Yukon that was parked nearby.

As they trekked across the cemetery, Alexandro walked up to them and said in Spanish to Hector, "*Tenemos que hablar.*" It meant, "We need to talk."

"I'll meet you in the truck in one minute, baby," Hector said to Cartier.

She nodded and proceeded toward the truck alone. For some reason, she had a very uncomfortable feeling with Alexandro and her man talking. He was a high-ranking affiliate in the gang with a harrowing demeanor and haughty look about him. He was a dangerous man to be around—a murderous and mindless thug. Alexandro was an ambitious *amigo* and feared in Miami.

Cartier walked toward the truck and noticed the black van parked outside the cemetery. She instantly knew it was the feds watching. Nervousness swept through her body, because when you had the feds on you, they were like stink on shit.

She jumped into the backseat of the gleaming Yukon and sighed heavily. From where she was seated, she watched Hector and Alexandro engrossed in conversation. *What did Alexandro have to speak to Hector about?* she wondered. From the first time she met that muthafucka, she knew he was nothing but trouble. There was something about him that she didn't like at all. She waited for a moment, and her eyes shifted back to the dark van.

"Muthafuckas!" she muttered.

As she waited, she started to think about Christian, but immediately pushed the thoughts away. She'd been through too many emotions in one day. Cartier needed to remain focused. Her woman's intuition was screaming at her—trouble was brewing somewhere. She didn't trust too many people. With so much going on around her, it was becoming hard to breathe.

Hector ended his conversation with Alexandro and walked toward the SUV. Cartier watched him. When he climbed inside the backseat, Cartier couldn't hold her tongue any longer. She didn't care what his reaction would be. She had to ask and then let her feelings about him become known.

"What did Alexandro want?" she asked.

"It's just business," he replied, being short with her.

"I don't trust him at all, Hector. You shouldn't either."

Hector looked at her. "What's your problem, baby? You think I need to hear your fuckin' mouth right now? I just buried a good friend of mine today—just shut the fuck up before you get me upset!" he barked.

Cartier exploded right back at him. "Look across the fuckin' street, stupid!" she pointed toward the van. "It's the feds watching us."

Hector stared at the dark van. He knew she was right. She was always on point.

He sat back in his seat. Things were becoming really heavy around him. He understood that so many people wanted to knock him down from his throne. Once again, the crown was getting heavy on his head. He had nothing to say, but he couldn't look worried.

"We gotta change up, baby," said Cartier. "We gotta do things different. And I have a few ideas to help us out."

Hector continued to sit back in his seat. The driver got behind the wheel and before he pulled away, Cartier was saying to him, "You can trust me, baby. I got your back because I love you so much. But if we don't modify our way of doing business, then all this will come to an end for us. I don't want you to go out like Sanchez."

"I don't either," he replied softly.

Cartier neared her body to his and was ready to wrap herself in his arms. She kissed his lips softly and said to him, "Let your queen put these muthafuckas in checkmate for you, baby. I'm smart, you know this. Take advantage of some of my ideas and we can build, and come up like a Fortune 500 company."

Hector was listening.

"First, you have to fully separate yourself from the day-to-day operations on the streets. You only deal with one man you trust, and put up a wall between you and everyone else. The less access to you, the better," Cartier lectured.

The SUV exited the cemetery; the dark van was following behind them. The driver had already been made aware that the feds were watching them. The van was three cars behind them. Everyone continued to remain calm. Cartier continued talking to her man, filling his head with proposition after proposition.

"You've been thinking, I see," said Hector.

"I'm always thinking...for us."

Hector nodded. One of her proposals was to encourage Hector to have his men stop promoting their purple gang colors and tattoos in everyone's faces. "When you stand out like that, it makes us an easy target, not just to the feds, but to our rivals. We cloak ourselves, and our rivals won't even see us coming," was her reasoning. Then she went on to talk about the prostitution ring and Hector's heavy gambling.

So far, Hector liked what he was hearing. Cartier was about her business and it was one of many reasons why he fell in love with her.

"I'll call a meeting and then tell my peoples about the changes," he said.

Cartier smiled. She was ecstatic that Hector was listening and finally ready to make changes.

Cartier stood without a sound behind Hector as he was about to address the notorious Ghost Ridas with some new changes. The spacious warehouse in Little Havana was swarming with gang members from aging O.G.'s to riotous youngsters who were ready to see some action—for some, it was fun to see the world burn. Being around the bloodshed was a thrill for them. There were hardcore looks on the men's faces while their leader stood before them looking sharp and astute in his tailored suit, polished shoes, and diamond pinky ring, sporting a gold Rolex. Hector oozed wealth and power. He was flanked by his lieutenants and ready to make his proposals known.

He lit a cigarette, took a deep drag, and waited for a moment. The chatter was loud amongst the gang. Hector wanted everyone's full attention. He took another pull from the cancer stick between his fingers, exhaled, and then shouted, "Everyone, shut the fuck up!"

The room of hardcore gangsters all of a sudden fell silent. He had everyone's undivided attention. They were ready for him to speak, assuming he was going to mention their deadly and ongoing war with the Miami Gotti Boys and come up with a devious game plan or some kind of methodical method to strike back hard at their rivals and try to kill as many as their foes possible. Whatever payback Hector had in mind, his men were ready to implement it on the streets. Over fifty men stood in the room waiting to hear what Hector had to say to them.

Clad in a sexy, black, short-sleeve minidress, Cartier was the only eye candy, the one woman in the room. The majority of the men already had a strong distaste for her, but she was far from being intimidated by anyone. Being Brooklyn-born and headstrong, she made it clear to everyone that she was here to stay. She stood behind Hector with her own corresponding frown, but inwardly, she smiled, knowing her ideas for the gang were about to come to light.

"We gonna have some changes with this gang from this day forward," Hector announced. "I've been thinking, and we need to start running this gang like a cartel, or a fuckin' company. We need to be better out there."

The men were confused. The bewildered look on their faces said, *What the fuck is he talking about?*

Hector continued with, "From now on, I want all y'all to stop promoting our gang colors out on the streets and stop flashing the gang signs and signatures everywhere."

The room erupted with upset and disagreement. It was clear that no one wanted to concur with Hector's sudden and ridiculous changes. They were all furious. His own lieutenants questioned it. Ghost Ridas were proud to flaunt their purple and black colors, display their gang tattoos and be a dangerous force to be reckoned with in Miami. They were one of the most dominant gangs in Miami. They'd been around for years, and were feared and respected even out of state. Now their leader was trying to take that away from them.

"What the fuck, Hector!" someone shouted from the crowd.

"Y'all muthafuckas listen the fuck up," Hector growled. "We at war out here."

"And you want us to back the fuck down?" Swagger M shouted.

"I'm not sayin' that Swagger M," Hector spat back.

"Then what the fuck are you sayin', Hector?"

"If you shut the fuck up and listen, then I'll get to my point."

"Ain't no fuckin' point, Hector. What the fuck is wrong wit' you?" Swagger M continued to squabble. "You got that bitch behind you tellin' you how to think now, ay. She the one wit' the swinging dick?"

Hector began to rush toward him, but was quickly held back by one of his lieutenants. It wasn't a good look to attack a top ranking gang member in front of everyone else, even if he was their leader. They had a code, and the Ghost Ridas respected that code.

So Hector retorted. "Watch ya fuckin' mouth, Swagger M. I already gave you one warning."

"Ay, fuck that. Our peoples is dying out there, and look at you, living in ya fuckin' penthouse suite wit' ya tailored suits, that self-centered bitch, and playin' ya away games wit' ya fuckin' businesses. You forgot who the fuck you is 'n' where you come from, *puta*? When was the last time you put in any work on the streets. Ay yo, you and ya bitch can both suck my fuckin' dick," Swagger M ranted.

The others were in shock. Hector and Swagger M had been like brothers back in the day. Now it was like they were going to kill each other.

"Ya out of line, Swagger M," Alexandro chimed.

"Ay, fuck that! He outta fuckin' line!" Swagger M snapped. "You became weak, Hector. It should have been you in that ground instead of Sanchez. Niggas in here might be scared to speak their mind 'bout it, but I ain't!"

It was the ultimate disrespect to Hector. He glared at Swagger M and was ready to tear him apart. Swagger M's mouth was about to have him bite off more than he could chew. Things became really edgy with each one in the room. Cartier was ready to tear into Swagger M also, but she knew her man was going to handle it. The situation escalated from idle threats to a natural disaster when Hector started to unbutton his suit jacket slowly. He reached for the .9mm holstered at his side and snatched it out. The pistol was aimed at Swagger M.

"Hector, what the fuck you doin' man?" one of his other lieutenants shouted.

"I'm tired of this *puta*'s disrespect. He needs to be put the fuck down like the dog his is," Hector retorted.

Swagger M didn't flinch. He returned Hector's hard stare and boldly shouted, "You think a gun in my fuckin' face scares me now? I'm Swagger M, muthafucka! You already know my pedigree, Hector. So fuck you and that dumb fuckin' bitch—"

*Bam! Bam! Bam! Bam!*

The bullets slammed into Swagger M's chest, pushing him off his feet and dead onto his back. Faces stood aghast in the room. Swagger M was lying dead by his peoples' feet with his eyes still open. Hector was stoic with the smoking gun in his hand. Everyone was dumbfounded by the sudden killing of an O.G. like Swagger M.

Calmly, Hector looked into the faces of a few gangsters surrounding him and exclaimed, "Anybody else got a fuckin' problem wit' my bitch and me, and wit' the way I'm running things?"

His harsh question fell against silence in the room. Seeing Swagger M dead on his back made them rethink their angst or dispute with their leader. Cartier had no words either. The action committed was inevitable. Swagger M was definitely trouble brewing for them, but to kill him in front of everyone could be added-on trouble.

"Hector, ay…you made ya fuckin' point! What the fuck," Alexandro cried out.

"Fuck that. Anyone else needs to speak the fuck up?" Hector shouted, becoming belligerent. "Because if so, say it the fuck now. But let it be clear, I run this shit! I'm the fuckin' power in this fuckin' room."

There was no feedback. Hector holstered his pistol and casually buttoned up his suit jacket. His cold, dark eyes showed no remorse for what he'd done. Cartier figured it was time to make their exit. She felt the sudden dissension in the room.

"Baby, let's go," she said to her man, trying to pull him away from the men that surrounded him.

Hector frowned. He refused to be taken down or have his position threatened. But the wheels started to spin and a machine was in motion. Cartier followed behind Hector. They exited the warehouse and hurried toward the parked SUV. They climbed into the backseat of the idling Escalade. In the backseat, Hector closed his eyes and became aloof.

"I think I fucked up," he said bleakly.

Yeah, he had. What he did to Swagger M made the Ghost Ridas concerned. To kill a member of your own gang, a man he once considered his brother, in cold blood like that would stir up uneasiness. If he could do Swagger M like that, then what was stopping him from doing any of them the same way? The last thing Hector needed was a civil war happening within the Ghost Ridas. They were all family to him—however, Swagger M was respected and loved, and so was Hector. It just seemed that nothing was going right.

Cartier tried to comfort him, but Hector was far too upset and disturbed. So she pulled away from him and stared out the window as the truck headed toward South Beach. Her mind was swimming with her own concerns. With trouble developing from so many directions, she needed to take a deep breath and think. She'd come too far to have things fucked up now, and the people responsible for killing her family still had to pay. Hector was a major part in her revenge, so he needed to pull it all together and rise back to the top.

# CHAPTER 8

## *Citi*

M arcus left Citi's pussy dripping wet and throbbing for more. It felt like lightening was exploding between her legs when she got up from the queen-size bed in her bedroom. It was their umpteenth sexual encounter in the past weeks, and Citi hadn't yet been disappointed. She couldn't get enough of his dick. The way Marcus ate out her tight little pussy and pounded his long, black flesh into her was fuckin' mind-blowing. She had picked the right one to start an affair with. Behind her mother's back, she was fucking the shit out of her man.

The dick was so good; it hurt when he was pounding her relentlessly, causing her to hold back tears while she somehow simultaneously hovered on the verge of an orgasm. Citi would be sore for hours, and that only served as a constant reminder of her illicit exploits with her mother's husband.

Citi became Marcus's little nasty whore, and she loved it. She would gaze up at him lustfully while sucking his dick. She didn't give a fuck. The nastier she was to him, the more turned on Marcus became. And when it came down to sucking dick, no one could ever argue about Citi's skills. Sometimes, Marcus would grab a handful of Citi's hair and jerk off, leaving her face dripping with his semen. Or he would eat her pussy out and then go kiss his wife, her moms, with his breath stinking of another woman's cum.

Citi would be with her mother and grin inwardly knowing her mother was clueless. In due time, she was about to lose her man. And in due time, if Citi kept giving herself to Marcus the way he loved it, then she would be the bitch by his side, not her moms.

Citi sat up from the bed and watched Marcus put his big, fleshy dick back into his pants and zip them up. He was done with her for the evening. "When I'm gonna see you again?" she asked.

"I'll see you tomorrow night," he said.

She smiled. "Can you make it sooner?"

"I'll see."

He walked out of her bedroom, leaving Citi behind to clean up the mess. She could still smell his cologne on her and feel her pussy throbbing. He left her in a foolish daze. She lingered in her bedroom for an hour, reminiscing about the things she did to him and vice versa. Thinking about it made her pussy wet and pulse even more. She became bored and decided to have some fun. She put on a T-shirt and jeans and went searching for her mother throughout the house. She found Ashanti in the kitchen talking on the phone and conducting business on her laptop while seated at the countertop. Ashanti was a subtle businesswoman. She walked up to her mother with an elated smile, knowing the taint of Marcus's cologne still lingered against her skin.

The one thing Citi could say about her mother: She was always on point, from her hairstyle and makeup to her wardrobe. Ashanti was a fly and beautiful woman. She stayed dressed down in Gucci, Dior, Chanel, Donna Karan, Prada, and so on. Her two walk-in closets in the master bedroom were as big as a small apartment. From her shoes to her dresses and jackets, she hardly wore the same outfit twice. She was rich and fabulous. The combined value of her jewelry totaled in the millions, and she drove around Miami styling in one of two cars, her red Maserati or her silver McLaren with vertical doors. Both high-end cars were gifts from

Marcus. Citi's moms was the epitome of living the lifestyle of the rich and famous. Being wife to Marcus had serious perks in Miami—clubbing, shopping, spas, and dining. Ashanti felt like she was the first lady to the city.

But Citi was ready to take her place and have her moms kicked to the curb. In the meantime, she was going to play nice to Ashanti—be a warm daughter, while she continued her illicit affair right under her mother's nose.

"Hey, Mom," Citi greeted.

"Citi, why the huge smile?" Ashanti asked.

"I met someone," she said.

"Oh really?" Ashanti replied with a raised eyebrow. "And what's happening with you and L? I haven't seen him around here lately."

"L is cool, but I was really never that into him like that. He helped me out in New York when that shit went down, but he was never really my type," she explained to her mother.

"So, who's this new man you've found?"

"He's someone close to home. He's fine, Mom. I mean really fine. And he has money."

Ashanti smiled. It felt good that her daughter was in her life and finally felt comfortable enough to come to her to have some good girl talk—that Ashanti could finally be a mother to her daughter. Their reunion several months back was bittersweet, almost disastrous. The two couldn't even be in the same room together without an argument happening. Cane was there to smooth things out, but the pain and wounds Citi felt from her mother not being around when she was young were going to take time to heal or for her to forgive. Citi had a few harsh words for her mother, and Ashanti repeatedly apologized for her long absence from Citi's life.

The two talked. Ashanti was happy that Citi found a new love. "I can't wait to meet him," she said.

"For some reason, I feel that you already have. He's like part of the family already," Citi said smugly.

Ashanti was confused by her daughter's statement. She shrugged it off and continued the girl talk with her daughter.

"Listen, tomorrow afternoon, let it be just you and me at the spa. We can get deep heated massages, get our nails and toes done, and just talk. Everything on me," Ashanti suggested.

Citi smiled. "I'm wit' it."

"It's a date then," Ashanti joked.

Ashanti went back to typing on her laptop. She didn't even smell her husband's cologne on Citi. Maybe it wasn't strong enough, or Ashanti didn't know what Marcus wore. But Citi wanted to be mischievous and get some kind of rise out of her mother. She went back into her bedroom with Marcus on her mind. She wanted him to touch her pussy again.

She was ready for a day out at the spa with her mother, especially if her mother was treating. Citi, being the spoiled brat that she was, only thought about herself. She had to have everything her way, or no way at all.

The luxury Day Spa in South Beach on Ocean Drive was what Citi and Ashanti both needed. Walking into the Encore Spa was like getting a peek inside *I Dream of Jeannie's* bottle. The spa's good luck ritual grants the wish of complete relaxation in 80 minutes. Ashanti spared no expensive. Everything was VIP for them, from dipping in the sanctuary spa's heated outdoor pools to having the top massage therapists at their beck and call. At the Watsu pool, the ladies floated weightlessly for an hour, while two therapists manipulated and stretched their bodies to release tension and blockage, focusing on reflex points in their hands, feet, and ears. The ladies then got rubbed down with oil and received a head-to-toe massage, topped off with an intensive moisturizing hand treatment, invigorating peppermint foot rub, and a clarifying wild limp scalp rinse that left their strands healthier and shinier.

As the ladies lay on their stomachs across the massage tables with the warming pads, in pure bliss and relaxation, clad only in towels underneath them while two muscular therapists treated them with an intense rubdown for the third time in one day, Ashanti stared at Citi and smiled.

"So, tell me more about this new guy you met," said Ashanti warmly.

"I think I'm in love wit' him," Citi replied.

"How did y'all meet?"

"It's a long story," Citi replied.

"We have nothing but time."

Citi gazed at her mother; she still had a luscious backside and a curvy figure. Her mother was still a beautiful woman and a MILF. The bitch was still in shape and not looking her age at all. It was hard to hate on her moms, but Citi did.

"I'll definitely introduce y'all one day. But the way he fucks me, shit…I can't get enough of it, lately," said Citi with a sly smile. "He got a really big dick, and he's dark-skinned with money and respect out here in Miami. Shit, I'm lovin' my baby right now."

"Sounds like my type of guy," replied Ashanti.

"He do, right?"

Ashanti smiled. She didn't mind the vulgar language her daughter used. She was a grown woman and been through a lot. As long as they were talking and still getting to know each other, Ashanti was ready to move on into a loving relationship with her daughter. The past was the past; it was the future she was more concerned about.

Citi continued talking about her mystery man. It was just too much fun. She decided to taunt Ashanti somewhat. She gave Ashanti minute details about him: his description, his occupation, the things he liked to do in the bedroom.

"He's in the game?" Ashanti asked.

"Yeah, I think."

"Just be careful with men in the game, Citi. I should know," Ashanti warned.

"But you still deal wit' them now," Citi shot back.

"Yeah, I know. I've dealt with them one too many times in my lifetime, from your father to Marcus. Yeah, they have the money to take care of you, but everything that glitters ain't gold, Citi. Ever since I was fourteen, the hustlers, the pimps, the thugs, and drug dealers were the only men I knew. My father, your grandfather, he was a pimp, and before he married your grandmother, she was his bottom bitch," Ashanti stated.

It was the first time she ever heard about her grandparents. Ashanti was ready to open up to her daughter about everything. There was so much she didn't know about her family. Citi was listening. Ashanti continued talking.

"When I met your father, he was so handsome and so smooth. I fell in love with him at first sight. He treated me like a queen. And he was nothing to play with in the streets. The respect that Curtis had everywhere, it turned me on. I got pregnant with Chris first, then Cane, and then you. Me and that man, we fucked like rabbits. But having children back to back like that, it did something to me. It changed me. I got scared, and I just left. I knew Curtis loved y'all greatly and he was going to take care of my babies. But I regret just leaving. I'm getting old, Citi. I needed to slow my ass down."

"You still look good for your age, Mom," Citi complimented.

It put a smile on Ashanti's face. She continued with, "I've been fortunate to find Marcus and have him in my life. The one thing about men like Marcus and your father, you just gotta fuck 'em with passion and love 'em right, and keep yourself fit, continue to be their eye candy, and respect them or their position, and they'll take care of you. Remember, there's always a bitch out there that's trying to replace you. So you try not to cause any headaches for men in the game—for men like Marcus and your father. They already have enough to worry about in the streets and shouldn't have to come home to a problem or another headache."

Citi was taking mental notes. The things her mother was saying to her were deep. She knew Ashanti always had wisdom. She'd been in the game long enough and been around enough thorough and big-shot niggas to know what she was talking about.

The deep massages continued along with the mother-and-daughter talk. Ashanti looked like she had a lot on her mind. She gazed at her daughter once again and spilled, "I think my husband is fuckin' with another bitch."

Citi was shocked. "What? Why you say that?"

"For the past few weeks he hasn't fucked me or even touched me the way he used to," she explained.

Citi was listening. "Marcus seemed to be a really good man. Shit, I like him." It was a slick comment, but her mother didn't pick up on it.

"I don't know, Citi…I love that man to death."

"You love him more than you loved Daddy?" Citi asked.

It was a hard question for Ashanti to answer. Ashanti fell silent for a moment. She was thinking. She locked eyes with her daughter and answered, "They're two different people. But I really loved your father, Citi. I did. This thing with Marcus is something much different."

"How different?" asked Citi with a raised brow.

"I don't know. It's just different. When I met Curtis, I was so much younger, so much in the streets and so wild. Now that I'm older, I don't take certain things for granted like I used to back then. Marcus is a much different man from your father, but I do miss your father a lot."

"I miss him, too," Citi said sadly.

She lingered on old thoughts about her father for a moment. Citi remembered how Curtis treated her like his little princess. He always protected her and was always there for her. The nostalgic feeling she felt, it almost brought tears to her eyes. But she immediately collected herself and came back to the present.

"Shit, with this man, I'm gonna be his everything, and if he has a bitch by his side, she'll soon be replaced, cuz I know I'm the baddest bitch out here," said Citi coldly.

"It's not always good to share a man, Citi. And word of advice, humble yourself before something or someone humbles you in a way you won't like," Ashanti stated.

Citi wasn't trying hear it. Fuck being humble, she thought. It was a dog-eat-dog world, and she was ready to devour everything in her path. She was ready to cut her own mother's throat to get what she wanted.

The two ended the day together having martinis at a local lounge. The spa was a blessing and Citi felt refreshed—like a brand-new woman! What would make her day more perfect, was Marcus. If she could get some dick tonight, she could go to bed feeling like she was in seventh heaven. Citi just couldn't stop thinking about his dick—the sex. She felt like a fiend. As she sat having drinks with Ashanti, she thought about Marcus the whole time, becoming a shady bitch—smiling in front of her mother's face while she was fucking her husband behind her back and plotting to have her replaced.

When they arrived back at the house, Ashanti wanted to rest, but Citi had other plans. They didn't see Marcus's Bentley parked out front in the circular driveway. Citi was ready to wait. She hugged Ashanti and kissed her on the cheek, saying she'd had a wonderful day, and walked into her bedroom to put on something more comfortable for the evening. The minute she turned on the lights, L sprung out at her and threw her against the wall. Citi was shocked by the sudden attack.

"What fuckin' games you playin' wit' me, Citi?!" L shouted.

Citi found herself on the floor hurt with L towering over her, scowling. L had his fists clenched and looked like a rabid dog.

"What the fuck, L! What is your fuckin' problem?" she shouted.

"You think I don't fuckin' know! Huh?" he screamed. "You fuckin' that nigga?"

"What?" Citi looked baffled. "What the fuck are you talkin' about?"

"I've seen y'all!"

"You've seen what?" Citi screamed back.

"You fuckin' that muthafucka! Marcus! You think I'm stupid, Citi?"

Citi stood up, aghast. She wasn't as careful with Marcus as she'd thought she was. L was furious. How was she going to play out this situation? The look in L's eyes was murderous.

"I loved you, Citi, and you playin' me?" L screamed.

"L, listen. You just don't understand, it's not what you think."

"What, him being between your fuckin' legs and stickin' his dick into you was a mistake? You think I'm stupid? You think I'm seeing things?" screamed L.

He had done enough talking. He rushed toward Citi and started striking her repeatedly. The first blow struck her across the head, making her dizzy; the second almost paralyzed her, hitting her in the temple, and she felt her face swelling up. She found herself helpless on the ground as L beat her viciously. She screamed for help, trying to defend herself from the rain of heavy blows coming down upon her.

"Get the fuck off me! Help…help!" Citi screamed.

"Fuck you, bitch! I fuckin' loved you, and you treat me like this! Fuck you! Fuck you!" L screamed out madly.

Citi felt herself about to black out. She felt the blood and bruises against her face. L was going to kill her. He was about to beat her to death. The coldness in his eyes indicated he wasn't going to stop until he saw her lifeless. Citi tried to fight back. She clawed and scratched at him and his swinging fists, and then tried to flee from the room, but her effort was fruitless. L was too powerful and too determined. He grabbed Citi abruptly and pulled her back ferociously by yanking the back of her hair like it was a rein on a horse. It felt like every root of her hair was being ripped out from her scalp.

"I'ma kill you, bitch!"

"Help me!"

All of a sudden, Cane came bursting into the bedroom, responding to Citi's pleas. When he saw his little sister cowering in the corner bloody and being beaten, he snapped.

"What the fuck you doin' to my fuckin' sister, nigga!" Cane shouted.

"Back the fuck up, Cane! This shit don't concern you," L shouted.

"Like hell it don't," Cane shouted back.

Cane didn't hesitate. He went charging for L like a bull seeing red and was ready to tear him apart. But L quickly snatched a pistol out his waistband and aimed it at Cane, shouting again, "I said back the fuck up!"

Cane stopped suddenly in his tracks. He glared at L and the pistol and exclaimed, "So, it's like that now, nigga? I thought we were cool?"

"Nigga, we were, until ya sister decided to play me and fuck some other nigga," he stated strongly.

"Yo, you a dead man, L…bet on that," Cane threatened.

"Oh, you ain't in no position to throw out threats, muthafucka!"

Cane continued to glare at L. He then averted his attention away from the culprit and looked at his sister. She was in very bad shape. He wanted to run over there and comfort Citi, but L still had him at gunpoint.

"What you gonna do wit' that, nigga…huh? You better kill me now, L, cuz if you don't, I'ma fuckin' find you and it ain't gonna be pretty."

L knew he had fucked up. His emotions had gotten the best of him. With the pistol still aimed at Cane, he knew it was best to make his exit while he could. L backed toward the doorway with his glare still locked on Cane. Before L left the room, he glanced down at Citi. She was in and out of consciousness. He had done a serious number on her.

"Fuck y'all! Come find me, nigga, cuz next time, I ain't gonna hesitate in squeezing," L threatened Cane.

"Neither will I," Cane snapped back.

L ran out. Cane wanted to chase after him, but he decided to see about his little sister. He ran over and shouted, "Citi, you okay? Talk to me." He pulled Citi into his arms and shouted, repeatedly, "Somebody help me!"

It only several minutes before others entered Citi's bedroom and saw the damage done. Ashanti also came rushing in and was horrified at what she saw. "Who did this to my baby?" she screamed.

"L," Cane said.

Ashanti found herself dumbfounded.

"Why?" she asked wildly.

"I don't even know, Ma, but I'm gonna definitely find out," Cane heatedly replied.

Cane went to get his gun and made a few phone calls to a few killers he knew. Ashanti was ready to rush her daughter to the hospital and then get to the bottom of things.

# CHAPTER 9

## *Cartier*

Heavy weed smoke lingered in the tricked-out Chevy Impala with the candy paint job and tinted windows. Each man in the ride took turns taking a pull from the burning blunt. The car moved through Little Haiti with rap music blaring inside. The three passengers were loving Future's new song, "Karate Chop," as the potent Kush flowed through their systems, taking its effect on them. They rhymed to the raw rap track and bobbed their heads.

Heavily armed and dangerous, the men meant nothing but trouble. Their colors and tattoos indicated that they were Miami Gotti Boys. Proud of the gang and their reckless ways, the men were celebrating their come-up in the game. Tonight was going to be a festival with whorish women, drugs, and drinking. Since Bones and Shotta's demise, their leadership was in the air.

The driver exhaled the smoke from his black lips and uttered, "Why you tryin' to see this bitch right now?"

"Cuz, nigga, she got my money 'n' some pussy. Shit, I'm 'bout to swing by 'n' collect fo' real, dawg. And she hittin' me up to come through," said the passenger. "This bitch can't get enough of me."

"Get that bitch to have her friends come through and we can party all night. We need to celebrate 'n' shit tonight," the rider in the backseat said.

"Man, y'all niggas tryin' to invade on my shit?" the passenger said jokingly. "The bitch is right though, and she got some good pussy."

"Man, both y'all niggas is some thirsty muthafuckas! We need to be 'bout this fuckin' business 'stead of chasing behind some bird bitch," the driver exclaimed.

"I am collecting, Mac. The bitch got a few stacks I need to pick up from her… that pussy is just interest, my nigga. Shit, knock out two birds wit' one stone."

"Yeah, whatever, nigga, just don't be takin' long 'n' have us waiting 'n' the car for you all fuckin' day. We gotta get that money out here 'n' shit. Y'all feel me?"

"Nigga, I already get my fuckin' ends," said the backseat passenger, pulling out a stack of money from his pocket and flashing it around.

"And you ain't the only muthafuckin' one, nigga!" the other passenger returned.

The men continued to smoke and laugh while the driver navigated his way toward their destination. The streets of Miami had been calm for several days now. No gang murders in five days, but many felt it was only the calm before the storm. The Miami Gotti Boys and the Ghost Ridas were on full alert in the streets. The men moved with caution—so many were dead on both sides.

The Impala came to a stop in front of a one-story, three-bedroom home with remnants of trash, junk, and an old car littering the front yard, making it clear they were in the hood. The passenger jumped out still laughing with his homeboys, a cigarette dangling from his lips.

"Y'all niggas is fuckin' stupid and crazy," he laughed. "But I ain't gonna be long, let me go holla at his bitch fo' a fuckin' minute."

"Nigga, hurry the fuck up! Shit, you think you the only one that wanna fuck a bitch today. Man, see if that bitch got any friends 'n' shit," the driver exclaimed.

"Yeah, who lookin' like the thirsty nigga now?"

"Ten minutes, Lock. You get that money, get you a fuckin' quickie 'n' get ya ass back to this car or me 'n' Tone gonna rush up 'n' that bitch 'n' gang rape ya bitch."

He laughed. "Yeah, whatever, nigga…and I ain't no minute man."

Lock walked toward the dilapidated looking home while taking a few pulls from his cancer stick with his .45 tucked in his waistband. He knocked a few times and waited. It didn't take long for a big-breasted, dark-skinned, hood rat bitch with a scarf tied around her head to answer the door.

"Damn, Lock, it took you long enough to fuckin' get here, nigga!" she hissed.

"Bitch, just open the fuckin' door 'n' let me slide in. I ain't fuckin' come by to just stand on the got-damn porch 'n' listen to you talk shit. You got my money 'n' pussy, right?"

She rolled her eyes and sucked her teeth. "Fuck you, Lock."

"Yeah, that's what I'm tryin' to do right now," Lock returned. He pushed his way past the woman and made his way inside.

"Damn Lock, why you gotta be so fuckin' rude?" she barked.

"Cuz I can be," he spat back.

The instant Lock stepped into the living room, he knew something was wrong. It was a setup. One of his homies, a fellow gang member, was tied up by his wrists and ankles in the living room, and gagged. He had been beaten badly and was stripped naked.

"What the fuck!" Lock shouted.

He went to reach for his pistol in his jeans, but he wasn't fast enough. The butt of a Glock went crashing against the back of his skull and the hard blow dropped him to his knees. Lock suddenly found himself surrounded by three Ghost Ridas. They were heavily armed while scowling down at their foe.

"Fuck y'all niggas!" Lock shouted.

"No, fuck you, *puta*!" one shouted back, with the .380 aimed at him.

His foes continued to assault him violently. They pistol-whipped him, using the handgun as a blunt weapon and wielding it like it was a baton until Lock's face turned a crimson color. He could barely stand up. The woman he came to see looked detached toward the brutal action she was witnessing, which indicated she was part of the setup. She stood behind the Mexican goons and watched with a smirk.

"Ay, he didn't come alone, right...execute them other *putas* in the fuckin' car," one gave the order.

Lock was glued to the floor in terrible pain and knowing his fate. He could only screw his face and scowl at his attackers. One Ghost Rida aimed the gun at his face and frowned. "This for Sanchez, ay, *puta*." He fired multiple shots into Lock's face, and flesh and brain matter exploded everywhere.

The Mexican shooter then turned to the second tied-up man and fired, pumping two shots into the back of his head. The woman stood stoic and watched him murder two people in cold blood. She wanted her money for the setup, but to her surprise, the shooter turned toward her with his gun elevated. The woman was taken aback—she uttered, "No! No!"

He quickly shot her in the face, leaving behind no witnesses. Inside the home, a bloody massacre was displayed.

Outside, Mac inhaled the burning blunt as he sat slouched behind the steering wheel. In a calm tone, he uttered to the passenger in the backseat, "This muthafucka better hurry the fuck up 'n' shit. You know we ain't tryin' to sit out here all fuckin' day."

The rider in the backseat nodded and agreed. His eyes were faded and his movement sluggish. The weed was burning slow and almost done. Unbeknownst to them, their high was about to come to an abrupt end, because the nightmare was just about to begin.

Hearing the unexpected sound, *chk-chk,* indicating a shotgun being cocked back, Mac and the passenger all of a sudden found their car surrounded by three heavily armed Mexican gunmen—scowling Ghost Ridas itching for payback for their fallen friends. Before the men in the car could even react, the slaughter began.

*Boom! Boom! Boom!*

The shotgun blast at close range tore the driver's head clean off, splattering blood and flesh all over dashboard and front seat. Two assault rifles opened fire, with a barrage of gunfire shredding into the vehicle and the passenger in the backseat. Riddled with bullets, the man jerked around violently until he was slumped over across the backseat looking like Swiss cheese with his face and body eaten up by machine-gunfire. It was a gruesome sight, but a strong message to their rivals. The five days of no bloodshed between the gangs came to a violent end. Four Miami Gotti Boys met a grizzly fate.

Cartier stood by the property she owned in North Miami. It was nothing but a vacant lot and an opportunity for her near the ocean. She had so many plans for the property—so many things she was ready to build. But first she had to get past the red tape the city had her tangled in, and next was this violent war with the gangs. Cartier had so much on her mind. She didn't want to stress herself, but there were one too many worries.

Civil unrest had developed within the Ghost Ridas. Since Swagger M's death, the gang members were talking, and Hector's reputation and credibility to lead was put into question. Anarchy was brewing. Cartier wanted to fix things, but Hector was making it harder. He was becoming unstable. Since he killed Swagger M, his mood changes were becoming more unpredictable and violent. Some nights, he would take out his frustration on Cartier.

She hid her black eye behind the dark shades. Last night, Hector had started drinking and his fists started flying. Out of nowhere, he attacked Cartier and tried to beat her down senseless, but she happened to escape from his vicious wrath and lock herself in the bathroom until he was able to calm down. She loved him, but she felt the walls crumbling stone by stone.

Cartier sighed heavily. She stared at her property and couldn't wait to get something developing. She had to escape South Beach, Hector, the Ghost Ridas, and everyone else. She needed some alone time. She needed to look at her future. She was ready to leave behind the bloodshed, the gangs, and anything that wasn't profitable. And since the meeting with her attorney Maxwell hadn't gone too well this morning, Cartier didn't know which way to turn. It seemed easier when she was on the streets killing people and making her money by any means necessary, and making tons of it. But when a bitch tried to go legit, everyone suddenly wanted to become an obstacle.

She lingered at the beginning of her acres of land. She saw a vision that could make her a very rich woman. But that vision came with a cost; bribes, and high-priced lawyers. And even with those variables, it was still difficult to get shit done. As she stood alone, transfixed by her vision, her cell phone rang. She quickly answered, seeing that it was Penny calling her. Penny was one of the very few O.G.'s from the gang who accepted her and gave her respect. He was good friends with Hector, and someone Cartier felt she could trust.

"Penny, talk to me," Cartier answered.

"We need to talk. Things are not looking good," said Penny.

"What you mean?"

"I mean, there's heavy dissension with some heavy O.G.'s about Hector's action the other night. They not taking what he did to Swagger

M very lightly," Penny warned.

"So what are you sayin'?" Cartier asked, alarm in her voice.

"Shit might get really ugly out here, meaning Hector might have to watch his back twenty-four seven," Penny frankly replied.

"Is that a threat to us, Penny?"

"I got love for Hector and you, Cartier, you know that, but they saying things about him that I don't even like to hear."

Cartier took a deep breath. Shit was definitely falling apart. She kept her composure even though the tears started falling underneath the shades. She and Hector had come too far to fall now. Swagger M was an asshole who was all-around trouble, and if the Ridas didn't see that, then Cartier felt they were looking for fault in the wrong place.

"Cartier, you still there?" Penny asked.

"I'll call you back."

She hung up and took another deep breath. Where she was at was so peaceful and quiet. North Miami was a suburban city located northeast of Miami-Dade County Florida, about ten miles north of Miami, on the Biscayne Bay. It was far enough away from her troubles that she could actually breathe and get some thinking done.

Cartier loitered near her property for almost an hour. She ignored phone calls from her lawyer, Penny, and others. She just wanted to be alone. After she felt somewhat unruffled, she turned on her red-bottoms and walked toward her Escalade. She climbed inside the car and her cell phone started to ring again. It was Penny calling back. She didn't want to pick up, but Penny kept calling indicating it was something urgent.

"What Penny?" she snapped.

"I can't reach Hector. Have you spoken to him recently?"

"Not since last night," she mentioned.

"My calls keeps goin' to voice mail. Everyone is on code red," said Penny. "Including you. Ay, shit is gettin' real out here, so you be careful, Cartier."

Cartier understood why things were so tense. She heard about the killings in Little Haiti. Four Miami Gotti Boys and a young woman were viciously murdered. It was headline news, along with front-page news, and created a media feeding frenzy. It felt like Miami's own St. Valentine's Day Massacre.

She started the ignition and made her way back to South Beach. Taking no chances, she removed the .380 from underneath her seat and set it on the passenger side. Keeping her pistol close was simple, and even though she was riding around in a bulletproof SUV, a gun was always that extra protection.

She made her way back toward her penthouse suite while trying to dial Hector's cell phone, but it kept going straight to voice mail. The butterflies began fluttering around in her stomach. Something bad was about to happen, and Cartier didn't know when or where. She spun her truck into the parking garage and hopped out. Rushing toward the elevator, she called Hector again, but his phone went straight to voice mail again. She hated when he never picked up. It was becoming a routine thing.

As the elevator ascended, her heart dropped, and when the elevator doors opened and she saw him standing there, Cartier stood aghast.

It had been several months since she'd last seen him. The two locked eyes. Detective Sharp was always a handsome man. He stood in front of Cartier wearing his standard chestnut fedora and blazer. His six-three frame and trimmed beard were impressive.

"Detective Sharp," Cartier uttered in disbelief. "What brings you here? And how did you find me?"

"It wasn't hard, Cartier. But we do need to talk," Sharp replied coolly.

Instantly, the worries swamped Cartier and her heart started to beat like drums at an African concert. Hector came to mind. Was he here to deliver her some bad news? Hector was dead, it had to be the only reason why his cell phone was going straight to voice mail.

"Is it Hector?" she asked frightfully.

"No, this is a personal visit," he responded.

Hearing him say that brought some much-needed relief to her soul. She exhaled. Detective Sharp stared at her. He noticed the worry in her eyes. "Can I come in?"

Cartier was unsure. Being around a cop and inviting him into your home was forbidden in her world, but Sharp looked like he wasn't taking no for an answer. Releasing a deep sigh, Cartier said to him, "You can come in and talk, but you can't stay long."

Sharp followed behind Cartier and entered the lavish penthouse suite that was made as if to comfort royalty. He was impressed as he looked around the sprawling structure, taking in the luxuries. It was a grand-looking place. He stood expressionless in the center of the living room, though.

"I would offer you something to drink, but it ain't that kind of party," Cartier said to him.

He smiled. "Yeah, police is always bad news around your kind."

"My kind?" Cartier returned with a raised eyebrow.

"I was just joking."

"Well, don't! And let's cut the bullshit, why are you here?"

Detective Sharp removed his chestnut fedora from his head, respecting her home, and looked at Cartier. Cartier's heart started to beat. When a detective came to visit you, it was never a good thing.

"It seems the dominions are falling in your direction," said Sharp.

"What do you mean by that?"

"You started something a few months back, and now it's coming back to bite you hard."

"I don't know what you're talking about."

"I'm not here to arrest you. You have greater troubles to worry about. What with the trouble you caused in my city, I shouldn't even be here right now. But I'm an officer of the law and I try to be a righteous man. I'm only here to warn you," Sharp said.

"Warn me about what?" Cartier asked with alarm.

"You think you can just murder people in this city and it won't come back to you? There's something out there called Karma, and it's a vicious bitch," said Sharp sternly.

"And you can tell that bitch I'm nothing to fuck wit' too! And about these murders, I don't know what the fuck you're talking about."

Sharp sighed. Cartier was a head case.

"I know what they did to your daughter, and it was wrong, but you can't always fight fire with fire. You know there's a saying: 'When you go looking for revenge, then you best dig two graves.'"

Cartier rolled her eyes. She wasn't in the mood to hear a cop lecture about revenge and other nonsense. The only thing he said to her that was sticking to her mind was the warning. She looked at him and frankly asked, "What are you trying to warn me about, Detective Sharp?"

"The man you murdered. Luis Juarez," Sharp uttered.

Hearing that name again made Cartier frozen inside, her heart skipping a beat. She kept her cool though and quickly replied with, "I don't know who you're talking about. And I sure didn't murder anyone. You have me mistaken, Detective."

"Cut the bullshit, Cartier. I'm a detective, and it's my job to investigate murders. Now, I know he was one of a few responsible for your daughter's brutal murder, and he probably deserved what came to him. But a report came across my desk earlier today with your name in it. Three of the Gonzalez cartel's primary killers just crossed the border into the States from Mexico. One was captured by customs' agents earlier and they found your picture in his possession. They're here to find and kill you, Cartier," detective Sharp warned.

Cartier looked unfazed by the news.

"Why are you telling me this, Detective?"

"I just thought you needed to know. The last thing I want in this city is another murder, especially yours. If I can prevent it, then I will. I'm just giving you this one courtesy," he said.

Cartier looked at him with no compassion. "Thank you."

Detective Sharp returned her spiky stare and said, "You're a beautiful woman with so much pain in your eyes, Cartier. I know a lot was taken from you, but don't let it take your soul also. I've been a detective and a cop for a very long time, and I see women like you get sucked into something that they can't pull themselves out of. This world, that pain, it will bury you in something nasty."

Cartier heard what he was saying, but she wasn't trying to listen. "I think it's time for you to go," she told the detective.

"I guess so," replied Sharp. He put his fedora back on his head and walked toward the door. Cartier was right behind him.

Detective Sharp stepped out into the hallway. His gut feeling told him that his cat-and-mouse relationship with Cartier was going to come to an abrupt end. He gave her the warning about the contract killers being in Miami, but now what ripple effect would this cause? Once he was completely in the hallway, Cartier shut the door behind him. He sighed and went on his way.

In the apartment, Cartier walked out onto the terrace and watched the city of Miami. She gripped the railing and became lost in her thoughts and emotions. She took a deep breath and out of the blue rushed toward the closest bathroom and dropped to her knees. She floated her face over the toilet and started to throw up. Thinking about the contract on her head made her sick. She lingered on her knees against the porcelain god for a moment. So much was happening and so much was on her mind.

Knowing a storm was coming, Cartier jumped from her knees and went into her bedroom. She removed a few high-end weapons from the safe in the wall and checked the ammunition. Displayed on her bed were an M-16, an M41A pulse rifle, two Uzis, and her personal favorite, a Heckler and Koch MP5. Fuck with a bitch if they wanted. The cartels weren't the only killers on the block with high-power weaponry. She was locked and loaded and tried to put the fear of death to the side. Revenge weighed heavily in her heart. The ones responsible for killing her family had to die. Cartier made a few phone calls and was readying herself for the storm coming. She refused to go down without a fight.

# CHAPTER 10

## Apple

Three kis of cocaine was nothing to sneeze at. Apple removed the kis that were concealed in a small duffel bag from the trunk of her Chevy and walked toward the brownstone. So far, it had been a good day. With the warmth of the sun coming down on her and the .9mm on her person, she couldn't help but to feel like that bitch. The block was quiet, and so was the low profile she was trying to maintain. Apple had only been in Harlem for two weeks, and already she was coming up. She and Row were a good team. With Apple's hundred thousand and Row's connection, they were able to acquire a few kis to push on the streets on a small scale. It was mainly to pay their bills, get some recognition from the right players, and expand once again. Apple needed a come-up. She needed to stick with her plan. She needed a hardcore team of killers to travel down to Miami with her and find her daughter. And in order for her to do that, she needed to build up her status in the streets heavily like before—real recognizes real.

Apple walked into the brownstone with the small duffel bag slung over her shoulder. She walked in on Row shirtless. He was in the kitchen talking on his cell phone, a small arsenal of handguns displayed on the table before him. Row's chiseled, slim frame displayed his tattoos and war scars. One particular scar stretched from the middle of his chest down to his abs, indicating where he had been shot multiple times once and survived. When Apple walked in, he turned and looked at her. He nodded and went back to his conversation. It was obvious that he was talking to some bitch.

Apple remained standoffish. She dropped the duffel bag near him and said, "Let's get to work."

"Give me a minute," he replied.

"Money over bitches, nigga, I thought you already knew that," said Apple with a grin.

Row flipped her the bird and continued his conversation. He wasn't getting any pussy from Apple, and he had needs. While Row continued to talk, Apple removed the kis from the duffel bag and placed them on the table. Each ki went for fifteen five. Apple was the front money. She still had a few resources in the underworld that she could depend on for a favor. She made some phone calls indicating she was back in town and in the game. Money talked—once she was able to show she was good for the cash, her peoples hooked her up with a good price, giving her two kis for fifteen five each, and the other on consignment. The product Apple had was pure and potent. Now it was time to make moves.

Apple's plan was to wholesale the two kis in the streets for anywhere from twenty-two thousand to thirty thousand. And the last ki, she was going to cut up and get that street profit. Even though she had a hundred thousand to her name, Apple needed to get her ends up—because $100K in Miami, while searching for her daughter, wasn't going to last long. The ballers were heavy down in the sunny state. Apple couldn't go anywhere looking like a fool or desperate.

In the drug world, there are no hard and fast rules for cocaine prices, as with anything that is bought and sold. The prices always fluctuated. Apple was ready to set her own rules, and she knew that with the quality of blow she had, niggas were going to pay whatever she charged. With so many new drugs out today to compete with—meth, heroin, weed, molly, and ecstasy, crack was a dying high, but still profitable.

Apple sat at the table and began going to work while Row walked into the next room, still chatting on the phone with some bitch. Apple rolled her eyes and got the materials she needed to produce crack cocaine for street distribution: baking soda, rubbing alcohol, distilled water, a glass beaker, and a lighter. Wearing a mask and latex gloves, she began mixing four parts of coke to one part of baking soda in the glass beaker. Then she began adding a few drops of distilled water to the mix; only enough to give the powder a muddy, sludge-like consistency. She made sure not to add too much water so the coke would harden up during the cooling process. Next, she drenched the cotton ball with rubbing alcohol in a thick metal dish.

The cooking process was simple for Apple. It was a trade she picked up on while being with Chico and his goons. She used to sit around and watch them cook up crack all the time just for fun, and she was a fast learner. She used the lighter to ignite the alcohol in the cotton ball. While the cotton ball was still burning, Apple heated up the coke-sludge by swirling the beaker above the tip of the flame. She continued swirling until the substance came to a boil. She then removed it from the flame to cool. When the substance cooled, it formed a clump of solid "rock-bubbles."

She added more distilled water to the beaker, enough to stand about one fourth of an inch above the hardened bubbles. She then reheated the substance in the beaker. When she saw the yellow mass floating in the center of the water while it was being thoroughly reheated, Apple nodded.

Row walked into the kitchen. He was still shirtless and finally off the phone. He looked at Apple and asked, "Who taught you how to cook?"

"Dumb-ass question," Apple replied.

Row walked over to inspect her masterpiece. He nodded. She had his approval. "Nice."

Apple continued cooking by swirling the beaker until the hardened bubbles melted into a yellow coke mass.

"You ready to get this money, I see," said Row.

She didn't respond to his comment. Apple remained focused on her cooking. While the two kis were going wholesale for a high amount, the last ki she was cooking could easily profit greatly for them on the streets. Row had gotten a few low-level soldiers to move the crack vials into the hands of the fiends.

While Apple sat at the table cutting the rocks into desired proportions, Row stood by the kitchen window gazing at the street. His block was always quiet, which he liked. And he didn't have too many nosy neighbors. As Row stared out the window, he suddenly noticed a gray G-class Benz with tinted windows drive by his home slowly. At first, he paid it no never mind, thinking it was only a passing vehicle. But as he lingered by the window, he noticed the same car creep pass his home again. Becoming suspicious, Row removed himself from the window and grabbed the .45 off the table.

"What's wrong?" Apple asked.

"Just being cautious, this gray Benz keeps driving by slow," he said.

Apple removed herself from the table and snatched up a pistol also. In her world, you couldn't take anything lightly. Everything was a threat, no matter how simple or innocent it may look. She went toward the window to look out but saw nothing.

"It's probably nothing, just a car looking for the right address."

Apple frowned. "Next time, try and get the tag numbers."

Row nodded.

The remainder of the day Apple cooked and made phone calls. She had two buyers from New Jersey that wanted the two kis for $25,000 apiece, netting her a profit of twenty thousand. With her package ready for street distribution, Row made the call to his young goons working the streets for him. It was time to grind. Somewhat exhausted, Apple removed herself from the room and said to Row, "I'll be in the shower."

"A'ight, just don't take long. We gotta make this move," he said.

She went up to the second floor and stripped away her clothing. She turned on the shower and adjusted the setting to lukewarm. While the shower ran, Apple stood naked, staring at herself in the mirror. Even though her scars were hardly visible, inside she was a tragic figure. She felt ugly and distorted. The pain from being a sex slave in Mexico still lingered in the deep recesses of her mind. Mentally she wasn't strong enough to shake it. And then it felt like her little sister, Nichols, was haunting her for some reason. Apple hadn't been to her sister's grave since the burial. She started to feel guilty about it. She felt like beauty and the beast wrapped up into one. It was easy to fix her appearance, restore her features—but to revamp her soul, to make Apple the meek, affable and lovely young twin with the golden smile that she once was long ago, it damn near felt impossible. Her soul felt like it was engulfed in darkness. Her mind felt like it was being ripped apart with rage and revenge.

She stepped into the shower and allowed the flowing water to cascade off her natural, curvy light brown skin. She closed her eyes and enjoyed how the spurt from the shower head crashed against her breasts. She chilled for a moment, dropping her head low with her palms flat against the shower walls and felt the energy of running water gush down on her like a waterfall. The shower became her temporary sanctuary. It was hard to wash away her problems, but she tried. And for one split moment, she missed Kola. Despite their turbulent relationship, they would always have that sisterly, twin bond. But Apple had her life back in the States, and Kola had her life in Colombia. And she knew they would never see each other again.

Apple stepped out of the shower and toweled off. This time she refused to look at her image in the mirror. She averted her reflection like it was some type of deadly plague.

Apple got dressed in a pair of blue jeans, white sneakers, a T-shirt, and a ball cap she wore low over her eyes—it was nothing revealing or eye catching. She tried to hide her identity somewhat and keep a low profile while she was in Harlem. She met Row downstairs in the kitchen. He was dressed and ready to hit the streets. They both armed themselves with automatic handguns. Apple picked up the duffel bag containing now two kis of coke and the street-ready product for the goons to make some sales to fiends.

Row stepped out the brownstone and loitered at the top of the stairs. His eyes ran up and down the block looking for anything suspicious. The slow passing Benz earlier had him feeling uneasy. He kept his residence a secret; he moved subtle, kept his circle tight, but you could never tell who was watching. It could have been nothing, or it could have been something serious—a rival, the feds. With his .45 concealed and tucked snugly in his waistband, he moved down the concrete stairs and headed toward his 650i coupe parked across the street from his home. Apple was right behind him. She placed the product in the trunk of the car and jumped into the passenger side of the coupe.

Newark, New Jersey was their first destination. Row drove across the G.W. Bridge with the sun slowly setting in the west. The traffic into Jersey was sparse, and they arrived in Newark in no time. Apple had arrangements with two local hoods, Micro and A-Rod, for the kis. They were on the come-up in the game, making a serious name for themselves in the mean, Jersey Streets. It was simple to buy from her. With Row being her protection and having her back, Apple didn't have any worries.

The meeting in Jersey went smoothly, and next was back to Harlem to meet up with Row's young goons to hand off a few G packs for street sales. Row steered his gleaming coupe back across the G.W. Bridge into the city again. Apple sat back in the passenger seat, trying to relax. The sun had faded into oblivion, making way for the night owls as the ghostly full moon hovered over the city like a huge Christmas ornament.

Apple stared up at the moon and said, "I guess the freaks are goin' to come out tonight, huh, Row?"

Row chuckled lightly. "I guess they are. Shit, as long as they don't fuck wit' me or you, then let 'em come."

He took a pull from the burning cancer stick and made his way onto the Harlem River Drive. Apple rode quietly for a moment. The nightly traffic on the Harlem River Drive was like a parking lot—break lights seemed to travel for miles.

"Shit!" Row uttered.

"Go around this shit. I ain't in the mood to sit in traffic," Apple said.

"I'm 'bout to."

Row did a sudden detour onto the side streets into the projects and made a few turns going south. Harlem was bustling and animated from block to block—old men seated at tables in front of aging shops playing dominos or cards, the young hoods flaunting their lavish rides on the streets with blaring music, the ladies moving about in groups displaying their sexy attire with their teasing smiles thrown back at the pack of hustlers who tried to gain their attention as they passed. It seemed like everybody was outside enjoying the balmy evening.

With Jay-Z and Kanye West playing from his ride, Row caught attention as he moved his BMW through the busy streets. His rims shone like mirrors and the paint job was flawless. Apple took a pull from Row's burning cigarette and gaped out the window. She reminisced about her earlier days growing up. Once, everybody had love for her—her, Kola, and Nichols. Now, they feared or hated her. With the brim to her ball cap pulled low over her eyes, she fixed her attention on certain people and places.

Row pulled up to the projects on West 133rd Street, right off of Amsterdam Avenue. Standing outside one of the buildings was his young pusher, Tee. Row stepped out of the car and called him over. Tee walked over to the coupe, bopping in his sagging jeans, fitted Yankees cap on backwards, little jewelry showing, and urban swag. His demeanor said that he was the one in charge of the block. With the .380 snug in his waistband and his shifty eyes watching out for trouble, Tee was the center of attention.

"Row! What's poppin', my nigga?" Tee greeted.

Row gave his little soldier dap, and then Tee's eyes went wandering to the passenger he had in the car with him. Apple looked back and growled, "Why the fuck you lookin' so hard?"

Tee scowled back and was ready to snap back with his own rude comment, but Row said, "Don't even do it to yourself, little nigga. You don't even know who she is or what she's about."

"I'm just sayin…I was just tryin'…"

"Just chill, Tee. Anyway, I got some work for you in the trunk," said Row.

"That's what's up," replied Tee, slapping and rubbing his hands together with eagerness.

Row popped the trunk of the car and removed the product that was concealed in a book bag. He handed it over to Tee. "You already know the arrangement, Tee."

"Yeah, I know. Shit, a nigga out here tryin' to get this money. I got these fiends bubbling right now for something. You already know how me and my crew do, Row, clockin' that dollar twenty-four-seven," Tee said glibly.

"Yeah, I know, I know. And y'all keep doin' it."

"No doubt."

The men dapped hands once again. Tee took the book bag and slung it over his shoulder and bopped back toward the building he was standing in front of. Row jumped back into his ride. There were no more transactions for the day. With the illegal content removed from the car, the two could breathe a little easier.

"We on the money, Apple," said Row with a smile.

He pulled away from the curb and headed south toward his brownstone, unaware that he was being followed. Row drove a few blocks toward his home with the music blaring. As Row made his way onto Eighth Avenue, the gray G-class Benz was one car behind them. Row looked in his rearview mirror and squinted. He thought he was seeing things, but he wasn't mistaken. It was the same vehicle from his block that was following him now. Reaching under his seat for his pistol, he cocked it back and continued to drive calmly. Apple became aware of his movements and looked back.

"What's up?" she asked.

"It's that Benz again. We being followed," he said.

"You sure?"

"I ain't stupid. This gray G-class has been on us since we left the brownstone."

Apple cocked back her pistol and took a deep breath. She was ready for anything. She'd been shot before, and it was an agonizing and traumatizing experience. She wasn't going through it again. It was going to be them before her. Row came to a stop at a red light. His eyes stayed in his rearview mirror. The Benz was approaching them slowly. He had a bad feeling. It could be anybody in the truck. He couldn't tell how many were inside.

His eyes followed the Benz as it came to a stop right behind them at the red light. Row and Apple could see a few men in the vehicle. The G-class sat up high and looked like a tank on chromed wheels. It wasn't pretty. Row was ready to run the red light, but traffic at the intersection was heavy. He kept watching in his rearview with the pistol in his hand—Apple, too. It was a tense moment. Their guts were screaming trouble, but from who? Was it the feds?

Now it seemed that they weren't trying to be subtle anymore.

The light turned green, and Row pulled off. The G-class was right behind them. Apple kept turning back, seeing the truck following them. She gripped the pistol in her hand tightly and frowned.

"Fuck these muthafuckas!" she growled.

When they came to a stop at red light at the following intersection, the chaos began. The Benz sped up next to them and came to an abrupt stop on Apple's side. With the windows down, automatic rifles and pistols extended from the Benz. Apple's eyes widened with fear. She screamed, "Shit! Go, Row! Get the fuck outta here!"

They opened fire on the 650i Coupe and a loud boom erupted in the streets. But Row's foot was already on the accelerator. He sped through the intersection and red light, just barely missing having an accident. The G-class did the same. It chased behind them. Row made a sharp right turn and sped down a narrow one-way street with the Benz trailing behind them. He blew through a red light and drove like he was in the Indy 500. Today wasn't going to be their day to die.

A few sharp turns and doing 65mph on the Harlem streets, Row managed to escape the Benz and death. They were also fortunate not to get pulled over by police. A moment later, Row pulled to the side to catch his breath and collect his thoughts. They had no idea who the men were, but they were a threat to him. The trouble was, they knew where he lived.

"Fuck, we can't go back to the house," said Row.

"I know," Apple agreed.

"Fuck!" he screamed, smashing his fist against the steering wheel.

Row looked at Apple and asked, "Were they after you?"

"I don't fuckin' know," Apple spat back.

"Apple, I've been doin' my thang for a while now, with no fuckin' trouble at all. But the minute you come back into my life, I got muthafuckas stalking my crib and trying to shoot up my ride on a public street. What the fuck is goin' on?"

"The minute I find out, then everyone's dead."

"I think someone knows that you're back in Harlem."

"Who? I've been chilling…"

"I don't know. Fuck!"

"We gonna handle this, Row. They missed, right? Now it's our turn to shoot back, and we ain't gonna miss at all," Apple said.

The following two weeks were cautious and busy for Apple. After the murder attempt on her life, she had Row's young soldiers hit the streets to find out anything about the G-class. She was adamant on finding the shooters and turning their lives into a living hell. Family, friends, whoever, no one was safe from her wrath. Apple wanted to hunt them down and destroy them. She was getting her weight and crew up again in Harlem. One goon to ride or die for her was turning into two, then three, and then she had a small following, a solid team of shooters. She had the reputation and the money. The hope of keeping a low profile in Harlem was gradually fading, and this worried Row. They had to change locations and increase their artillery, and he remembered the damage Apple caused last time.

Apple's eyes were still on the prize. She was constantly thinking about Miami and finding her daughter.

It didn't take long for word to get back to Apple about the G-class. Paying five thousand for information had people coming to Apple every day. The Benz belonged to Tatty, one of Chico's former lieutenants. It appeared he had a serious grudge against Apple, somehow found out that she was back in town, and decided to strike. But the attempt on her life was sloppy—too sloppy. Apple remembered Tatty. She'd never liked him. She never trusted him. Now she had a reason to kill him. Apple put up another five stacks to find out where Tatty laid his head. Wherever she found him would be where he took his last breath.

Two days later, she had what she needed. Row took a pull from his Newport as he sat slouched in the couch. With the gun on his lap, he continued to smoke and said nonchalantly to Apple, "How you wanna get this nigga?"

"Viciously." Apple replied.

Row smirked. "What happened to the low profile you suppose to keep?"

"Fuck that…once this muthafucka is dead, then I can relax."

Row didn't say another word. He stood up, cocked back the hammer in his grip, and proceeded toward the exit. He was ready for things to get ugly, and he was down for whatever. Apple loved the way he moved. She snatched up her pistols and was right behind Row. They weren't coming back until Tatty and whoever he had with him were slaughtered like pigs.

Tatty had a cozy residence in Yonkers, New York. It was a few miles away from Harlem, bordering the Bronx, two miles north of Manhattan. Apple and Row found themselves moving through the suburbs, not too far from I-87/Major Deegan Expressway. Row was behind the wheel of Apple's Chevy as it passed through on the residential blocks slowly. Apple eyed every address she went by. Each home looked like it belonged in some well-to-do family sitcom, like *The Brady Bunch*. The owners were so privileged and blessed. *So sickening,* Apple thought.

It was twilight in the skies, the block quiet like a cemetery. The Charger came to a stop in front of a two-story home nestled amongst the others in the picturesque community with the manicured front yards and paved driveways. Apple sat in the passenger seat and lit a cigarette. She gazed at the house for a moment. It was dark, but there was no G-class parked in the driveway. Whether someone was home or not, she was going inside, and she was ready to do like one of Biggie's rhymes—duct tape his wife and kids, pistol-whip his bitch.

"This is it, right?" she asked Row.

"Yeah. My peoples that got back to me are always accurate," he replied.

With her eyes fixed on the house, she studied everything, aware of her surroundings like a hawk, ready to charge in and exterminate everyone.

"How you wanna do this?" asked Row.

Apple emitted a pressing sigh. She decided to wait around for a moment—woman's instincts. She didn't want to miss her shot like they did theirs.

An hour passed with them watching the house in the shadows from a small distance. It was almost midnight when activity started. With Apple becoming impatient, in the nick of time, the G-class pulled into the driveway. Seeing two silhouettes in the front seats, Apple perched at the edge of her seat and watched their every movement. Tatty jumped out from the passenger side, but the driver stayed inside. Standing in the doorway was a beautiful woman with long, raven-black hair and a huge smile to see her man arriving. She was in a house robe and fuzzy slippers.

It was no time for games or hesitation. Apple was ready to show Tatty what being a real gangster was about—how to strike, shoot, and not miss. She quickly got out of the car with two pistols in her hands. She moved in the shadows like a ninja, keeping out her target's line of sight. Row wasn't too far behind her. She trotted their way, and when Tatty reached out to hug his lady hello, Apple lunged at them from the darkness and opened fire with the two .9mms in her hands.

*Bak! Bak! Bak! Bak! Bak!*

The first shot tore the back of Tatty's head open, and it viciously dropped him in front of the black-haired woman. She screamed, but it was short-lived; two shots to her head shut the bitch up and left her lying there dead next to her man. Before the driver could retaliate, Row was on him.

*Pop! Pop! Pop!*

He received three shots into his slim frame—two in the head and one in the neck. It was over like that. Row and Apple ran toward their car before the neighbors' lights flicked on and faces came to windows to be nosy.

They were gone like a thief in the night.

"So much for you keeping a low profile," Row said.

No response from Apple. With the smoking guns still in her hands, she looked out the window and exhaled. Nobody was going to fuck with her—nobody.

# CHAPTER 11

*Citi*

Citi sat by her bedroom window, thinking. L had betrayed her. He fucked her up pretty badly, and she wanted payback. But she was scared. L saw her with Marcus. He could easily spill the beans to her mother and spoil her plans. She couldn't allow that to happen. She was in love with Marcus, not L. Cane had every thug in Miami looking for L. Cane was ready to shoot first, and fuck questions. The nigga had put his hands on Cane's little sister, and there was no forgiving that.

It was a quiet afternoon. Citi removed herself from the window and went over to the mirror, looking at her reflection. The bruises were healing. It had been a week since she'd been with Marcus—a week was too long. Her body yearned for him, but business and other affairs had taken him away for the moment.

She went back to the window. When she saw Marcus's car turning into the circular driveway, she smiled broadly. She watched him climb out his car, looking ravishing in his dark suit and blue tie as he headed inside. The first place he was going was his office. It was business, always business. Citi rushed out of her bedroom; she wanted to greet him downstairs before he could lock himself away in the office and be alone. When she got to the foot of the stairs, Ashanti had already beaten her to the punch. She was hugging Marcus and kissing him like a loving wife should. Citi's smile turned into a frown. She wanted to say, *Bitch, get your hands off my man,* but she kept her cool.

"You need anything, Citi?" Ashanti asked.

"No, I don't," Citi replied, sourly.

Citi eyed Marcus and continued to frown at her mother. Yeah, they were married, but Marcus was her man. She loved him. Ashanti didn't know how to fuck him like she did. Marcus carried the same blank look on his handsome face. It seemed he had a lot on his mind.

"How was business today, baby?"

Marcus pulled away from his wife's loving hold. "The fuckin' same. I'll be in my office." He marched down the hallway.

Feeling unloved, Ashanti took a deep breath. There had to be another woman in her man's life, she just didn't know who. She then turned her attention to Citi. Fixing her hurt look into one of concern for her daughter, she asked, "How are you feeling today?"

"I'm fine," Citi replied.

Ashanti approached her daughter, but Citi wasn't in the mood to talk to her mother about anything. She stepped back from Ashanti and said, "Just leave me alone, Mom. I'm okay."

"Are you sure?" Ashanti asked.

"Yes."

Ashanti didn't want to push her daughter. It was understandable that she was in a foul mood. She had been assaulted by the man she once trusted. It was going to take time for her to come around. Citi folded her arms across her chest; Ashanti just wanted her daughter to be fine.

"Citi, if you need me, I'll be in my office and then I have to head out. I have a lot to do today. You know I'm starting another business soon."

Citi didn't want to hear about another one of her mother's businesses. Ashanti already had the hair salon at South Pointe and an upcoming entertainment and modeling agency in South Beach that was doing okay.

The start-up money came from Marcus, and now Ashanti was running around town like she was the female Donald Trump. It gave her something to do.

Citi wanted something to do—she wanted to do Marcus, and she wanted to be in her mother's shoes. She envied her mother every single day, watching her run the household and run her businesses, always on her cell phone, making vital moves, with access to the checkbooks and the credit cards at the ready.

Citi was used to being the princess, spoiled by her father. And now to watch her mother being the spoiled one, the woman who'd abandoned her for so many years and left her family to rot and fend for themselves all on their own back in New York—it truly bothered Citi. She had to watch someone else receive all the attention and adulation, and it was more than she could take.

"Well, I see you're not too talkative today," Ashanti said.

Citi wanted to say something sarcastic, but she held her tongue and went the other way, leaving her mother standing in the room, perplexed.

"What is wrong with that girl?" Ashanti asked herself.

Citi went into her bedroom, closed the door, and shut the blinds. She plopped down on her queen-size bed, spread her legs, closed her eyes, and shoved her hand down her panties and gradually started to play with herself. She just needed to escape somewhere, and fingering her clit made her travel somewhere nice. She cooed as her wetness saturated her fingertips. She had Marcus on her mind. She envisioned him naked and climbing on top of her, her legs wrapping around him like a cocoon. She could feel his large penis penetrating her as she played with her pussy. She cupped her breast and pinched her nipple. Sounds of pleasure escaped from her quivering lips.

Hearing a car door slam shut interrupted her pleasurable moment. Citi rushed from the bed and moved toward the window, fearing Marcus was leaving again. She pulled back the blinds only to see it was her mother leaving the premises. She sighed with relief and smiled.

*Let that bitch be gone all night*, she thought.

Ashanti drove away in her Maserati, leaving Citi alone with her husband once again.

Citi got decent and walked out of her bedroom. The house was quiet; the staff had retired for the day. Citi moved toward Marcus's office. It was situated at the rear of the house near the backyard and pool. When she got to the door, she took a deep breath. She knocked and felt her heart beating fast like drums. With her mother away, she felt the urge to play with her boo thang.

She knew Marcus was stressed out; she saw his nasty reaction to Ashanti. He barely wanted to touch her. Citi knew she would be able to relieve her man from his worries; it was what a real bitch did for her man. It was too bad that her mother didn't know the art of seduction. Citi was ready to be there for him. But before the fun happened, she needed to reveal the truth about that night with L. She was filled with concern, but it needed to be told and exposed.

"Who is it?" Marcus's voice boomed from the other side.

Citi knew he was busy. His office was his safe haven away from the gritty, cutthroat world of Miami, and even from his family. When Marcus wanted to be left alone, it was like a death sentence to interrupt him during his moment of solitude.

"It's me, Citi," she said.

"I don't have any time for you, so leave, Citi," he shouted.

"I need to talk to you about somethin' important."

"Citi, I'm in no mood right now," he growled.

"You need to hear what I have to say, because this can't wait," she exclaimed.

The office door opened up and Marcus stepped toward her, upset.

He didn't want to be bothered, especially by a salacious young girl who was always hot in the panties. He wasn't in the mood for sex; it was obvious from his reaction. He had business to handle. However, Citi was adamant in getting his attention, and now she had it. He looked at her unpleasantly. With Marcus, she couldn't sugarcoat what she needed to tell him. Her stepfather's time was valuable and you dared not waste it by beating around the bush.

"What do you have to tell me that's important?" Marcus asked pointedly. "And it better be important."

"It's about the night Bones and Shotta were killed," she mentioned. "I know who did it."

She had his attention now.

Marcus's frown grew heavier. "You better not be lying to me, Citi. This is serious shit," he warned.

"I'm not lying, Marcus."

"Then let's talk," he said, taking a step to the side and allowing her into his office.

When the door shut, Marcus stood closely behind Citi. She turned around. He looked at her healing bruises for a moment. He figured L was long gone by now, probably back to New York. Marcus once had love for him, but no one violated his family or his home. He didn't care who you were. The threat against L was doubled, coming from Cane and Marcus. Cane went about things his way while Marcus went about finding L his way. They figured with pressure coming from both sides, the muthafucka would soon turn up and crack like a walnut in vise grips.

"Only monsters beat young ladies like this," Marcus said, taking her small chin into his hand and examining her like he was a doctor.

Citi loved the way he was touching her. In her mind, only a man in love with her would truly care. The way he touched her where she was hurting made Citi feel like she was someone special.

"We'll find him," Marcus assured her.

Citi smiled. It was now hard to tell him. She already had Marcus ready to kill for her. The contract on L's life had been sent out. The goons were looking everywhere in Miami. And for Citi, it was a thrill and an alluring high to have a man like Marcus ready to kill for her.

"Now, what's so important that you had to tell me about Bones and Shotta? You were there in the club when it happened, so fuckin' speak your mind, Citi," Marcus demanded with his cold, black eyes fixed on Citi.

She sighed heavily, her smile and thrilling feeling fleeting. She had already opened her mouth. Now the truth needed to come out. She couldn't just come up with some bullshit story to tell her stepfather.

Citi looked into Marcus's cold and expressionless eyes. "L did it."

Marcus seemed dumbfounded by the news. "Fuck you mean, L did it? Explain yourself, Citi. This is not a fuckin' joke," Marcus growled through clenched teeth.

The box had been opened; now the contents needed to come out. Citi needed to explain the story in such a way that she didn't look bad in his eyes. "L and Bones got into it on the dance floor and a fight broke out," she said.

"And what was the fight about in the first place? L and Bones had no reason to interact with each other. That's a vague description of the incident, Citi. I need more to go on. What really happened?" Marcus asked with much suspicion to her story.

"I don't know," she lied.

Marcus wasn't buying it. His eyes sunk into Citi like quicksand and he began to press her even harder. "You're telling me that you were there and you don't know why two men that have no dealings with each other suddenly got into it? For some reason I don't believe you at all."

Citi swallowed hard. Her stepfather's eyes were burning a hole into her. His fierce look was always intimidating. He already knew she was hiding the full truth. She sighed heavily once more, and was ready to let everything go.

"They were fighting over me. I was dancing, kinda tipsy, and tryin' to have a good time. Bones came over to me and I got smart and really nasty wit' him. L was defending me, protecting my honor. The two fought, a big fight broke out, and they jumped on him. L wouldn't let it go, so at the end of the fight, he waited around for them to leave the club and he shot them both down. That's the truth, Marcus. I swear," Citi insisted.

She didn't see it coming. Marcus slapped her so hard, Citi spun around in a circle and fell over, hitting the floor. He contradicted his statement from earlier about monsters beating on young, beautiful women. He was a monster himself.

"You dumb, fuckin' bitch," Marcus exclaimed. "You should have told me this shit the night it happened. Why keep this from me?"

Citi hugged the floor. She was too frightened to get up right away. Marcus towered over her in rage.

"I'm sorry, baby. I was just so scared to tell you," she cried out.

"You should have told me that someone in my own house did this. Now I look like a fuckin' fool." Marcus was seething heavily.

He glared down at Citi and was ready to put his hands on her again, but he restrained himself. He needed a drink. He went over to where he kept bottles of alcohol and picked up a twelve-ounce bottle of vodka and poured a glass. He took a few sips while Citi remained glued to the floor. He walked back over to her and looked down.

"L. We're going to find him no matter where he's hiding, and I'm going to personally fuck his shit up," Marcus said calmly.

Citi didn't respond to his comment. She didn't know what to say or do. It was obvious that Marcus was upset and she didn't want to cause any more trouble for him and herself. The tears started to fall like a waterfall from her eyes. It felt like her heart was being ripped from her chest. She picked herself up from the floor and wiped her face with the back of her hands. She knew she had fucked up.

"I can make it up to you, baby," Citi said faintly.

"Make it up to me?" he questioned.

She was ready to suck his dick right there in his office. She was ready to give him the best blow job he ever had, until her lips were numb. She had to make it up to him somehow or someway. But Marcus was unpredictable and dangerous, so there was no telling what might come next from him. He frowned at her and exclaimed, "Get the fuck out my office."

Citi wanted to apologize again, but she figured it was best to leave. She was already on his bad side and you don't debate with a man of his power. You just leave when you are told to leave. She rushed out of his office and ran toward her bedroom. For Citi, it felt like things were falling apart around her. Now she felt her mother had one up on her and it was a sickening feeling.

She stayed behind in her bedroom for a long moment. The butterflies and nauseating feeling in her stomach weren't getting any better. Citi hid under the covers and couldn't stop crying. She couldn't lose Marcus's love; she thought it was love, that he loved her, too.

A half-hour later, Citi heard another car door slam outside her bedroom window. She went toward the window; it was Marcus, leaving. He rushed from the house and got into his Benz. Something was about to go down. She felt it. Citi didn't leave the bedroom window until Marcus's Benz disappeared from her sight. The only thing Citi could do was hope he would forgive her and that they could continue on with their intense sex sessions. She would die if Marcus coldly ignored her and didn't want to be with her anymore. It was a thought that made Citi sick and made her do a beeline to the bathroom and throw up. She was in love, and living without him was impossible.

Cane and his goons pulled up to the hole in the wall spot on Martin Luther King Blvd/62nd Street. They were armed and dangerous. Cane jumped out of the white Lexus with the .45 in his hand and the look to murder someone showing in his eyes. He was flanked by two thugs who were ready to kill for him. He had gotten word that L was trying to leave town and was hiding out at the Sugar Shack until he received the funds needed to go back to New York.

L had been hiding out there for a week now, staying low in a back room and making phone calls to New York. The owner of the place subtly gave him up. Even though he was L's distant cousin, he didn't want any problems with Cane or Marcus. Problems with them two meant your life was about to be over.

Cane looked at his two soldiers and gruffly said, "Yo, we go in here and we fuck this nigga up. Drop that nigga where you see him."

"No doubt," one goon replied.

They walked toward the club refusing to conceal their pistols. They were there to make a very strong statement. Cane was ready to explode like firecrackers going off during the fourth of July.

But before they could set foot in the raunchy looking establishment, a glinting black Cadillac STS came to a sudden stop near them in the parking lot. Three ominous-looking men jumped out and hurried toward Cane to confront him. Cane was ready to open fire, but he quickly recognized them. They were Marcus's henchmen, and they didn't look too happy.

Cane glared at them and shouted, "What the fuck y'all doin' here?"

"Marcus wants him brought back alive," one of the men stated.

"Nah, fuck that, this nigga dies tonight," Cane shouted back.

"You don't call the shots, Cane. Marcus wants him alive, so he comes back with us alive," the man said sternly.

"So, this nigga could put his hands on my fuckin' sister and he ain't supposed to die? You fuckin' serious, nigga? Y'all just gonna allow him to disrespect my family like that?"

Marcus's henchmen weren't at all concerned about what Cane had to say. They were immune to his emotions and only there to do a job for the boss.

"You have a dispute with the boss, then you call him. But don't get in our way," the man warned.

Cane was infuriated by the sudden change of situation, but he had to reluctantly back down. He scowled, letting the men go by him and into the club. With the .45 still in his hand, he took aim at the back of someone's head and pretended to fire. "Bang!" he mouthed. Too bad the shot wasn't real.

Security at the door gave Marcus's men no problems. Their status was already known. Like authority figures, they hurried through the nightclub with the blaring rap music, rudely pushing past the patrons and making their way to the back of the venue.

They reached a narrow and badly lit foyer which led to stairs into the basement. The area was off-limits to everyone except the owner and a few trusted workers.

Marching down the stairs, the three henchmen removed their automatic pistols from their holsters and cocked back the hammers, readying themselves for anything. L was scared and possibly armed. Derrick, the owner of the nightclub, led the way. He brought them to a brown door: "He's in there."

The men nodded. Derrick took a few steps back away from the door and allowed the killers to handle their business. They kicked in the door with brute force and rushed into the room, catching L completely off guard. He jumped from the chair he was in and tried to reach for the pistol near him, but he was too late. They were on L like white on rice, beating him to the ground with their fists and guns.

"Get the fuck off me! I ain't do shit!" L screamed.

"Shut the fuck up!" one of the men shouted.

L tried to fight back, but he was overpowered with his face pushed against the floor and his body feeling like it was on fire from the hits he received. He could barely move. They subdued him to the ground and continued to assault him until his face was covered in blood. He was barely conscious when they dragged him out the back, away from nosy stares in the club. They exited toward the parking lot.

Cane and his gun-toting thugs still lingered in the area. When Cane saw them dragging L to the Cadillac, he scowled, rushed over to the activity, and raised his pistol at the man. He wanted to shoot him dead right there. But Marcus's thugs were ready to prevent it from happening.

"I said back the fuck down, Cane!" one henchman shouted.

Seething with rage, Cane kept his weapon aimed at his target. His eyes were blood red, and his itchy finger lingered on the trigger. He was dying to squeeze and let the bullets fly. No one was going to tell him what to do.

"Fuck that! Nigga put hands on my sister, and y'all walkin' him the fuck out!" Cane shouted.

"I said back the fuck down, Cane!" the man reiterated strongly, but this time aiming his Glock at Cane's head.

"So, it's like that now?"

"I'm not going to warn you again. Put the fuckin' gun down!"

Boxed into a corner, Cane lowered the gun. The man also lowered his Glock from Cane's face, but tension still remained. Cane watched them stuff L into the Cadillac's trunk and shut it. He had been badly beaten, and it angered Cane that he'd had no part in the punishment.

"Y'all some fucked-up niggas. I need a piece of him, too," Cane growled.

They ignored his comment, and all three climbed into the Cadillac STS. The ignition started and the car drove off.

Cane felt disrespected. He looked at his two goons and said, "I'm supposed to just sit back and take this shit? Fuck outta here!"

His violent cowboys were quiet; their moment of action was gone with the wind. They climbed back into the Lexus and hurried toward Marcus's estate.

The blows rained down heavily on L, drawing blood from his jaw and bruising his face. L sat bonded to a chair with his arms folded behind him and his hands tied tightly. He could barely move. Every part of him was swollen, bloody, or black and blue. There were half a dozen sullen men standing around him in the room.

Marcus just wanted to severely punish him. He wanted to get his hands dirty on this one and torture L. The young nigga from New York needed to know how things worked in Miami. He continued to punch L with the brass knuckles clamped around his right hand. The last punch knocked out two teeth and cut his lip.

"You lied to me, L. I don't like liars," Marcus exclaimed.

"Fuck you!" L shouted.

"Did you just say fuck me, muthafucka?" Marcus shouted angrily. "Who the fuck you think you're talking to, muthafucka?"

Marcus grabbed L by his hair and yanked his neck back so roughly, you almost heard it snap and then pop. The boss then got into L's face, his spit landing on L's beaten face. "Welcome to Miami, nigga, hope you enjoyed the city," Marcus taunted.

He continued to beat L's face in with the brass knuckles. He started to make his face look like putty. L felt like he was about to choke on his own blood.

"You made a serious problem for me, L, when you killed Bones and

Shotta. You created some drama in my city, made me lose fuckin' money because of this ongoing war with the Miami Gotti Boys and the Ghost Ridas, and you laid hands on my stepdaughter. You gotta be one crazy asshole, nigga. You fucked up and didn't think I would find out about it. I fuckin' run this city, nigga. I'm god here. I know about everything that goes on. I own you, nigga!" Marcus heavily growled.

The blows continued, this time to his body. Marcus attacked L's ribs repeatedly until he felt a few break under the pressure. L howled from the severe pain burning on the inside of him while Marcus was breathing heavy. It was becoming a workout to punish a man with fists.

"You have my city swimming in rapid bloodshed because of your ignorance. This isn't Harlem, muthafucka, this is Miami," Marcus exclaimed.

L knew he was a dead man anyway, so he decided not to go out like a punk.

"You fuckin' hypocrite!" L spat.

"Did you say something li'l nigga?"

L coughed heavily. He spit out blood and could hardly speak coherently. Marcus glared at his handiwork. His own fists were swollen, bloody and bruised. He was clad in a wife-beater, his physique a phenomenon. The hits against L were like being pounded by a sledgehammer.

Marcus looked at his thugs and joked, "This is one tough muthafucka, I'll tell you that."

His men laughed.

"I'll give y'all this; y'all niggas from New York can sure take a beating. Usually, when I hit a nigga this hard and for this long, they don't last... tell 'em, Chuck."

"They don't," Chuck replied.

L continued to cough.

"Speak muthafucka!" Marcus shouted.

"I...I loved her..." L said incoherently.

"You loved who?" asked Marcus.

L didn't answer right away. He felt himself slipping in and out of consciousness.

"Talk, muthafucka!" Marcus punched him again.

L woke back up and glared at Marcus.

"Citi, you took her from me. You turned her against me. I saw you fuckin' her," L informed him.

Marcus chuckled. "You're honestly tripping over this young bitch? A piece of ass? She ain't anything but some good pussy to me, muthafucka. I had the mother; it was only right for me to know what the daughter feels like, too. You know what, you're a fuckin' idiot, and I can't have idiots around me. I thought you were built differently, L…but you ain't, nigga. You ain't one of us, and never will be."

He was done punishing L. Marcus reached for the .9mm and pressed the tip of the barrel to L's forehead. L didn't flinch. He glared at Marcus and was ready to die. Citi had played him. She used him, and it was a mistake following her down to Miami.

With his last breath, L spit his blood at Marcus. The glob of bloody spit landed on Marcus's face like a birthmark.

"Fuck you, Marcus, you gonna get yours," L spat.

Marcus became enraged and disgusted. He wiped the bloody spit from his face and attacked L with the gun. He brutally pistol-whipped him and then thrust the gun at his forehead again and squeezed.

*Bam! Bam!*

Two bullets were put into L's forehead, leaving him slumped in the chair. Marcus stood over the body with no emotion, the smoking gun in his hand, his point clearly demonstrated to his men.

"What the fuck, Marcus?! I wanted a piece of him. He was mine!"

Cane rushed into the room with his pistol gripped tightly and was ready to take deadly action. But Marcus instantly shut things down.

"Fall the fuck back, Cane!" Marcus warned.

"Nah, fuck that, he was mines to deal wit'!" Cane shouted.

"Who the fuck you think you're talking to like that, Cane? Remember where you are. This is my fuckin' house and my city. You do things my way, not yours. You understand?" Marcus stated sharply.

Cane didn't respond. So Marcus had to shout it louder for him to hear. "Do you fuckin' understand me, Cane? You fuckin' better!"

"Yeah, I understand," Cane replied bitterly.

He looked over at L's body drooping in the chair and then he glared at Marcus. Seething, Cane knew he couldn't win. He missed the news about Marcus fucking his little sister, because if he had heard that statement coming from L's mouth, without any hesitation, Cane would have put a bullet in Marcus's head right there. He loved Citi to death, and he would protect her at any cost, especially with their father dead and their older brother Chris doing time back in New York.

"Since you want him so bad, Cane, then you clean up the mess and do with him as you please," Marcus instructed.

"What?"

"You heard what the fuck I said. Clean this shit up, and then come see me for further instruction."

It was a slap in the face to Cane. Marcus was publicly trying to humiliate him in front of his men. Marcus was his mother's husband; Black Mamba of Miami—but none of that mattered if Cane shot him dead.

Marcus pushed past Cane and exited the room. His henchmen followed. Cane was left there sulking and feeling cheated. When the room was empty, he walked over to the body and grunted. Miami was never his home, and he didn't have any ties there. Nobody was going to run Cane or make a bitch out of him. He always had respect for Marcus, but the Black Mamba made a huge mistake when he tried to embarrass Cane in front of his peers. Cane didn't take that act lightly.

# CHAPTER 12

## Apple

Apple walked into the Starbucks on the corner of 125th Street and Lenox Avenue on high alert with her head low. She needed her caffeine and a few snacks. The place always had a crowd of diversified customers ready to pay high prices for some coffee. The line wasn't long, thank God; Apple had places to go and things to do. She remained undercover, mostly moving during the evening hours. Wearing her usual attire—sweats and a fitted ball cap worn low over her eyes—she awaited her turn. Things looked normal to her. However, she kept her pistol close, safety off, just in case shit went down.

She ordered a cappuccino and a croissant. After ordering and stepping back from the counter, she noticed the newspaper in front of her. The ghastly murders in Yonkers had made the front page and were on the evening news. She read the headline. The woman she'd shot was four months pregnant. Apple hadn't been able to tell because of the robe the woman had on. The community was in uproar and disgusted by it. They wanted to see arrests quickly made. Someone had to be held accountable for shooting a woman who was four months pregnant.

For Apple, it was good riddance to bitch-ass niggas like Tatty. *What the fuck kind of name was Tatty?* Apple thought. She smirked. She remained cavalier, but he high-profile murders were creating too much attention, and she was already on the feds' radar, probably one of the top ten most wanted on the FBI's list. She needed to go underground, maybe get out of town for a while.

Apple picked up her order and was ready to leave the Starbucks, but she noticed a man looking at her—watching almost every move closely. He was seated at one of the tables near the window with today's newspaper in front of him, sipping hot coffee and munching a donut. His baseball cap and sweats were almost identical to hers. He was a handsome black man, with nice brown skin and a grayish goatee. He seemed to be in his early forties. It was obvious that she had his full attention. Her suspicion grew. Was he police or an undercover FBI agent? How did they find her so fast? Apple tried to remain calm. Was she caught up in a sting?

His eyes remained on her. He wasn't trying to be duplicitous about it either. It was almost like he wanted her to know he was watching her. Apple took a deep breath. She didn't make a quick exit from the Starbucks. She decided to go into the ladies' bathroom. Once inside, she removed her pistol and tossed it into the trash can. If he was a cop and they were ready to bust her, she didn't want to get caught with it. Apple had to keep playing her part if she wanted to stay out of prison. Her name was Lisa Johnson and she had the passport and license that said so. Period. She looked into the mirror. She didn't even recognize herself, so how could a cop? Her ride was parked around the corner, and Row was in New Jersey handling business.

*Fuck it*, Apple said to herself. "Let's do this."

She exited the bathroom; the stranger watching her wasn't seated there anymore. She looked around. He was nowhere to be found. What was going on? Apple hurried out of the Starbucks, leaving her purchase on the countertop. An employee called out to her, shouting, "Miss, you forgot your order. Miss…"

Apple ignored him. Once outside, before she could take three steps, he approached her.

"Can I buy you another cup of coffee?" he asked, quietly .

Apple was spooked. She thought at any moment, swarms of police cars were going to come out of nowhere and lock her up, and she was going to spend the rest of her life in jail. She looked around nervously.

"I'm okay," she replied, trying to move away from him briskly.

"Are you sure? Let's go for a walk then," he suggested.

"I walk alone."

"Well, now you don't," said the stranger stubbornly.

Apple was unarmed and alone. *What is this about?* she thought.

"My name is Jonathan." He held out his hand for a handshake. "And may I have the pleasure of knowing your name?"

Apple was now really confused. He stood in front of her, blocking her way. He was taller than he'd appeared in the Starbucks. He seemed very distinguished and educated. Apple quickly sized him up. She figured he couldn't be a cop; they didn't take this long to arrest their perps, and they didn't give out handshakes and first names.

"I'm Lisa," she lied.

"Lisa, that's a very nice name. You caught my eye in the Starbucks. I saw you in the hat and sweats, and I find you to be a very beautiful woman. Do you run, or work out?"

"Sometimes," she continued to lie.

"Well, maybe you and I can go running someday. I just came running from Central Park." he mentioned.

*What's his motive?* Apple wondered. He wasn't her type at all. He wasn't a threat to her anymore, and now Jonathan seemed more like a cornball when he talked. He was eyeing her because he was attracted to her. Apple was ready to disappear from his sight. She found no use for him.

"I live in a brownstone not too far from here," he said.

"Jonathan, you don't know me and I sure don't know you," Apple said.

"Well, maybe we can get to know each other someday," he replied.

"That probably will never happen."

"And why not? Is it because of my age?"

"I just have a lot going on right now, and I'm not too trusting of strangers coming into my life," she stated.

"I see," he replied downheartedly. "So how about a cup of coffee or lunch one afternoon? Just one cup and conversation with you. That's all I'm asking for."

He was pushing it. Apple was ready to explode on him, but his cell phone rang. "Excuse me, I need to take this," he said, answering the phone call.

Apple was ready to walk away, but suddenly she found his conversation over the phone interesting.

"Hey, Counselor, I finally get you to call back," said Jonathan.

Apple delayed leaving. She started to ear hustle.

"I already took care of the dilemma. He agreed to a hundred thousand. I spoke to Paul Gibson earlier, and the papers are being drawn up as we speak. Yes. Yes. I'll give you my deposition first thing Monday morning. I'll have my assistant draft the paperwork needed and then we'll proceed with litigations first thing next week," Jonathan said.

Apple continued to listen.

"Yes, it will get done. I'll have my people on that right away. Okay, you have a good day, too. Bye." Jonathan hung up and smiled at Apple.

"If you don't mind me asking, what is it that you do?" she asked.

He continued to smile at her. "I'm an attorney."

"You are, huh?"

"Yes. I'm a former district attorney with the Brooklyn DA's office. But now I run my own profitable civil law firm in Manhattan."

Apple found that to be very interesting and suddenly found him to be useful. She was no longer in a rush to leave. She stepped closer to Jonathan and said to him, "You still want to have that cup of coffee?"

He could only smile.

Jonathan Waken was his full name, and his lavish brownstone on the upper west side of Harlem, near Riverside Drive was something out of a "best homes" magazine. Apple was impressed. When Apple walked into the home, an apple-cinnamon flavor immediately nourished her nose. As he showed her around the place, Apple took in the countless degrees hanging on his walls: two masters' degrees from Colombia University and a bachelor's degree from Harvard, along with a doctorate—countless awards and certificates.

Jonathan owned the whole brownstone—three floors of luxury. From the small foyer, they entered the great room that doubled as a kitchen and a living room, dominated by a huge, black granite-topped island. The great room included a sitting area with a fireplace and a huge 60-inch plasma television screen, as well as a dining room table and chairs.

There were two big mirrors on the side of each wall. The golden living room set sat beautifully on the tan carpet. Down the hallway to her right was his office. Everything was in polished cherry wood.

It was a slice of heaven, but Apple had seen better and bigger homes before, from Eduardo's sprawling estate to her own home upstate when she was dealing with Chico. Men treated her like royalty; she just didn't let Jonathan know that. He believed she was Lisa from Harlem—it was the partial truth about her life.

Jonathan went over to his minibar and poured himself a glass of scotch. He offered Apple a drink, but she declined. She hardly knew him and needed to remain alert. Jonathan downed his scotch and they continued to talk. Surprisingly, she was enjoying the conversation with him. He was highly intelligent, educated, and not as much of a cornball as she'd thought he was. Apple figured she could use him for information. He appeared to have some clout with the bigwigs, lawyers, and politicians in New York. Knowing Jonathan would definitely have its advantages.

"I need a shower. You can make yourself at home," said Jonathan.

Apple planned to.

"You have access to anything you like in here. The TV remote and DVDs are over there on the shelf, music is to your right, and anything in the kitchen is yours if you get hungry," Jonathan said.

Apple smiled. "Are you always this welcoming to strangers in your life?"

"No, but there's something about you that I like."

"You're not a serial killer, are you? Because I do know how to defend myself," she joked.

Jonathan laughed. "No, far from it. I should be the one worried about you, because you are the one in my home; my sanctuary. And I do carry pistols."

"Oh, really?"

"But I'm a good guy, just attracted to a beautiful, young woman," he added.

"I see."

"But I'll be in the shower. I won't take long."

"Take your time," said Apple.

"Just don't steal anything."

"I'm no thief," she replied dryly.

She watched Jonathan walk away and into the bathroom. She snooped around his home briefly, and everything seemed okay. Her fear of being set up weakened. She browsed through his CD collection and saw that he was into reggae and pop music heavily. There weren't too many rap or R&B CDs for her to listen to. Apple turned and stared at the bathroom Jonathan had disappeared into. She headed that way, slowly stripping away her clothing and leaving a trail to the bathroom door. She could hear the shower running and when she turned the knob, the door was unlocked. It probably indicated that he was hoping that she would join him soon.

Apple slowly entered the master bathroom. She could see Jonathan's silhouette behind the glass shower door. Apple proceeded forward. She pulled back the shower door and took in Jonathan's nudeness. He wasn't a bit startled. He only smiled and said, "I was wondering when you were going to join me."

She smiled and stepped into the steam-filled shower. His physique wasn't magnificent, or eye catching, but mere average. He didn't have any definition or muscles to him, but a hairy chest and flat stomach. His penis size was also average. Apple knew she could work with him. His body wasn't the best or the sexiest, but his clout and status made up for it.

Jonathan pulled Apple into his arms underneath the streaming water that cascaded off of them. Their lips collided with fever and his hands journeyed across her body, massaging her round, succulent ass and cupping her sweet tits. Their bodies were pressed together like a wet pretzel. Apple reached down and grabbed Jonathan's penis. His arousal grew to a painful edge as she slowly jerked him off. She rubbed her palm over his head and started stroking him with more vigor. Jonathan moaned with eagerness. Apple was ready to give him an evening that he wouldn't forget. She gripped the back of his neck tightly and yanked him toward her. Her mouth latched onto his once more and she pressed her nude, wet front to his. Apple's lovely body molded to his, and he felt her free hand continuing to grope his painful erection. She gave him a gentle squeeze and several arousing strokes while she kissed him passionately.

Ready to do the unthinkable, she lowered herself onto her knees and took his erection into her mouth. Apple moaned, and the moan vibrated Jonathan's dick between her lips. He shoved her head hard against his dick, feeling the head of his prick sink past her tongue and into Apple's young throat. She sucked and swallowed, the motions of her throat coaxing the orgasm out of Jonathan's balls. Apple moaned again with Jonathan's head thrown back and his eyes shutting tight from the unbelievable blow job he was receiving. He was now thrusting into her mouth; both of his hands were wound through her hair and pressing into the back of her skull. Every now and then, her thumb would roll across the top of the head, collecting the precum.

"Oh shit! Oh, that feels so good," he groaned.

Apple's full, juicy lips moved back and forth on his dick. A single tear ran down from the side of Jonathan's eyes with his head leaned forward. His eyes were opened and they were glued to the woman that was sucking his dick, expertly. He couldn't take the intense oral bliss any longer. He needed to feel her insides.

Apple removed herself from her knees. Jonathan lifted Apple's leg and gently slid his penis inside her tight pussy, with the water surging against them. Her hands were pressed against the wall, both her legs now wrapped around his waist. Her pussy opened up when Jonathan's hips thrust forward, impaling her with his dick. Apple groaned at the motion.

"Ooooh, damn, your pussy feels so good. Ooooh, you feel so good," Jonathan cried out.

He pulled her onto his sex. His eyes closed as he felt her juices saturating his entire manhood. The pussy was so good to him, that he wasn't even going to last a minute. Jonathan's hands started tensing into fists as his whole body went rigid feeling the explosion inside him about to happen.

"I'm gonna cum!" he cried out.

"Pull out," said Apple.

A few more strokes inside her tight, clenching vagina and he was going to burst like a geyser. His loud grunting and moaning indicated that he wasn't complaining about the feeling of her tender, firm pussy wrapped around his dick. He shut his eyes and thrust hard and deep inside her. He continued to grunt and right before his nut, he pulled out from her warm and wet insides and shot off his white, sticky load onto the shower floor. It came out of him like water shooting out from a garden hose. His mouth opened wide with excited lust.

"Shit!" he uttered, feeling spent.

She gave him what he needed, great sex. They washed away their uncleanness afterwards and stepped out of the shower. Jonathan felt more alive than before. He needed to release himself and Apple was the perfect remedy—spontaneous sex was always the best sex.

The two continued to relax and talk more. Apple started to feel more at home in his place. He knew so much and was so ambitious. The plus was when she found out he planned on running for district attorney of New York. She would do well to be under his arm. But her past could easily get in the way, and how much pull did Jonathan Waken truly have? When shit hit the fan, would he be able to prevent her from receiving lengthy jail time?

Round two continued in Jonathan's bedroom, where he stretched Apple out across his king size bed and dug deep into her pussy. He loved every minute of it. Late in the evening, Apple knew she was going to spend the night. She wanted to know more about her new friend.


Apple woke up the next morning to find Jonathan wasn't in bed with her. It had been an exhilarating night. He was something new in her life, something different. She wasn't in a rush to go back to her own place, so she figured she would chill and talk with Jonathan some more. The more they talked and shared things, the more interested she became in him. She donned a long T-shirt and left the bedroom to explore the house. The parquet flooring sprawled everywhere inside the house, and the warmth of the home caused a small tingle to travel down her spine.

She went from room to room searching for Jonathan. She explored all of the first floor and then journeyed upwards onto the second floor. Where the first floor was more homelike, the second floor's décor seemed more like stepping into a Manhattan office. Printers and fax machines lined the hallway, and each room had a different style. Literally, someone had brought their work home.

Apple found Jonathan in the last room on her right. He was seated in a high-backed leather chair behind a polished mahogany desk and talking business over the phone. She peeked in, Jonathan waved her inside. He smiled and continued his talk.

"Yeah, Henry, I understand that…and your point is?" he waited for a response. "I don't see it that way."

Apple stepped farther into the office. The walls were an eggshell color and there were more diplomas and admissions certificates on the walls. There was plant life around, an expensive looking Ariel rug, and a grandfather clock in the room. On his desk were a giant computer screen, a business-card holder, and a photo of a young man who appeared to be in his early twenties. She assumed it was his son.

"It depends on your definition of it, Henry," Jonathan continued. "C'mon, it is possible under the equity law. Yeah, legal opinion is currently divided over this matter…uh huh, yeah…yes, I read about the Act and let's put it this way, the section can be interpreted in either way."

Apple stood in the office and waited patiently for him to finish his talk. She didn't understand what the conversation was about, but it seemed really important. Law talk went over her head—in one ear and out the other. The only thing she knew was the streets, how to kill people, drugs, and pain.

"I'll talk to you later about this, Henry. I have company at the moment, and I can't be rude," said Jonathan.

He hung up and then stood up from his high-backed chair to greet Apple with a hug and kiss. "I see you're finally awake. Did you sleep well last night?"

"I did."

"Are you hungry?"

"I'm starving."

"Good, then I'll treat you to breakfast in the city. I know a wonderful place that serves the best eggs and pancakes."

"Sound delicious."

Jonathan was so lively and down to earth. It felt like he didn't want her to leave his side. After breakfast, he wanted to take her shopping in the city. Apple went along pretending to be a charity case, someone he wanted to treat and take care of, for some reason. She had her own money, but she was ready to spend his—if he wanted to be the fool and allow it to happen.

Jonathan took Apple shopping, purchasing a few things from Fifth Avenue, and then they went to get lunch. The café in SoHo was a friendly place with a small upstairs balcony and a good selection of salads, toasted sandwiches, and fruit juices. It was a tranquil place for a meal and a relaxed place to converse. It was nestled in the bustling downtown area, away from Harlem. With the weather nice and sunny, Apple was all smiles with Jonathan. Clad in her new linen dress and heels, she didn't appear to be the venomous woman so many knew her to be, but a pleasant woman having lunch in SoHo.

Their day continued with a walk through Central Park and touring the Midtown area. Later on they enjoyed Times Square and a nice dinner at Sparks Steak House on 46th Street. And then, at night, it was another intense sexual session at his brownstone. She needed someplace to lie low for a while. Jonathan's place was perfect.

By day, Apple was off running her flourishing drug empire, and at night, she was with Jonathan, becoming intimate with her new lover, enjoying her wild affair with her new lawyer friend. The pussy was so good to him that he was falling in love with her. Putting her plan into action after three weeks of fucking his brains out, she started to secretly videotape their conversations and sexual exploits.

Unbeknownst to Jonathan, while he was away doing business, Apple had set up wireless spy cameras and mini microphones in his bedroom, his office, the living room, and other major areas throughout the house where they either had sex or talked, or where he discussed private matters via phone. It was nothing personal, only business. Jonathan didn't know what type of woman he was dealing with.

The sex videos and conversations gave Apple the upper hand. Since Jonathan was a prominent New York attorney, it would be easy to blackmail him for money, but what Apple truly wanted was information. Her time was running out. With her daughter on her mind constantly, she was ready to act—it was time to confront her lawyer and reveal her real motives.

It was a chilly summer night when Apple pulled up to Jonathan's brownstone with one of her gun-toting goons in the car with her. Sin was her personal beast in the streets. He was a vicious muthafucka with a strong appetite for violence and murder.

"You want me to go in wit' you, fuck this nigga up and get what you need from him?" Sin asked gruffly.

"Not now. I just want to have a talk with him," said Apple.

Sin nodded, but he was ready to strike.

Apple stepped out of the car wearing an A-line dress, heels, and concealing a .380 in her purse. She walked up the concrete stairs and rang the bell. Jonathan answered the door right away with a huge smile and his blue button-down opened up, revealing his hairy chest.

"Hey Lisa," he greeted. "You look gorgeous, baby."

Apple's expression was the opposite of his. She was frowning. Jonathan immediately picked up on her cold demeanor.

"Is everything okay?" he asked.

"We need to talk," she said briskly.

"Okay, come in."

Apple walked inside, but before he could close his front door, Jonathan noticed the dark silhouette in Apple's car. He found himself confused. Sin glared at him. Men like him were lunch for Sin.

Jonathan's smile had changed into worry. "Who's the man inside your car?" he asked.

"Right now, he's none of ya business," Apple replied coldly. "And my name is not Lisa."

"So, you've been lying to me."

"Let's talk in your office. I need your help wit' somethin'," she said.

"First, before we do anything, what is your real name?" he asked.

Apple felt hesitant in giving him her real name, but he was nice to her. She figured it wouldn't hurt. "My name is Apple."

"Apple," Jonathan replied incredulously.

"Yes."

"So why did you lie to me in the first place?"

"It's a long story, Jonathan, so let's talk in your office," she suggested.

Jonathan headed toward his back office on the first floor looking dumbfounded by everything that suddenly happened. The woman he was in love with was not the woman he thought she was. When they entered the office, Apple shut the door and told him to take a seat behind his desk. When he did so, she said to him, "I'm not gonna lie to you, I have a .380 in my purse and Sin outside is a stone-cold killer."

"Why are you doing this to me?" Jonathan asked with contempt.

"Because I need your help and I don't know no other way in getting it."

"What kind of help? You can talk to me, Li...I mean, Apple."

Apple took a seat in the chair opposite of him. She locked eyes with Jonathan. He remained calm, leaning back in his leather chair and waiting for the woman he was in love with to tell her tale.

"First off, I have a wicked past and a daughter, and I don't have much time," she started. "I'm from the streets, and the things I've done and seen will probably scare you."

"Try me," he said coolly.

She had Jonathan's undivided attention. He was listening. Apple went in, telling Jonathan her story, and as she spoke, he remained nonchalant. She didn't know why she was all of a sudden telling him everything, but things just started to flow out of her like she was purging herself. Jonathan's attitude was somewhat trustworthy and there was something about him that she really liked.

She told him her war stories and how Peaches had been taken from her in Mexico. When she was finished talking, Jonathan continued with his nonchalant attitude. To her surprise, he wasn't all that shocked by her tale. She figured he'd be ready to call 911 and turn her in, even though she would shoot him down before he could do so. However, Jonathan leaned back in his chair again and looked at Apple. It was almost like he had his own dirty little secret to reveal of his own.

"You lived an interesting life," he said. "But since you told me so much about yourself, I need to be honest with you and let you know some things about me."

Apple was listening. Something changed within Jonathan, his demeanor stoic, his easygoing way hardening somewhat.

"Not everything is always what it appears to be. Me, I grew up in an environment like yours…Brownsville, Brooklyn, born and raised back in the seventies and eighties. I once ran with this fierce drug crew when I was fifteen, sold crack, and shot a man once. Fortunately for me, I got out with the help of family and received a scholarship to Harvard because of my academics. I was always smart growing up, and I got lucky. And let me tell you something—climbing the ladder of success when it comes to politics and becoming an attorney is an aggressive and ruthless thing,

Apple. So don't let the good looks, nice smile and cool attitude fool you. I changed for the better. Believe me, your world and mine, they're something similar—the only difference is, I wear a suit and carry a briefcase to work, and you and yours handle business wholesale and with a gun.

"But let's cut past the bullshit, Apple. I'm in love with you, whether you know it or not…so what is it that you need from me?" he added.

"I need you to help find my daughter. I'm desperate and I figured you would have the resources to at least point me in the right direction."

"Okay, here's what I can do for you, come to my Manhattan office tomorrow afternoon and I'll have my paralegals dig up as much information on your daughter as possible," he said.

Apple smiled.

"And Apple, one more thing," Jonathan started.

Before Apple could stand, he said to her, "Don't ever lie to me. And don't ever threaten me. My clout in this city doesn't only extend to the politicians and lawyers, but a lot more dangerous underworld figures who owe me tons of favors."

Apple was listening. It was ironic how Jonathan's meek character had, out of the blue, changed into this dodgy mystery man. He'd also had *her* fooled. Apple stood, seeing Jonathan in a whole new light; she had to respect him. The cornball, nice-guy routine was only an act. She wasn't the only one who could put one on.

Before Apple could exit the office, Jonathan stood and said to her, "And what about the footage of us?"

Apple was speechless. She didn't mention anything about the sex tapes and conversations she had on them. How did he know?

"Don't play me for a fool, Apple. You think you can come into my home and set up cameras and mics undetected and I won't find out about it? I didn't get this far in my career by being stupid. I'm the one who does the blackmailing to get what I want," he declared.

Apple smiled. "I'm impressed."

"You should be," he replied dryly.

"I'll have the footage sent to you."

"I would appreciate that," Jonathan replied calmly.

Apple exited the brownstone with Sin still seated in the car. When she got behind the steering wheel, Sin looked at her and asked, "So, what you wanna do wit' this clown? He gonna see the end of my pistol or what?"

Apple looked at her beast and said, "Let him be, he's good peoples."

"What?" Sin roared.

"I said chill, Sin. He looked out for me," she said to him.

"A'ight, whatever!"

Apple pulled away from the brownstone with anticipation of meeting Jonathan tomorrow at his Manhattan office. She had this gut feeling that Jonathan's resources were going to point her in the right direction.

The next afternoon, Apple was at Jonathan's Midtown office with butterflies in her stomach. Clad in a pair of blue jeans and T-shirt, she looked more like a concerned mother trying to find her child than a ruthless killer and drug kingpin. She came alone and walked into the towering steel building that seemed to stretch toward the stratosphere. Inside, she signed in and proceeded toward Jonathan's office on the fifteenth floor.

Jonathan immediately had his two paralegals get on the telephone and contact a few of his alias. They telephoned DAs, police captains, politicians, and finally hit the Internet and searched for anything pertaining to missing children. His intel had them focus on the Mexican region first and then research illicit baby-selling operations. The two women were good at what they did, and it didn't take long for them to find out that there was a major baby-selling ring going on in Miami. Miami and the Mexican cartels had strong ties with each other. The Gonzalez cartel had much control over the baby-selling ring; it was one of their many sub-operations in trafficking that was profitable. The search for Peaches was leading Apple down to Miami.

At once, Apple thought about Cartier. She was excited about the news. Jonathan was a blessing to her. She thanked him and definitely owed him a huge favor. She left his office with more determination to leave New York and travel down to Miami.

Once inside her car, she searched for Cartier's number, knowing that her friend and her boyfriend, Hector, were running shit in Miami. Also, when Cartier had reached out to her several months back, Apple had given her the muscle she needed to defend herself when she was in trouble. It was now time for Cartier to return the favor. It was truly needed.

Time was critical; there was none to waste. Apple dialed Cartier straightaway. Sitting behind the wheel of Row's cocaine-colored BMW m5, parked by Riverside Drive on the West Side, she waited for Cartier to answer. The bitch had better answer. The last thing Apple wanted was problems.

The phone rang a few times and Cartier picked up. Apple wasted no time beating around the bush. Once she heard her friend's voice, she said, "I'm coming down to Miami, Cartier."

"What for?" Cartier replied brashly.

"What you mean, what for? You act like you ain't happy to hear from me," Apple spat.

"Apple, I have a lot going on down here right now, and you coming down here ain't gonna make things better for me."

"You forget who helped you out when you was drowning in trouble? I sent you a good soldier and cash. Don't fuckin' play me like this, Cartier. You owe me."

"Owe you what?" Cartier exclaimed. "My daughter is still dead."

"And now I need ya help to find my daughter!"

"I said now's not a good time."

"You on some ratchet bullshit right now for real for real," Apple exclaimed. "So it's gonna be like this? You on top wit' ya man now, thinkin' you running things down there and you gonna forget about your own peoples in New York? Me and my sister looked out for you—"

"That was a long time ago, Apple. And besides, Miami is too hot right now. We at war with a rival gang and you better off staying up top."

"So, you don't want me there, is that what ya sayin'?"

"I'm sayin' you coming down here is a bad fuckin' time."

Apple was fuming. If she could, she would have reached through the phone and choked the shit out of Cartier. With or without her approval, she was still going down to Miami with two of her goons.

"I'm gonna remember this, Cartier…don't make an enemy out of me, cuz I swear, I'm not the bitch you want to go against, and you'll regret this day," Apple warned.

Cartier was about to reply with some harsh words of her own, but then she stopped herself. While Apple was still ranting, Cartier had to rethink about the situation. It wasn't the best thing to make any more enemies. And she did owe Apple a favor. Cartier's reply was strictly strategic. Although Apple felt she was the baddest bitch around, the saying that there wasn't any shook hands in Brook-land was especially true when it came to Cartier. Apple and her threats weren't a real threat to Cartier. However, Kola and Eduardo, was another matter. Cartier wasn't trying to go up against those two. Especially since she was already at war with the Gonzalez cartel and most of the Ghost Ridas.

One on one, Cartier knew without a gun she would fuck Apple up because she was nice with her hands. Apple could never scrap. But with a pistol in either girl's hand and it was a toss-up on who would come out as the victor.

"Listen, my bad. I just have a lot on my mind. I didn't mean to come at you like that," she apologized. "But before this conversation goes further, don't you ever fuckin' threaten me again. Do we have an understanding?"

"It's cool." Apple didn't like being challenged and told what she could and could not do, but for the sake of having an ally and not an enemy, she acquiesced.

"Good, then we straight. Come through and Hector and I will do what we can to help you get your daughter back. But I gotta keep it gully—I'm hot out here so you might be walking into an ambush meant for me."

"An ambush?"

"That's real talk. I'm on the Gonzalez cartel's hit list."

Apple's voice elevated. "Did you say Gonzalez cartel?"

"Yeah, why what's up? You heard of them?"

"I'm lookin' for them cuz those muthafuckas might know where Peaches is at."

"Well they got money on my head, so you don't have to go looking, not if you rock wit me."

"How much is the contract on ya head?"

"I don't know. But there are two killers out here looking for me."

"And I'll bring two killers of my own down there. All you have to do is supply weapons, ammunition, and transportation," said Apple.

Cartier liked the sound of that. Knowing Apple's pedigree, she could use the assistance of a deadly friend from New York. She didn't have anyone she could trust in South Beach. With Hector and his crew, along with Apple and her men, it was extra muscle, and they would be able to hunt down the Gonzalez cartel together and get Apple's baby back. It sounded like a good idea via phone.

"I'll book three plane tickets right away for me and my goons, and we'll be in Miami by the weekend," said Apple. "And we gonna give that city a special kind of hell to remember us by. But in return, I need your help to find Peaches."

Cartier agreed.

Apple hung up feeling a step closer to finding her daughter. She knew the perfect two goons to travel down to Miami with, Row and Sin. They were each a special kind of wicked when it came to murder and gunplay. Miami was about to have one hell of a rude awakening.

# CHAPTER 13

## *Cartier*

Cartier woke up to find Hector seated at the foot of the bed. At first she was startled. He was naked and hunched over, staring at the wall in silence. He seemed spaced out, thinking about something important. Neither of them had really been able to get any sleep last night; there were more gruesome murders that hit home. The Miami Gotti Boys came back heavily with revenge and gunned down three of Hector's primary lieutenants—each man torn apart by high-powered rifles as they left a nightclub, their faces and torsos eaten up by machine-gunfire.

Everyone was drowning in blood. Miami was a raging battleground of gang warfare, where every corner from South Beach to Little Haiti was under threat of murder and violence. Even the tourists were being impacted by the gang violence plaguing the city. People were becoming scared to come see Miami. South Beach was becoming known as "violent beach" and compared with the roaring eighties, when crime and murder were high. It seemed like the police and mayor had no clue on how to stop the mayhem.

Cartier remained quiet while Hector stood up to answer his cell phone. He remained naked while he walked around the bedroom.

"Penny, talk to me," she heard him say.

Knowing it was Penny on the other end, Cartier became curious to hear what the conversation was about. The dissension within the Ghost Ridas since Hector had killed Swagger M was becoming worse. It was soon to be civil war within the gang, and the timing couldn't have been worse. Penny was trying to defuse the conflict Hector suddenly had with some members that wanted to see him go.

"You know what, fuck 'em…my brother built Ghost Ridas from the blood than ran through his veins and when he was murdered I took over! We are Ghost Ridas! I am Ghost Ridas for life! *I todavía ejecutar esta mierda…*" Hector shouted.

Paying Cartier no attention, he left the bedroom still naked and walked into the next room near the terrace with his voice still booming through the cell phone. Hector was clearly upset and ready to go to war with his own gang. It would be a huge mistake. They already had enough on their plate between the Gonzalez cartel, the Miami Gotti Boys, and the feds; this would be suicide for them. Penny was trying to advise him to keep the peace and maybe step down from leadership, but Hector's pride was too big for him to back down. He was the don, and he wasn't going to be punked by anyone.

Cartier removed herself from the bed. She had her own worries. Her talk with Apple the other day was troubling. She wasn't happy to hear from her at all. She didn't have time to hear about her predicament and her missing baby. Apple was bad news waiting to happen, but then Cartier felt it would probably be good to have the extra muscle around and to see a familiar face from New York again. Hector became more distanced from her every day. And it was a favor owed, because Apple *had* sent down a soldier when she needed the extra help. Not to mention, with the contract on her head put out by the Gonzalez cartel, she needed some backup.

Cartier could still hear Hector talking loudly to Penny. He was standing butt-naked on the terrace, pacing back and forth with his penis swinging. It was another beautiful day on South Beach, but things were far from picturesque in their chaotic world.

"Ay, fuck them *putas* Penny...my own family wanna war wit' me, then let 'em, ay?" Hector shouted.

Cartier donned her long, white robe and went to join Hector out on the terrace. She was truly worried. She knew Penny was trying to give Hector some solid advice, but Hector refused to listen. Hector hung up and tossed his phone. Cartier wanted to wrap her arms around her man, but he was clearly frustrated.

"What did Penny say to you?" she asked.

Hector turned to her with a grimace. "Fuck everybody!" he said.

"Baby, let's just leave Miami for a while, go somewhere and chill out," she suggested.

"What?" Hector barked.

"We can go somewhere west. We have enough money to last us for a long while..."

Hector charged toward her unexpectedly and wrapped his hand around her slim neck. He squeezed tightly while glaring at her. Cartier tried to fight him off of her, but he was too strong. He moved her toward the railing, pushed her halfway over and was threatening to throw her off. He was becoming a lunatic.

As he choked her, he shouted, "So I'm supposed to run like some scared *puta*, it's that what you're tellin' me? This is my fuckin' home and my fuckin' family. I don't run from no one! You understand me?!"

Cartier gasped. Hector loosened his grip around her neck and she fell to her knees, coughing and gasping for air.

"I'm not goin' anywhere. You understand me, Cartier? If my own peoples want to bring war to my doorstep, then let 'em! Let 'em fuckin' come!" he screamed madly.

Hector stormed away. Cartier stood up. She collected herself quickly and frowned. She saw the insanity in his eyes. He was losing it. She felt like he was really going to kill her. The tears fell, and the heartache was overwhelming. She took a deep breath and joined Hector in the bedroom. He was getting dressed and moving about. There were two chrome Desert Eagles on the bed.

"Hurry up and get dressed. We gotta make some moves," said Hector.

Cartier was hesitant. She watched Hector move around the bedroom removing large amounts of cash and other items from the closet and the drawers and placing everything on the bed.

"What are we gonna do?" she asked.

"I got everything under control," he said.

He pulled out a duffel bag and started to place the cash inside. There had to be about $250,000 in several stacks. Cartier wondered what he was going to do with the money.

"I said get dressed, Cartier. I gotta make some moves and I need you to come with me," Hector said loudly.

She sighed and removed her robe, letting it fall from around her shoulders and lay meshed around her ankles. Her nakedness suffused the bedroom. Hector stopped what he was doing for a moment and eyed her. She was a beautiful creature with a body to kill for. They hadn't had sex in a while.

"What?" Cartier asked.

"Nothing…I'm sorry about earlier. I didn't mean to go off on you, baby. You're beautiful to me, and I love you. I just have a lot on my mind," he said sincerely.

Cartier was silent. She looked at Hector and nodded. She understood his position. They both were in the fire with no extinguisher. She walked up and placed her arms around her man. They kissed passionately for a moment. Hector began groping her lovely figure, palming her round, phat ass and loving how the warmth of her body was pressed against his. Their breaths were heavy against each other. Cartier felt that special tingle between her legs, her pussy becoming wet from his touch. She wanted him. She wanted to feel his penis inside of her. But suddenly Hector pushed her away and said, "We don't have time right now. I gotta meet some peoples."

Cartier released a heavy sigh of frustration. It had been a while since she had some dick inside of her. She was loyal to her man, but the war had consumed most of his time. Last night was the first night in a long time since they'd actually slept in the same bed. Hector was too busy in the streets handling his business or conducting other affairs. Cartier had her own thing going, too, but there was always time for sex, in her book. She needed to release some pent-up frustration. Hector was only focused on one thing at the moment—the streets.

Quickly, Cartier got dressed and followed her man out of the penthouse. They were both armed with automatics and took the elevator down to the parking garage where they were met by one of Hector's street goons, Samsung.

The trio piled into Hector's Yukon with Samsung driving, and the SUV merged onto the sunny streets of South Beach. Hector was on the phone with Penny. Penny was determined to ease the tension and somehow keep Hector alive. He was like a consigliore to Hector and other gang members. Penny was smart, methodical and highly respected.

While Hector was on the phone with Penny, Cartier gazed out the window. Her mind drifted toward the hit on her life taken out by the Gonzalez cartel. Knowing that there were two contract killers out there somewhere, lurking and watching, sent chills down her spine. She didn't know who they were or when they would strike, but she refused to hide in a hole like some frightened little animal. She didn't tell Hector about the contract on her life. She figured he already had enough on his plate.

In her purse was a loaded .9mm. and underneath their backseat was a Heckler & Koch, and the driver, Samsung, carried a Desert Eagle on him, and also in the SUV were a sawed-off shotgun and an Uzi. Every vehicle Hector or Cartier rode in was armor plated with run-flat tires, thick, bulletproof windows, and secret compartments for weaponry and other items.

The Yukon moved down Collins Avenue with Hector still chatting on his cell phone with Penny. The streets were cool and unruffled for the moment. Dozens of tourists and locals were out shopping, mingling, and minding their business, taking advantage of the sunny day and the pricy shops that lined the street. Cartier was quiet.

Finally, Hector hung up. He seemed cooler now. His talk with Penny was creating some results.

"What's goin' on? What is Penny sayin' to you?"

"Later this evening, we gonna have a sit-down with a few members that have a problem with me and try to work things out without the violence," he said.

"You sure?"

"Penny's reaching out now, making the phone calls to the right people. He got my back on this."

Cartier wanted to smile, but for some reason, she was unsure of things. She just needed to have faith and remain calm.

"You hungry?" Hector asked.

"Yes, I am."

"A'ight, we'll get something to eat. Samsung," Hector called out.

"Yeah, Hector?"

"Stop off at the nearest café. Me and my baby wanna get something to eat." Samsung nodded. "I got you."

Samsung drove a few blocks north and came to a stop at the Front Porch Café on Ocean Drive. Samsung stepped out first and opened the door for Hector and Cartier. The pair walked toward the classy café that had the best smoothies in Miami.

The café had its regular morning-to-afternoon crowd coming and going. People were smiling, laughing, and enjoying another sun-drenched day. Keeping close to each other, Hector went to get them a table outside, while Samsung remained by the Yukon keeping an eye out on things. He stood vigilant, making sure there weren't any threats looming about.

Hector and Cartier took a seat at one of the outdoor bistro tables and for a moment, they focused only on food. The two made small talk. Cartier wanted to forget about everything that had gone on during the past several weeks. She sat looking nonchalant, sipping on a flavorsome smoothie.

Cartier sighed and glanced at Samsung. He was still posted by the gleaming black Yukon looking like one of the president's Secret Service details. He scowled most of the time. The bulge underneath his jacket indicated he was armed and dangerous.

Hector was on the phone with Penny for the duration of their meal, their talk imperative. He remained calm, not exploding in public while conversing about his beef with his own peoples.

Cartier made a few phone calls of her own. They mostly were about business with her property in North Miami. She spoke to her lawyer again and he stated he had some good news to tell her about her property and the permits she applied for. She just wanted things to look up. They arranged to meet at his office sometime after 5 p.m.

"You ready?" Hector asked.

She nodded.

Hector removed a small wad of hundreds and fifties from his pocket and dropped a fifty-dollar bill on the table to pay for the thirty-dollar tab. He stood up and nodded to Samsung that they were ready to leave, which meant to get the car ready. Cartier followed behind him.

"Where to now?" she asked.

"We gotta meet with Penny before this sit-down with my peoples. He got something…*No puedo creer esta mierda—*"

And then it happened out of the blue. It was loud and deafening.

*Boom! Boom!*

Cartier found her face splattered with his blood. There was screaming, and panic ensued—dozens of shoes and sneakers fleeing the bloody scene. Cartier became frantic quickly. Hector was sprawled out in front of her with two monster-size holes in his chest. Three shooters came out of nowhere in the public quarter and executed her man like they were in a video game.

Samsung tried to react fast after seeing Hector cut down by the shotgun blast with the .50 caliber gripped in his hand, but the minute he had one foot out the driver door against the concrete, a barrage of bullets shredded into him maliciously. Glass shattered with his blood leaking all over the seats and concrete. Samsung dropped face-first between the curb and the Yukon.

Cartier screamed and found herself helpless. From the black, green and gold colors, it appeared that the Miami Gotti Boys had finally caught up with them. Their faces were covered with black bandannas and hoodies. Cartier tried to run, but toppled over a chair, crashing onto her side, and found herself on her back, defenseless. Her purse with her pistol slid into a different direction. One of the shooters rushed toward her with a Ruger in his hand. Scowling, he aimed at her head and fired. But nothing. He fired again, and the same outcome happened. His gun had jammed. Cartier found herself wide-eyed and terrified.

"C'mon, forget that bitch, let's go," one of his homies called out.

Cartier locked eyes with the shooter who attempted to murder her like she was some dog in the streets. Instantly, she noticed the tattoo on his hand with the gun. It was a Ghost Ridas symbol—a purple and black skull on fire.

"Lucky bitch," he shouted, before running off.

Cartier wanted to exhale, but it felt like she couldn't breathe.

Everything happened so fast. With the shooters gone, she picked herself up from the concrete right away and ran toward her fallen king.

"Hector!" she screamed.

She dropped to his side and scooped his limp frame into her arms, his blood staining her dress and skin. The tears started to fall uncontrollably. His eyes were closed, his chest ripped apart from the two shotgun blasts at close range. His breath, silent.

"Hector! Hector, get up, baby! Get the fuck up," Cartier screamed, cradling her man tightly in her arms and rocking back and forth. "Someone call 911!"

Bystanders stood around her in awe. It was something out of a movie they witnessed. Their paradise was once again torn apart and shattered by gang violence. Sirens blared in the distance. The beautiful sun-drenched day suddenly transformed into an ominous storm. Cartier cried her eyes out—her pain echoing everywhere.

The news of Hector's death traveled fast. Within an hour, dozens of outraged Ghost Ridas were at the crime scene, but they couldn't get close to their fallen leader due to the strong police restriction. Yellow crime-scene tape looped around the entire street guarded by heavy police presence.

The media had shown up to cover the high-profile slaying of a brutal drug kingpin, and detectives were combing the area, taking statements and talking to witnesses of the cruel murder. When civilians learned of the identity of the man murdered, chills moved down their spines. They were so close to the bloody horrors they'd been watching on the news.

Cartier was distraught as Detective Sharp tried taking a statement from her. Her tear stained face looked off into the distance. She was angry. She couldn't believe he was dead. The only thing on her mind was revenge.

"Let us help you, Cartier," said Detective Sharp.

But there was nothing Detective Sharp could say or do to help her. She was shaken up. If the shooter's gun hadn't jammed, then there would have been three dead victims. But she was no snitch and the last thing she needed was a cop in her business. Hector's and Samsung's bodies still lay sprawled out on the ground covered with a white, bloody sheet.

"You need to talk to me, Cartier. Who were the shooters? Cartier, who were the shooters? Let us help you," Sharp continued to press.

Cartier remained stone-cold silent—her eyes showing separation from her reality. They were taking everything from her. They were pushing her over the edge; with her feeling she had nothing else left. The detective was in her ear, but the only thing Cartier could focus on was Hector's bullet riddled and lifeless body spread out in front of her like human trash and how she was going to murder every last one of the muthafuckas responsible—starting from the betrayal from Hector's own peoples down to the Gonzalez cartel.

The Ghost Ridas flooded the block with their nasty scowls and foul language. They were ready to cause a riot and fight with police. Hector was dead, and the majority were heartbroken and saddened, while a small percentage saw it coming. However, for them, it was painful to see one of their brethren taken from them in such a wicked way.

Penny pulled up to the scene in his purple Audi a7. The minute he stepped out his vehicle, members from his crew swarmed toward him. They were looking for answers and more payback. Another high-ranking member was gunned down. Who was next to lead— Penny or Alexandro? Penny wasn't rushing to take leadership in his gang, knowing that "uneasy lies the head that wears a crown."

Penny—standing only five-nine with his dark, deep-set eyes, slim frame and his head bald as a baby's bum—was someone you didn't want to mess with. What he lacked in height and weight, he made up for with his ferocious reputation, along with his cleverness in surviving and knowing the streets and the game like the back of his hand. He was an aging O.G. in his mid-thirties with smooth, brown skin and neatly trimmed goatee peppered with small tufts of gray. He was a gangster who had an air of power about him, but he was also distinguished.

While members wanted to talk to him, Penny looked over at the crime scene with a visage of contempt. He gave an exasperated sigh and looked for Cartier. He saw her talking to the detective. He could only wait until the police did their job before he could start his.

Several hours later, Cartier stepped out of the precinct. Penny was parked out front, waiting to give her a ride. The day had been tragic, and the pain was still fresh. Cartier locked eyes with Penny, and when she got closer to him, she went berserk and started attacking him.

"Did you do it, Penny?" she screamed, as she smacked him repeatedly upside his head. "Did you have him killed? Huh? Was it you?"

Cartier was hysterical. One of Penny's goons rushed to pull Cartier back, but Penny stopped him and pushed her off of himself. "Ay, chill the fuck out, Cartier! I had nothing to do with it. I thought it was the Miami Gotti Boys that came at y'all."

"No, it was one of y'all. I saw the tattoo on one of the shooters...a purple and black skull on fire."

Penny was extremely upset.

"How did they know where to find us? You're the only one he's been on the phone with all morning," she exclaimed.

"I don't know. But I'm gonna find out," said Penny. "Hector was my brother; I was trying to prevent this from happening."

"How did this happen?" she cried out.

"Just get in the car, Cartier. I'm gonna handle this. Trust me," said Penny. He wanted to remove himself from in front of the police precinct and talk somewhere else where it was safe.

Cartier climbed into the backseat with her face still filled with grief. They had been questioning her for hours and finally decided to let her go. She gave them nothing. She was ready to hit the streets and avenge the wrong done to her.

Penny took her back to his three-bedroom apartment in East Little Havana to stay until the heat blew over. Hector's death was definitely going to put Miami deeper into the frying pan with repeated bloodshed. Once inside, Penny told her to relax and make herself feel at home. Cartier didn't have a home anymore. While Penny got on the horn to make some phone calls, Cartier found herself on his couch sobbing her eyes out. She missed Hector already. Now, she felt really alone. Hector was that wall of protection from her foes, and with him gone, her life was gravely in danger.

Visions of Head resurfaced. The last time she'd seen him he'd unexpectedly come to her house in Palm Beach, Florida. Cartier turned Head away for this exact reason. Too many of her loved ones were murdered because of her. Cartier knew she was going to go up against the Gonzalez cartel for her family murders and didn't want Head to be another casualty of war. He deserved better. He had already risked his life for her on too many occasions, and telling him that she didn't love him was, in her own way, showing that she did. He told her that if she allowed him to walk out her door, that he was never coming back. Ever. She could still see the deep pain and hurt in his eyes when she told him to bounce.

Cartier knew she was in hiding with the last few people she could trust. She had to move wisely, because one mistake could cost her her life.

# CHAPTER 14

## *Citi*

Citi gripped the thick dick with both hands and shoved it down her throat heatedly. She was butt-naked in his office. The door was locked, their sexual episode uninterrupted. Her nipples were hard as stones with the heat that had built up inside of her. Marcus cooed and grunted, feeling her fleshy lips wrap around his penis, sliding back and forth. He leaned against his giant granite desk with his pants around his ankles, fucking Citi's mouth like it was a pussy. She could feel her juices leaking out of her and running down between her thighs and ass cheeks. Marcus had her so wet and horny.

Marcus grabbed the back of her skull and pushed her face deeper into his pelvis, causing Citi to deep-throat inches of hard dick. She handled it like a professional. His cock was kissed and then sucked into Citi's pink folds. Her heat wrapped around his hard shaft as he let his own lust jerk his hips forward quickly. As she sucked his big dick, Citi's thumb worked her own naked clit, and with the intense sensation, her moans vibrated against his dick, causing Marcus to shudder and grabbed her hair tightly.

"Ooooh yeah, suck that dick…suck it!" he groaned.

"You like it?"

"Oh yeah…suck it! Fuckin' suck it!"

He rubbed his hands all over her sweet brown curves, pinching her hard nipples, pulling her long hair. While she let her nails trace down his shivering sides, her breasts rolled seductively over his hard, rising cock flesh, begging it to stand and be delivered. She caressed his sac gently, massaging, as her lips caught the mushroom tip of his thickening pole and her tongue flicked away, making Marcus gasp and catch his breath, and once again shudder from the blissful feeling of wet lips and a pleasing tongue engulfing him proudly. His eyes were watering and he could hardly speak. Citi felt the pressure building within him. She stopped, squeezed his balls, and purred. "Cum for me, lover."

The pressure hit its boiling point and Marcus exploded, releasing his semen onto Citi's awaiting face and tongue. She proudly accepted his sticky, wet liquid inside her mouth like it was a tasty drink. After his forceful nut, Marcus quickly pulled up his pants and fastened them. He was done. Citi stood from her knees. Her clothes were scattered all over the office like she had been caught in a whirlwind.

Citi wiped Marcus's cum from her mouth and stared at him. She wanted more from him, but he continued to remain detached toward her. She picked up her clothing and started to get dressed. While Citi fastened her jeans, Marcus got on his office phone and gestured for her to leave his office. Though his actions were telling her it was time for her to go, she wasn't ready to leave his side yet. For the past few days, she had been feeling disrespected by him. She was trying to get him to leave her mother, protesting that she would be better for him, but Marcus treated her like a concubine, and it was starting to bother Citi more and more.

Marcus leaned back in his leather chair. He was on the phone discussing the recent death of Hector. Citi hesitated by the door, with envy and strife developing inside of her. Their illicit affair started two months ago, but it was becoming obvious to her that he wasn't going to leave Ashanti for her. He only saw her as a young jump-off—his personal cum collector. Marcus gave his attention to the caller on the other end, while Citi stood there like a wounded puppy.

"Marcus, can we talk?" Citi asked.

"Not now, Citi," he refuted.

"So, it's like that, Marcus? You just gonna fuck me and have me suck your dick, and I can't talk to you, even get a fuckin' minute of your time after everything I gave you…even L?!" she spat.

Marcus paused for a moment on the office phone and glared at Citi, and through clenched teeth, he reiterated, "I said not now, Citi! I'm on the fuckin' phone, get the fuck out!"

Citi was crushed. She tried to hold back her tears, but his words hurt. She became defiant. She couldn't tolerate just having him part-time anymore. Fuck you, Marcus!" she shouted. "I'm tired of this shit! You either gonna tell my mother about us, or I fuckin' will. You ain't gonna keep playin' me, or us, like this."

Marcus cut his eyes over at Citi. He curtailed his conversation and hung up. The frigid glare of a killer shot back at Citi. He stood up and scowled at his young stepdaughter. Citi became frightened to the core. She knew she'd fucked up. This time, it felt like her mouth bit off more than she could chew. It was the wrong thing to say to a murderous kingpin like Marcus.

Moving from around his desk Marcus quickly approached Citi in a hostile manner. Before she could make her escape out the double doors, Marcus had his hands clamped around her neck and powerfully tossed her across the room. Citi went flying through the air like a paper plane. Now, she was going to see the Black Mamba, and it wasn't going to be pretty.

"You dare threaten me, you little fuckin' whore!" he screamed.

Marcus crouched down and clamped his hands around her thin neck again and squeezed violently. Her eyes started to bulge, and every breath in her body felt like it was becoming stale. She tried to fight him back, but his strength was crushing her. He picked her up off her feet by her neck like it was nothing, lifting the petite girl in the air like a ragdoll. Her feet dangled like she was being hanged, and her body becoming limp between his hands.

Citi knew he was going to kill her. It was the Black Mamba showing; Marcus was long gone. But he unclamped his hands from around her frail neck and she dropped at his feet. She gasped for air, clutching her neck. Marcus took a step back from her and glared at his victim. He could have killed her, but he didn't. Citi still remained frightened though.

"It's time for you to leave my home. I don't want to ever see you again," he told her.

Citi became wide-eyed. *Leave his home?* She stood up and pleaded with Marcus. "I can't leave, please…I'm sorry, Marcus. I'm sorry. Please don't do this to me," she groveled, but Marcus remained disconnected.

"You're dangerous to play around with. I think Ashanti suspects something, and you were fun while it lasted, but this affair between us, it comes to an end," he said sternly. "Today."

Citi eyes were flooded with tears. She had made a mistake. She didn't know her place, but she didn't want to lose him completely—especially not to the woman she loathed. It wasn't fair.

"I can do better, baby. I'm sorry I came at you like that. I wasn't thinkin' rational," she continued to grovel. "Please, give me a second chance. I'll be your side bitch, your mistress, whatever. I'll suck your dick, baby, until my mouth gets numb."

Marcus pushed her away from him with disgust. He was adamant. He was done with her. She was more headache than pleasure. He had other important matters to worry about.

Citi however, was completely heartbroken. While Marcus was treating her like day-old trash, she was ready to do the unthinkable, probably take her life and his. But it was a fleeting thought. She stood in his office disheartened. Her clothes were in disarray, her face stained with tears and anguish.

Marcus was sick of looking at her and hearing her pathetic groveling. To make his point really clear, he slid back the top drawer to his desk and removed a Glock 19. He pointed it at Citi and she stood frozen like her feet were in cement—like a deer caught in blinding headlights. She was wide-eyed and speechless. It felt like her life was flashing before her eyes.

"I'm done playing games with you, Citi. I want you out of my house," he demanded.

Citi sobbed. He really didn't care for her anymore.

"I'll leave, but I have nothing," she said to him.

He remained quiet. The gun was still trained at her body. It was a frightening position to be in, knowing that he was a stone-cold killer and that her life was in his hands. Citi turned and hurried out of his office with tears of anguish.

"Stupid little bitch," muttered Marcus.

The minute Citi was out his office, she ran into Cane. He noticed his little sister's heartbreak and tears, and immediately became worried.

"Sis, what the fuck happened to you now? Why you crying?" he asked with great concern.

She didn't respond to him. She had no words to say. She just wanted to disappear somewhere and never come back.

"Talk to me, Citi, who fuckin' wit' you?" he said.

Citi snapped at him. She pushed him away and screamed, "Leave me the fuck alone!"

She ran off, leaving Cane dumbfounded. Somebody did something to his little sister, and he was going to find out who. It didn't take him long to put two and two together. When he noticed Marcus coming out of his office with a smirk and his shirt unbuttoned, Cane exploded. He already knew what had gone down with him and Citi, and it disgusted him.

Cane, being the temperamental goon that he was, didn't hesitate to confront the nigga. He rushed over and shouted, "Nigga, what the fuck you did to my sister?"

Marcus scowled and harshly replied, "Cane, back the fuck down."

"What? Fuck you, Marcus!" Cane retorted.

He didn't care about Marcus's power or his loyalty to the man that was supposed to love him like a son; once you hurt or put hands on his little sister, all that shit went out the door. Cane was ready to attack, but Ashanti's sudden presence slightly neutralized the heated circumstances.

"What's going on here?" she asked, looking into both men's eyes.

"Ask this muthafucka, Ma…he did something to Citi," Cane uttered.

Ashanti cut her eyes at Marcus. He remained expressionless. His wife looked at him waiting for answers.

"What happened to my daughter, Marcus?" she asked with suspicion in her voice.

"Don't fuckin' question me, Ashanti," Marcus barked back.

"Nigga, don't be fuckin' talkin' to my moms like that. You fuckin' crazy, nigga?!" Cane screamed.

"Tell your son to back down, Ashanti, before he bites the hands that feeds him," Marcus warned.

"Fuck ya hand," Cane retorted.

Both men were seething. Cane got into Marcus's face, but Ashanti pulled her son back. Knowing they both were stone-cold killers, it wasn't going to get any better. Ashanti was ready to get to the bottom of things, though. For a while she speculated that her husband was having an affair with another woman, but now the woman he was having an affair was probably right under her nose, and right here under her own roof. She hated to think that it was her own daughter—if so, then the bitch done crossed the wrong boundaries, because that was a smack in her face and disrespect to her on so many levels.

Ashanti calmed the tension between her son and her husband. She had other things on her mind. Cane backed down, but the damage had already been done. He was ready to kill Marcus. He knew his stepfather was fucking his little sister, there was no denying it. Before Cane walked away, extremely teed off, he shouted at Marcus, "I ain't fuckin' L, muthafucka!"

"Yeah, I bet you ain't," Marcus replied angrily.

Ashanti already knew her son's life was in grave danger. She tried to reason with Marcus, but he was too upset for her to talk any rational sense into him. But her biggest gripe was Citi. She was ready to do some investigation of her own, and find out the truth.

The next few days were filled with tension and uneasiness. Cane disappeared, and Ashanti had her own worries to deal with. Marcus also had his hands filled with troublesome things. Citi was in her own daze— saddened and distraught. She locked herself in her bedroom and tried to stay unseen from her mother. It felt like Pandora's Box had been opened and all kinds of shit was flying out.

But unbeknownst to everyone else, Marcus had secretly told Citi that he had purchased a three-bedroom penthouse in South Beach, overlooking the ocean, and he would give her a $10,000 stipend per month for her to spend as she pleased. The only stipulation was that she had to stay away from him and her mother. Citi was somewhat content with the arrangement. Things were going to hell in her home anyway. Marcus just wanted to get rid of her, and even though killing her would have been easy to do, in his heart, she was still his stepdaughter and he had some love for her.

The Miami evening with the sun behind the horizon brought a chill to the air, but the streets weren't so calm. With tensions escalating in every fraction of the city, some of the biggest gangsters found themselves jumping at their own shadows and moving with steady caution. One wrong move could be fatal for them. With the death of Hector, the Ghost Ridas were out in full force, doing some headhunting of their rivals. It was shoot and kill on sight. The Miami Gotti Boys were also on high alert, and the other gangs caught in the midst of this deadly war knew to keep themselves armed and dangerous.

Marcus and Jameson, his bodyguard/driver, rode down Miami Avenue in downtown Miami in his polished black Maybach. Marcus sat in the backseat with his cell phone glued to his ear. With business his focus, he puffed on the Cuban cigar between his lips and couldn't wait until he arrived at Perricone's marketplace in the downtown area. He yearned for their Italian classics, like homemade potato gnocci and cioppino right alongside some good, thick Italian sandwiches. Perricone's was one of his favorite restaurants in South Florida. The ambiance was terrific with their outdoor dining in a garden café, and it was easy to relax with a glass of wine and let your cares slip away.

But Marcus had way too many cares to just easily have them slip away. His city was at war. He had enemies who wanted to see him gone. And then he had problems in his own home. Cane had been missing for several days now, but he didn't think anything of it, and Marcus and Ashanti had been going at war, their relationship becoming turbulent. Citi was the problem; he figured he'd already done his part by giving his stepdaughter a place of her own.

The Maybach pulled up to the posh eatery on Southeast 10th Street. There was already a crowd of people waiting to enter the place—without reservations, it was nearly impossible to receive seating. Marcus arrived for a prearranged meeting.

Under the canopy of stars, he stepped out of his high-end vehicle clad in an expensive, three-piece Tom Ford suit with a fedora on his head and cigar clutched between his fingers. He oozed power and commanded respect with his broad shoulders and frigid glare. His presence was heavy.

Jameson exited the vehicle too. He stood six-three with a bald head, and his grim aura made people turn away quickly, intimidated. The two were ready to enter the eatery like the gangsters that they were, but Marcus always thought of himself as a businessman first. Marcus chomped on his cigar and walked ahead with Jameson following behind him.

"I love this place," Marcus told Jameson.

Jameson nodded. He didn't say much. He mostly listened to his boss and hurt people; never much of a talker, more of a bruiser.

Before they could get close to the place, the unthinkable happened—it was a setup. As Marcus puffed on his cigar, talking to his man and about to walk into his prearranged meeting, a hit team wearing all black was waiting near the restaurant entrance. The hit team included Cane and three of his closest thugs. The gunmen ran up, and before Marcus could blink, they shot him and Jameson several times with pistols and shotguns. The sudden explosions from several high-caliber guns created a wave of panic.

"Yeah, muthafucka…what now?!" Cane screamed as he personally pumped round after round into his stepfather.

Blood sprayed and bodies dropped. Marcus's solid frame took in heavy gunfire, shaking up his insides like acid was dissolving him as he slowly dropped to his knees with his cigar still dangling from his lips. Cane locked eyes with his victim and smirked. Marcus couldn't believe it. He'd underestimated Cane. The urban cowboy had struck first and didn't miss.

Towering over his victim, Cane pressed the pistol to his head, while Marcus slowly was succumbing to his injuries. He had been shot sixteen times, but he still had some breath in him. He didn't topple over yet.

"This is for my little sister, muthafucka!" Cane shouted through clenched teeth.

He pressed the pistol against Marcus's forehead.

"I told you, I ain't fuckin' L, muthafucka!" Cane growled and squeezed.

The bullet ripped through Marcus's head and tore out brain matter and flesh. The boss finally toppled over. Witnesses were screaming and fleeing the scene, horrified by the appalling act committed at such a public venue. Cane stood over the body of a notorious underworld figure and felt no remorse at all. His family had been dishonored and Cane needed to do something about it, and he did. The killing emulated the mafia hit of Paul Castellano in front of Sparks Steak House back in '85.

Cane rushed toward the parked car and climbed into the backseat. Tires screeched as the Ford made a sharp U-turn and sped away. Shocked bystanders slowly emerged from where they'd hidden when the gunshots took place and stood over a dying Marcus. Surprisingly, after sixteen shots and being shot in the head, he was still alive.

"Call 911!" a bystander screamed.

The Ford raced away from the scene with Cane smiling. Cane wasn't a fool though; he knew he had to leave Miami for good. He and his crew had just murdered the Black Mamba in cold blood, and his men would definitely be out looking for payback. As the driver sped down the highway, Cane wiped every last one of the guns clean of their fingerprints and tossed them in the ocean. Then by sunup, he was ghost.

Ashanti rushed through the doors of Mercy Hospital with her face in anguish. She had gotten news an hour ago about Marcus. He was barely alive, in critical condition and in ICU. The doctors performed immediate surgery on him, but they had to induce him into a coma until the swelling in his brain and other areas went down. It was a miracle that he was still alive for this long after being shot sixteen times and once in the head, but they didn't expect him to survive the next twenty-four hours. His family was holding a vigil outside the hospital and his henchmen were readying themselves for war and retaliation. The carnage had finally hit home and Marcus became the latest victim of the growing violence in the city.

Ashanti was determined to see her husband, but doctors told her he couldn't have any visitors just yet. The news of Marcus being gunned down had spread throughout the city like wildfire—first Hector and now him. It was obvious that no matter how high your status was in the underworld, everyone had a target on their backs.

When Ashanti finally got to see her husband with tubes hanging from his mouth, his right hand resting on his chest near the twin heart-monitor leads stuck to his pectorals, she felt like spitting in his face. She'd found out about his nasty affair with her daughter. She once heard the gossip from men talking around the house, but she refused to believe it. But now, it was confirmed. She had been played for a fool by her daughter and Marcus. It sickened her that Citi had betrayed their relationship. She tried so hard to be a mother to her daughter. But it was obvious that Citi was only using her, smiling in her face while stabbing her in the back. To add insult to injury, when the word had gotten back to her that her own son, Cane, was responsible for the shooting; it gave dysfunctional family a whole new meaning. Cane was on the lam, probably heading back to New York. Marcus's goons were going to kill him and his peoples.

Ashanti stood by her dying husband's bedside and cursed him.

"You fuckin' bastard! How dare you disrespect me like that?" she hissed. "My fuckin' daughter."

But he was comatose and chances were that he wouldn't last the night. She could only stare angrily at him. There was some love for him, but she truly felt he deserved every bullet he got inside of him. She was angry at

Cane for the shooting, but she could forgive her son. Her daughter, on the other hand, was a sneaky, conniving little bitch, and she had to be taught a valuable lesson. Ashanti had been around for too long to be played a fool by the one she gave birth to. Citi was still learning the game, while she was a veteran. Ashanti was now the commander-in-chief. Her name was on paperwork, bank accounts, and plenty of other vital documents. She wasn't going anywhere. She couldn't say the same for her daughter.

After returning from the hospital, Ashanti was on a war path. She burst through the front doors of her home with a scowl. Her mission was to find Citi and exile that little bitch. She wanted her daughter gone. She couldn't stand the sight of her. Flanked by two of her own goons, she burst into Citi's bedroom and caused wreckage. Citi was caught off guard by the sudden entry. She was in her panties and bra when her mother rushed toward her, screaming, "I want you the fuck out of here, now!" and snatched Citi by her long hair and pulled her off the bed.

Citi screamed. "Get the fuck off me!"

Her mother was strong and vicious. "You think you can outsmart me, you little dumb bitch? I know this fuckin' game like the back of my hand. You think you can come into my home, fuck my husband and smile in my face, and I wouldn't find out?!" she barked.

The blows came out of anger. Citi cried out. She tried to defend herself, but her mother was like lightening. Her fists landed on her daughter heavily, striking her temple, her face and her jaw. Citi felt embarrassed as her mother pounced on top of her like she was some stranger on the street. The two tall goons could only watch, their eyes fixed on Citi's scantily clad flesh and yearning to have a piece of that ass. They envied Marcus; he'd had both of these beautiful women.

"Get the fuck off me! Get off me…get off me!" Citi screamed out.

Her hair was in disarray, and her bra strap had ripped, revealing her dark nipples, and she'd acquired more bruises to her face. Ashanti was panting with her fists still clenched and scowling at her daughter.

"You have forty-eight hours to leave this place and the fuckin' state, you scandalous, retarded bitch. I tried to love you. I tried to make up for my past and my mistake by being there for you, and you do me like this," said Ashanti despondently.

"Fuck you! You were never a fuckin' mother to me! I always hated you. Ya not my mom…you are a fuckin' bitch! I hate you!"

"Then hate me from afar, Citi. You leave here now, because I would hate to bury my own daughter," Ashanti replied hardheartedly.

Citi was sobbing and embarrassed. She didn't know what to do. Ashanti was kicking her out with only the clothes on her back. She knew her mother was serious. Her eyes were frigid and black toward her. She was adamant.

"You have forty-eight hours, bitch. Don't fuckin' try me," Ashanti said coldly.

She spun on her heels and made her exit. Citi was left howling in her bedroom. She needed someone to run to, but everyone was gone. Cane was nowhere to be found, and she had no friends in Miami. Citi felt alone, not knowing what to do or where to go. She took a chance, fucked up, and now it was costing her greatly.

# CHAPTER 15

## *Apple & Cartier*

Penny walked into the dim lounge on Seventh Street in the West Little Havana, flanked by one of his trusted soldiers. He was there to meet with Alexandro. The meeting place was common ground for both of them—it was a frequent chill-out spot for many Ghost Ridas members. Once Penny heard from Cartier on the down-low that it was his own gang that took his friend's life, he was determined to get to the bottom of things. He did his own investigation. With Hector dead, either he or Alexandro was next to lead the gang. Penny knew he didn't put the hit out on his friend, so that only left Alexandro.

Penny walked into the lounge with a hard scowl. Everyone respected him. Everyone knew not to fuck with him. He had clout in all places, but there was still dissension within the gang, even after Hector's death. There were those who were still loyal to Hector and Penny, and wanted to avenge their boss's death by any means necessary, and then there were those who followed Alexandro, and felt the gang should go into a different and more ruthless direction.

Alexandro was younger, vicious, and hungry enough to do whatever was necessary to keep the gang's fierce and notorious name ringing out. The Ghost Ridas were his family, and he was determined that no one was going to tarnish their ferocious, pit-bull reputation in the streets.

Alexandro and a few hardcore members felt that Hector had to go because he was hindering what they once stood for—fear and respect.

Penny moved through the lounge with his lone thug, and the other gang members greeted the O.G. with hellos and respect. But he was only there on business—to confront Alexandro about his thoughtless action.

The two proceeded toward a back room, which was authorized only for certain members to enter. Penny was one of those members. There was a broad-shouldered, tatted up, scowling Mexican thug protecting the door. Penny walked toward him without missing a beat. He locked eyes with the man and said sternly, "You gonna get the fuck out my way, *puta*?"

The man scowled harder. His loyalty was to Alexandro, but Penny was a major figure in the gang.

"I gotta check wit' Alexandro, Penny…no disrespect to you," he replied.

"So, he the boss now?"

The man shrugged like a mindless goon. The thug Penny came with scowled back at the tall goon and lifted his shirt, revealing the chrome .9mm tucked snugly in his waistband. "Ay, *puta*, you gonna disrespect an O.G. like that? You fuckin' crazy, ay?" he exclaimed.

"Ay, nah…no disrespect to Penny," he meekly replied.

"Then move the fuck out our way, *puta*."

Not having a choice, he sidestepped away from the door entrance and allowed Penny and his thug to enter. Everyone was watching, anticipating something going down. When Penny entered the room, weed smoke lingered in the air, music was playing, and Alexandro was seated on the couch sandwiched between two big-breasted, whorish women. He was accompanied by other sullen gang members.

"Penny, what's up?" Alexandro greeted with a smile.

"We need to talk," said Penny. He looked around the room and added,

"Alone."

"You don't feel comfortable wit' ya own homies, Penny? I thought we were all family in this room," Alexandro called out.

"I haven't been feeling too much of anything lately," he replied.

Alexandro sighed with his cold look fixed on Penny. It was obvious to the room that there were some ill feelings between the two. Penny stood tall, his reputation preceding him. No one wanted to be in the crossfire between these two men. Penny was adamant when he said he wanted to speak alone with Alexandro. Alexandro looked reluctant, but decided it was best to give Penny what he wanted.

"Y'all *perras largate*," he said to his two whores; they hesitated to leave. Alexandro shouted it again, "Y'all fuckin' deaf? I said y'all bitches get the fuck out!"

They jumped up from his side like the couch had caught on fire and hurried out of the room. The men stayed behind. Penny looked at everyone else and said, "Everyone!"

Alexandro didn't like taking orders from anyone, but he swallowed his ego and nodded for his men to leave the room also. When they left, he turned to Penny's lone thug and said, "Yours too."

Penny nodded to his man. Like the loyal soldier he was, he exited the room without a peep, leaving his boss to handle his business. When the door shut, and the two men were alone in the back room, Penny decided not to sugarcoat a damn thing. He walked toward Alexandro, and asked with a frown, "Did you have somethin' to do wit' Hector's death?"

Alexandro looked puzzled. "What?"

Penny frowned harder. "Ay, *ser real conmigo*…don't fuckin' lie to me, Alexandro."

"Where you hear nonsense like that from? Who the fuck you been talkin' to? That bitch, Cartier?" Alexandro exclaimed.

"Don't worry about it; I just want the fuckin' truth."

"The truth, Hector's dead and instead of you tryin' to revenge his death by killing the *putas* responsible, the Miami Gotti Boys, you fuckin' confronts me! Are you fuckin' serious? *Él era mi hermano también!*"

Penny fixed his eyes on Alexandro. Alexandro didn't break a sweat.

Penny had his doubts. Alexandro was an ambitious muthafucka who yearned to be the one on top. It was definitely in his character to use the situation with Swagger M and to throw salt on Hector's credibility to get what he wanted. Penny didn't have any solid evidence to back up his speculations, but he wasn't going to stop until he found some.

"You done trying to bring down one of your fellow brothers, ay?" said Alexandro matter-of-factly. "Who side you on, ours or theirs?"

Penny didn't respond. In his gut, he knew there was foul play within their ranks. He was trying to work out the situation before Hector was killed, but somehow, fate intervened, or someone overreacted. The two continued to have harsh words with each other in Spanish, and Penny was about to lose his cool. Alexandro was an arrogant and naïve dude.

"Enjoy the top, Alexandro, cuz there's only one way to go from there and that's the bottom. I will continue to look into this, because things just don't seem right," said Penny.

"You barkin' up the wrong fuckin' tree! I'm Ghost Ridas, ay, fo' life. Ain't no changin' that, *puta*…" he shouted.

Penny was done talking. He left the room, leaving Alexandro startled. However, Alexandro knew he had to take care of the problem, before the problem took care of him. He glared at Penny, and when he disappeared from his sight, Alexandro called in two of his top enforcers and shut the door to have a few words with them in private.

Penny climbed into his Audi and lingered behind the steering wheel for a moment. He had a lot of thinking to do. He wanted to get on the phone and call Cartier, but it was getting late. She was still staying at his place, under his protection. The streets were no longer safe for anyone; even he had to move with caution and keep a low profile. When he heard about Marcus, the Black Mamba, being gunned down in front of the Perricone's Marketplace, a chilly feeling swept over him. The Black Mamba was like the king of all kings in Miami, and if someone had gotten to him so easily, Miami was becoming the Dodge City of the east—hell on earth.

Penny drove home underneath a star-studded sky. The weather was warm, but the streets were so cold. Armed with a .45 and a Glock 17, Penny wasn't taking any chances getting caught slipping. It was hell everywhere in Miami, and with his friends violently losing their lives, he felt the Grim Reaper might be coming after him next. It was becoming hard to trust people; everybody was out for self or taking sides. The Ghost Ridas were being ripped apart by civil war—and Alexandro was the man behind the chaos. Penny smelt it.

He came to a stop in front of his apartment complex in East Little Havana. It was after midnight when he climbed out of his Audi and walked toward his apartment under the cover of night with his pistols near his reach. For once, the streets felt quiet, but quiet streets didn't mean safe streets. He entered the lobby and walked toward the stairway, removing his pistol and keeping it handy, cocked back and ready for anything. An uneasy feeling came over him. Was Cartier alright? He was about to call the landline when he remembered that Cartier had her friend, Apple, flying in tomorrow morning. She was staying at one of her undisclosed properties where they'd all be safe.

Penny moved up the stairway with his .45 in his hand. He walked up to the third floor. His apartment building was quiet, clean, and neighbors weren't in his business. It was one of the reasons why he loved living there. Not too many people knew where Penny rested his head. The fewer, the better.

However, the second Penny exited the stairway onto the third floor he jolted from the swift attack of a sharp blade sinking into his stomach.

His attacker repeatedly thrust the sharp blade into his abdomen and flesh. Penny found himself helpless. The gun dropped from his hand and he keeled over from the pain. He dropped to his knees, feeling his life slipping away from him. He looked up at this attacker, clinging to the man, and saw the man was in a ski-mask. He didn't doubt that it was one of his own that came at him.

"Die, muthafucka!" his attacker said.

Penny found himself lying on his back, with multiple stab wounds to his stomach. He clutched his wound, his hands coated with blood. The man took off running. Penny's breathing was becoming sparse, his life little by little fading from him. And then soon, he was dead, mere feet away from his apartment door.

Apple, Sin, and Row flew into Miami International airport early that morning. The trio moved off the American Airlines flight and into the bustling airport. Not carrying much luggage and aching to meet up with Cartier, they hurried through the busy terminal and outside into The Sunshine State. Apple was ready to hit the town like a raging bull, her first priority to get the rundown from her friend and load themselves up with heavy artillery.

It was Apple's first time in Miami. She remembered her sister coming down here not too long ago and doing big things for a minute with the right peoples, but then she got caught up, snitched on, and stabbed in prison, and came back to New York. She wasn't going to go running home like Kola; she wasn't afraid of Miami. She was ready to show out and let the city know who the fuck she was and what her dogs were about. In Apple's eyes, Miami was the country, and the country wasn't ready for a die-hard, city bitch like herself.

After the crew waited about ten minutes, Cartier pulled up in a gray Chrysler minivan with tinted windows. She was alone. Apple greeted her friend with a hug, and the trio climbed inside the van.

Once they pulled off, Cartier started to explain the situation to Apple. She was no longer sitting on the throne; her man was dead. The hit that took out Hector cost her everything, but she still had three men out of three dozen that were riding with her to avenge Hector's death. She explained that they were loyal to Cartier because they knew Hector loved her.

Apple was listening, fuming. She depended on Cartier's position to help find her daughter. It seemed like the trip was becoming a waste of time. But she refused to go home empty-handed.

"I got three men that are loyal to me, but that's not enough muscle to go after this muthafucka," Cartier exclaimed.

"Who's the muthafucka?" asked Apple.

"His name is Alexandro. They saying he's the new leader of the Ghost Ridas. Since Hector's death, he's taken over every meth lab in the city, the prostitution ring, the coke…everything, the whole gamut. He started to turn my man's gang against him, brought down his credibility, and soon afterwards, Hector was murdered," Cartier stated.

Thinking back to his death made chills go down her spine. She continued with, "Hector was supposed to sit down Alexandro and a few others the day when he was murdered. Alexandro never liked me in the first place. Now, between them and the contract on my head by the Gonzalez cartel, I feel trapped into a corner," she said.

Cartier hadn't really slept in days. She felt like a driver in the Indy 500; one slip up could send her crashing and burning into a wall. She had a strong feeling that Alexandro was behind Hector's murder, but it was only speculation. She felt that with Penny by her side, the truth was going to come out. But she was impatient, and ready to kill every last person who had betrayed her, talked shit about her, or even looked at her wrong since the day she arrived in Miami.

"I'm here now, Cartier. Fuck these niggas out here! We gonna get ya revenge," Apple declared. "You got what we asked for, right?"

"Yeah, I have some stuff in the back, and everything else is at the stash house I'm staying at," Cartier said.

"A'ight, we gonna take things over from here. This fuckin' city ain't gonna even see me and my goons coming," Apple said chillingly.

Cartier navigated her way through the city streets, going north. She drove on the expressway in the low-key minivan, heading toward North Miami where she had been laying her head in one of the properties she owned. It was a three-bedroom, ranch style home by the bay. The area was quiet and nestled between hundreds of others homes that resembled hers in so many ways.

Cartier pulled into the driveway of the home and everyone poured out of the van. Right away, everyone was met by two Ghost Ridas goons that were staying with her, Taps and Rico, both die-hard gangsters who were loyal to Hector and respected Penny. They each had love and respect for Cartier, and wanted to see her come out okay, even if it meant going against their own crew. Neither had any love for Alexandro.

Cartier started the introductions, and everyone became cool with each other. But it wasn't the time to mingle. It was war. Cartier noticed the look on Taps's and Rico's faces. They looked heartbroken about something. Taps eyes were watery, and so were Rico's. It seemed like they were holding their emotions in about something. While Apple and her men went into the home, Taps and Rico remained outside.

"We gotta talk, Cartier," Rico said with his voice heavy with sorrow.

Cartier knew it wasn't going to be good news. The past few days had been nerve-racking and hell-bent. She took a deep breath and said to Rico, "Just fuckin' say it."

Rico looked choked up, but he came out and said it. "Penny's dead."

Cartier felt like she was about to have a panic attack. She wasn't expecting to hear him say that. She stood bewildered, and then the anger started to creep inside her. Rico continued with, "They caught him at his apartment, stabbed him to death."

Penny was the one man left that she truly trusted. With him gone, it was the last of the realness and a dying breed. Everything seemed to be in shambles. Cartier didn't have time to cast off any tears for Penny. She held back the reaction, sucked in the pain, and refocused on her revenge. Taps and Rico felt the same way. Penny and Hector, over the years, had been like fathers to the two young gangbangers.

They entered the home and started to make Apple and her goons feel welcome. The first thing Apple wanted to know was where the guns were. Taps and Rico went into a back room and started to remove an arsenal for their guests. They had everything from Uzis, assault rifles, grenades, automatic pistols, and shotguns—the two gangbangers even pulled out a rocket launcher. The front room started to look like a gun shop had exploded, raining down every type of gun in the book.

"Damn, what the fuck are y'all two, Rambo?" Row joked.

The two gangbangers smiled devilishly. Rico replied, "We don't like to miss."

"I fuckin' hear that," Row replied.

With the only muscle they had in Miami, Apple and Cartier had to strategize their next move and put the pieces back together so they could get strong enough to go after their foes, including the Gonzalez cartel. Apple wanted to go after the Gonzalez cartel first. Cartier wanted to hunt after Alexandro. They both had their own objectives, but they each were ready to kill together.

With Taps, Rico, Sin, and Row teaming up with them, they had to hit hard and hit fast. It was now or never.

The outside of King of Diamonds was flooded with ladies and ballers leaving the club at the wee hours in the morning. The parking lot was overflowing with high-end cars—Porsches, Maybachs, Ferraris, Lamborghinis, and Mercedes decorating the night. The ladies strutted with the shot-callers and ballers in their stilettos and miniskirts. Blaring music, laughter and chitchat echoed from car to car. It was as much of a party outside in the parking lot as it was in the club.

Waiting patiently in a pearl-colored Lexus and looking for the right signal were Sin and Rico, partnered up and armed to the tee. They shared a cigarette and kept a keen eye out on their target: A tall, lanky gangbanger named Links, a member of Ghost Ridas who'd sided with Alexandro. He strutted from the club with a beautiful, scantily clad, curvaceous stripper under his arm. They walked toward his tricked-out Chevy, parked in the lot. The men watched Links escort his newfound pussy for the night into the passenger side and rush around to the driver's side. He seemed eager to get the fun started.

Rico took the last pull from the burning cigarette, flicked it out the window and said to Sin, "Let's fuckin' do this."

He started the car and began following the Chevy out of the parking lot and onto the highway. The Chevy pulled into a cheesy motel off I-95. The sun was slowly rising over the city, burning off the chill of the night air as the Lexus slyly followed behind the Chevy. The duo observed Links and his whorish companion exit the car and head toward the motel lobby. It was obvious what they were there to do. Rico and Sin stepped out of the car with their pistols concealed on their persons. Like two hit-men from the movie *Pulp Fiction,* they coolly walked toward the motel lobby and saw Links pay the clerk in cash and receive a keycard.

When Links walked away from the lobby, the duo entered. They confronted the clerk, a long-limbed, freckled and pale-faced young kid.

Sin shoved the gun into his face and the clerk became wide-eyed like he was about to pee on himself.

"What room did they go into?" Sin growled at the kid.

Shaking like a leaf, the clerk didn't give them any problems. "Room 204…the second floor," he stammered.

Rico stood behind Sin, remaining calm.

"You gonna make us a copy of that room key, right?" said Rico with composure.

The clerk nodded rapidly.

"Cool."

The clerk didn't hesitate to make a duplicate keycard for the two goons. He handed it over to Sin with a shaky hand. When Sin snatched the key, Rico stepped toward the kid and sneered at him.

"Look, *puta*, give us your ID."

The frightened clerk snatched out his wallet and removed his driver's license.

Rico took it and then said to the kid, "When we leave here, you ain't gonna call 911, right?"

"No…I won't," he replied, his voice trembling with fear.

"I know you won't; we now know who you are and where you live," replied Rico, looking at the address on his license.

They left the kid peeing in his pants and took the stairs up to the second floor. Room 204 was right by the stairway. With their guns drawn and keycard in their hand, the men had the element of surprise. Rico carefully slipped the keycard into the lock and when the red light changed to green, both men rushed into the room like hurricane wind.

Links was shocked by the sudden entry and was literally caught with his pants down. The stripper he was with started to scream, but Sin shoved his huge cannon in her face and warned her to *shut the fuck up*.

"What the fúck, Rico? What the fuck is goin' on here?" Links shouted.

Rico wasn't interested in verbal explanations. He smashed the butt of his gun across Links's head and caused his victim to stagger back from the harsh blow and fall against the bed.

"Now we need to talk, Links," Rico demanded.

Holding his head from the blow, Links grimaced at Rico and shouted, "Fuck you!"

Rico didn't hesitate to pistol-whip him while Sin held the bitch on the bed at gunpoint. Links's face quickly coated with blood. Rico pulled him off the bed and informed him that they were taking a ride somewhere. They dragged him and the girl through the lobby, stuffed them in the trunk, and drove off.

A few miles from the motel, the trunk opened up with to reveal Links and his stripper gagged, bound, and squirming. Apple and Cartier gazed down at their intended victims. It was time for questions and answers. Sin and Rico removed Links and his stripper friend from the trunk and forced them into the discreet location. In one of the isolated rooms in the vacant storefront on the quiet strip, the stripper was immediately shot to death, and Links was tortured with a blowtorch to his crotch and vise grips pulling out teeth and nails until he revealed vital information about Alexandro. When he was no longer useful, and his skin started to smell like burnt flesh, Cartier put three hot rounds into his skull. It was some payback for Hector and Penny.

# CHAPTER 16

## *Citi*

Clad in a purple silk robe with a G-string underneath, Citi slowly disrobed herself for her new customer. Her sensuous curves and beautiful brown skin glistened under the room light. She had gone from riches to rags, from being a spoiled princess living in the big house to having to turn tricks at an escort house to survive. It was degrading and beneath her, but with Ashanti adamant at seeing her daughter's downfall and not taking her mother's threat too lightly, she needed a ruse—a temporary haven until she could figure things out.

A week after Ashanti put Citi out she had a change of heart. It was no longer good enough for her daughter to remain breathing—not after fucking her husband. Ashanti just couldn't shake the nightmares she'd have of Marcus eating her daughter's pussy and then coming smiling up in her face. The images nearly drove Ashanti to a nervous breakdown. A stripper was the messenger who told Citi that a bounty was put on her head. The thought terrified her when she found out just how close she came to being murdered. The last place her mother would look for her would be in a whorehouse. But her stay there wasn't free, it came at a cost—her body. She went from sleeping with a handsome kingpin to fucking a gangster for a roof over her head.

"Yeah, take that shit off," he said while licking his lips and staring at

Citi like a hungry lion eyeing a wandering, small prey.

Citi did. Her robe fell to her feet and her panties came off next. The horny man seated in front of her couldn't wait to lay his hands all over her and put his dick inside her sweet goodies. She was the stepdaughter of a slain kingpin—a natural prize to have under his control.

Citi looked at Alexandro with a slight smile, her nakedness glowing like a light bulb in the dark. He was ready to ravage her sweet, curvy body from head to toe like a fat kid eating chocolate. Citi was his personal whore in the house where many other ladies turned tricks on the daily; however, she was only his to play with. In her predicament, she had no choice; she was trapped in a corner that was falling apart. Cane was nowhere to be found and she couldn't get in contact with him. When she heard the news about Marcus, she broke down in tears. She really loved him. But the real disaster was that the things he'd promised her, everything, was all gone so suddenly, like a Thanksgiving meal at the Fat Boys' house. No one had her back except Alexandro—the tatted up, violent thug who was now running the Ghost Ridas. Citi had caught his eyes when she was wandering on the streets. Alexandro approached her and offered her a place to stay.

The past several days hadn't been her best, but she was somewhere okay. She had caught some feelings for Alexandro since she'd started staying in the home. He was cute and the man in charge. He looked out for her, in a way. He took her in, put a roof over her head, and took her under his wing—for a cost, however. Nothing was free. The power he did have was slightly impressive. But she was no fool, knowing men like Alexandro didn't last too long in the game. One reason: He was too reckless and didn't have what it took to become a true don. He was immature and a hothead. He ran a violent gang, but her father and Marcus had run an empire. He lacked the quality to have longevity in the game. Yes, Alexandro was feared, but he wasn't respected. Men like her father and Marcus demanded both. Their qualities and smarts had made them legends.

Citi had to settle when everything was ripped away from her—work her way from the bottom to the top. It was something she'd never had to do before. She grew up with a silver spoon in her mouth. Being penniless and homeless made her desperate, and being desperate made her do things that were completely outside her character. It was embarrassing, yes, but in the streets, it was survival—at least, until she made her move.

Citi waited for Alexandro to make his move—to take from her what so many men yearned for—pussy. The lust in his eyes displayed his strong desire to have the daughter of a former don suck and fuck him. He took a swig of the vodka in his hand and stood up. He smiled at his pretty young thing and unzipped his pants. He took another swig from the bottle and pulled out his rising cock.

Citi wasn't impressed. Her attitude remained impassive. He jerked himself off to some extent and smiled at Citi, saying to her, "Ay, go 'head girl, do ya thang wit' it. It ain't gonna suck itself."

Citi took a deep breath. He had an okay size—Mexican sure wasn't better. She leaned forward and slowly took the mushroom tip into her mouth. Alexandro cooed, feeling the pleasures below. She shoved his dick further down her throat, her juicy, full lips blanketing his average width and feeling his hard flesh pulsating in her mouth.

"Ooooh, that feels so good. Ooooh, yeah," he groaned with his hand entangled in her hair.

Citi continued to suck him off, feeling the heat of his penis and his precum swirling around in her mouth. Alexandro gripped the back of her head and shoved her face further into his pelvis, causing Citi to perform a deep-throat action. His balls banged against her chin. On her knees for this Mexican thug was a serious downgrade for her. He closed his eyes and found himself in bliss.

"Ay, I wanna fuck," Alexandro said, pulling his dick from her mouth.

Citi stood up. She didn't want to, but in her position, what choice did she have? Alexandro curved her over the chair with her legs spread and thrust inside her pussy, raw. Citi gasped, her fists clenched around the cushion of the chair, her pussy opening up like a small doorway. As Alexandro pounded into her roughly, the tears started to fall from her eyes. This is what she had become, dropping from royalty to a whore. Her mother still had it all. She was living in a sprawling dynasty while Citi had nothing—not even a pot to piss in. The situation angered her, and the only thing that kept Citi from killing herself was getting revenge against Ashanti and seeing the bitch fall from her high horse. The thought of that bitch winning drove her to the brink of insanity.

"Damn, ya pussy is so good…so good, so good," he chanted.

Citi felt him digging inside of her vigorously like an earthworm tunneling through dirt. His hands were all over the place, cupping her swinging tits, palming her round, protruding ass. His dick drowned inside her juicy wetness as he gripped her hips and damn near fell in love with everything about her. Being inside of her didn't take him long. He was soon coming. His cock swelled with anticipation, and when he felt his nut brewing, he pulled out and shot his white load on the small of her back. It was the best he'd ever had.

He huffed and tossed Citi a towel and told her to clean up. A knocking at the door made Alexandro turn his head and reach for his gun.

"Who?" he shouted.

"Alex, it's me, Smiley. We got that thing in an hour."

"A'ight, give me a minute." He pulled up and fastened his jeans, feeling very satisfied.

After she was done cleaning the sperm off her back, Citi threw back on her robe and took a seat in front of Alexandro.

"Ay, you did good today, baby. I like ya style. You fuck wit' me 'n' you ain't gotta worry 'bout nobody else fuckin' wit' you," said Alexandro.

Citi was silent. She heard him, and wanted to believe him. She needed some protection at the moment. Dealing with the Mexicans was her temporary haven. Alexandro had said his peace and busted his nut. He opened the door and Smiley walked in. Smiley stood six-foot-three and weighed 260 pounds. He was a moving tank—an iron giant. He stared at Citi and then looked at Alexandro.

"Ay, you good here?" he asked Alex.

"Yeah, I'm good," Alexandro replied.

Smiley gazed at Citi for a moment before he left the room, taking in her natural beauty. The goons wanted a slice of her heaven, too, but Alexandro prevented her from being passed around. He had promised her that she would be only for himself. No one else in the world could have her. She was his addiction.

"I'll be back sometime tonight. Like always, make yourself at home. And if you leave, I have the power to find and kill you," he said coldly.

Citi didn't plan on going anywhere. In some awkward way, she kind of felt indebted to him, despite the way he spoke to and treated her. He was a necessary growing pain. When Alexandro left, Citi could only close her eyes and think about the one thing that fueled her anger and strength the most—Ashanti.

She dozed off and woke up to gunshots going off and screaming outside the room. In a panic, Citi donned her robe and stared at the door. She had nothing to protect herself with. She heard yelling and more gunshots. When Citi emerged from the back room, she saw two women and four scowling goons holding one of Alexandro's henchmen at gunpoint. Two bodies were already lying on the ground. The other whores in the room were frozen to the ground at gunpoint. Citi didn't recognize either one of the ladies. The one with the short, blonde hair raised her pistol at Conrad, a Ghost Ridas soldier, and threatened to blow his brains out. He stood defiant, scowling at the intruders.

"Where the fuck is he?" she shouted.

"Fuck y'all bitches! You know who spot this is?" he spat through his clenched teeth.

"Yeah, it's the fuckin' reason why we here," the blonde responded, and then *Bak!* The man's brains and blood were splattered against the wall behind him. The whores screamed and panicked, but the goons had them under control. The Uzis gripped in their hands made everyone cooperate fully.

Citi was shocked and tried to duck back into the room to hide, but she was too late. Cartier had seen her. The two locked eyes and Apple became the threat. She rushed over with her pistol aimed at Citi and shouted, "Bitch, who the fuck you lookin' at?"

Citi was wide-eyed and scared; she tried to remain calm, though—becoming speechless. Apple glared at her. She was ready to snatch away the girl's life in a heartbeat. Cartier intervened, saying to her partner in crime, "No, not here…not her."

"Why not?" Apple growled.

Cartier fixed her eyes on Citi; there was something familiar about her. Apple was ready to murder Citi, becoming paranoid and thinking she was some undercover federal agent. There was something about Citi that she didn't like. The pretty, young bitch was just too calm.

"I think this bitch is a cop," she hollered with the gun trained at Citi's head.

"Nah, she's no cop, but I know her from somewhere," Cartier chimed.

Citi kept her exterior cool, but she was terrified on the inside. Her life was in the hands of these two crazy bitches. Where did they come from? What did they want? It was clear as day they were looking for Alexandro and they wanted to kill him. But how many bodies did they plan on leaving behind? The survivors in the room were anticipating the worst. The women had come in shooting, killing the men first. They already had gotten their message across.

Cartier stared hard at Citi, trying to place her face, but it wasn't coming to her fast enough. "I know you from somewhere," said Cartier.

Citi didn't respond. She frowned, wishing Cane was by her side to protect her. But this time, it was only her. With Apple itching to pull the trigger, Cartier was still trying to figure things out. It was eating away at her, trying to place where she knew Citi from.

"If you can't place her face, then fuck it, I'll make her a fuckin' memory," Apple said.

It was then that Cartier remembered how she knew the young girl. They had met a few months back at one of Hector's events. She was with another cartel, the Black Mamba and his crew. And if her memory served her right, she was the daughter or stepdaughter of the Black Mamba. Everyone had heard about his recent death. Cartier became puzzled, though, as to why she was in such a degrading place, hanging out with gangbangers and selling her ass.

"You're Black Mamba's daughter, right?" Cartier asked.

"Who the fuck is the Black Mamba?" Apple questioned.

Citi was reluctant to answer. Her heart pounded heavily. She didn't know what was going to happen to her. Marcus was deceased, and now the streets had become a vacuum for violence. Other crews, other cartels wanted in, to take over what Marcus, Hector, and Penny had left behind. Citi found herself on the receiving end of the violence.

"We're not gonna hurt you. I promise," Cartier said genuinely.

"You know this bitch, Cartier?" Apple asked.

"Somewhat…" said Cartier. "What's your name?"

Finally, she spoke. "Citi…everyone calls me Citi."

"Where you from? Cuz you ain't from this town." Cartier recognized her Northern accent.

"Jamaica, Queens," Citi replied, hesitantly.

"Brooklyn," Cartier stated.

Apple gave a head nod. "Harlem."

"You know why we are here, right?" said Cartier.

"You want Alexandro," Citi replied.

"You fuck wit' him?"

"I do," Citi admitted.

Cartier seemed disgusted by it. It didn't make any sense on how a woman in her position could fall so low. She allowed Citi to tell her story.

Citi explained why she was in this place, telling Cartier about the hit on her life from her own mother, and how she needed to get in contact with her older brother, Cane. Cartier decided Citi could be useful to them. Citi had an ax to grind with her mother, and if Citi was willing to help them set up Alexandro, then they would help her get revenge on her mother.

Cartier wanted to know who gave the hit out to murder Hector. She knew it was Alexandro, and she wanted to see him dead. Also, Alexandro had a list of cartel members and associates that would be very useful to her, and with two contract killers trying to hunt her down in Miami, her time was running out.

And thus, the trio created a pact—their own cartel bent on retribution and destruction.

# CHAPTER 17

❦

## *Citi, Apple, Cartier*

Alexandro was outraged by the invasion in his place and the slaughter of three of his men. *How did it happen?* Citi was there to console him and gave him the false details and explained how she survived by hiding in the closet when rivals came in and gunned everyone down. It was carnage. Alexandro was out for blood, but his fate had already been set in motion.

They moved to a new, more discreet location near the airport, not too far from the swamplands. War was raging heavily, and the streets were aflame—the violence burning heavily like a wildfire, taking out everything in its path. Everybody was killing each other, and the Ghost Ridas were caught in the eye of the storm—an apocalypse, now. Then there was a new force in town; someone was helping Cartier kill heavily. Whoever it was, their reputation was growing. It angered Alexandro that the bitch wasn't dead yet.

Alexandro decided to keep out of sight for a while. He stayed shacked up with Citi and only gave orders to two of his trusted lieutenants. Other than that, he remained low-key. So many rivals were out for blood, and the pressure was building up.

Alexandro lay naked across the bed while Citi poured him a drink—Henny and Sprite. They had just finished fucking, and now it was time to relax. Citi had a different agenda than relaxing with her newfound man. She wanted him to get comfortable, and some good pussy and alcohol had Alexandro feeling like he was on cloud nine.

Citi straddled her man as she gave him his cup. Alexandro was stressed with a lot on his mind. He downed the drink like it was water and frowned. Recent information had him paranoid; there was a full federal investigation going on, and his inside source told him that federal indictments were about to be handed out to him and over a dozen lieutenants in the violent gang.

Citi continued to straddle her man and make him feel at ease. Her pussy rubbed against his manhood gently. The hour was late. He was feeling comfy and drowsy. Unbeknownst to Alexandro, his drink was drugged, a mixture of sodium thiopental aka truth serum that she purchased from a health food store and a few crushed sedatives.

"You know you can talk to me about anything, baby," Citi cooed in his ear.

"Talk to you about what?" he replied sharply.

The effects of the concoction hadn't settled in yet. She was patiently waiting. He was going to slip up, and she was going to catch the truth.

"I see you doin' ya thang, the one on top. How that happened?"

"Ay, fuck you mean how that happened? I do my thang. What you questioning it fo'?"

"I was just curious. I grew up around powerful men, and I can see you becoming one of them."

At her statement, Alexandro instantly caught an attitude. "Fuck you talkin' about? I ain't becoming powerful. I *am* powerful, bitch. I'm the nigga not to fuck wit," he barked.

"I didn't mean to disrespect you. You are powerful, baby. I just keep hearing ya men talk about Hector—"

"Fuck Hector!" Alexandro shouted. "Hector was a fuckin' fool!"

"He was?"

"Yeah, he was…" Alexandro said. His speech started to slur.

"Did you kill him?"

"The nigga got what was comin' to him, that's all I gotta say. There's a changing of the guard goin' on in Miami, from Hector to your stepfather…" said Alexandro.

Hearing him speak about Marcus piqued her interest even more.

"What about my stepfather?" she asked.

"He's just another nigga whose reign on top was too damn long," Alexandro said.

"Who set him up?" she shouted.

Alexandro laughed. "Bitch, you need to look into ya own circle fo' that…"

"Who set him up?" she screamed.

The concoction hadn't settled into his system fully yet—he was still aware of what was going on. He pushed Citi off of him and stood up, scowling. He glared at Citi and realized what was happening.

"Bitch, you tryin' to set me up?" he shouted.

"I just want the fuckin' truth!"

Alexandro raised his hand and gave Citi a backhand smack across her face. She flew across the bed. He rushed over to her and pulled her by the hair. "Who's tryin' to set me up?" he screamed.

She didn't answer. He struck her again, this time with his fist. Blood spewed from her mouth, as her jaw felt like it was on fire, and she landed on her side. The blow was hard and damn near knocked her out cold. Citi refused to black out though. She stood, looking dark, and heatedly exclaimed, "You better not ever put ya fuckin' hands on me again, or I'll fuckin' kill you."

"Bitch… what?" Alexandro stammered.

He started to feel dizzy and weak. He stumbled, grabbing for the bed to keep his balance. He stared at Citi, knowing something was wrong. He exclaimed, "You can't kill me, you dumb bitch. I'm ya only protection out there. Who you have, huh? You can try and kill me, but you fuckin' can't!"

Citi snarled back, "Do you think I can't kill you because I'm not built for murder, or because you think I actually love you?"

Alexandro's face twisted into rage. He was ready to rip her into pieces. He stepped forward, but stumbled. He then uttered, "I know you can't kill me, because no one can. I can't die."

He was becoming delusional. He was talking crazy. When he tried to attack Citi again, he abruptly fell to the floor and passed out on his stomach. The concoction had fully settled into his system. Citi stood over him with her face warped in resentment. Finally, the predator became the prey. It would be too easy to kill him while he lay flat on his face. He was vulnerable for once. But it wasn't her revenge to take. She had made a promise, and she was going to keep her promise. When he awoke, he was going to see true evil and cruelty.

The next morning, Alexandro was rudely awakened by having cold water thrown in his face. He stirred roughly and cursed loudly. "What the fuck!"

When Alexandro finally was able to open his eyes and observe his surroundings, the first thing he saw was Citi. Angry, he tried to attack her, but found himself butt-naked and tied tightly to a chair. He couldn't move. He was defenseless—and he wasn't alone. Cartier, Apple, and Citi stood around him. They glared at him like he was the antichrist. Cartier despised him, and she wanted to see him suffer greatly. But first, she needed information from him.

When Alexandro realized what was going on, he cursed, "Fuck y'all bitches!"

Then the horror settled in for Alexandro when he saw the heads of one his lieutenants and his own mother displayed in front of him like an art project—their faces frozen, in a horrific death—eyes frightfully opened and expressions twisted. With his eyes widened in shock, he tried to free himself from his restraints and madly cried out.

"Fuck y'all bitches, man! That was my moms...y'all ain't had to go there! I'MA FUCKIN' KILL EVERY LAST ONE OF Y'ALL!!" he wildly screamed.

Apple pistol-whipped him repeatedly and told him to shut the fuck up. Blood coated the side of his face with his eyes still carrying rage. He was in the hands of wickedness. He fought the restraints once more, violently trying to free himself from the chair, grunting and jerking, but it was hopeless—it felt like he was being held down by heavy boulders.

Cartier came into his view. She smirked. He was now hers to play with. They locked eyes, their hatred for each other manifested like a public show. Alexandro began breathing heavily. His eyes averted from her and noticed the intimidating apparatus in her hands. He scowled harder, trying to remain the tough guy.

"You remember me, right, Alexandro?" Cartier said to him coolly.

"Fuck you, bitch!"

"Fuck me, you wish...but we gonna talk."

"Fuck you!!!"

"Alexandro, we can do this the easy way, or the fuckin' hard way," she spat.

"Fuck you, you dumb bitch! I wish they would have killed you along wit' Hector," he screamed out.

That set off Cartier, and her look transformed into that of a raging bitch. She lit the small blowtorch in her hand, and the hot, blue flame came alive. Alexandro fixed his eyes on the flame as it came closer to his person. It didn't take a rocket scientist to understand what was coming next. She wasn't trying to scare him either. This was real. She neared the flame to his face, and he cringed.

"Who killed my man?" she questioned through clenched teeth.

He refused to talk. Cartier needed to give him some incentive. She sneered and neared the blowtorch to his naked, exposed balls and dick. Alexandro cringed away even harder, but there was nothing he could do. When the flame started to singe his balls, he jerked violently from the excessive pain and hollered loudly—it sounded like an animal. It sounded inhuman.

"Who killed him? Was it you? Just admit it, Alexandro, just give me fuckin' names," Cartier exclaimed.

He still was defiant. Cartier placed the flame to his dick this time, and the howling was even louder, blasting through the room like a cold, winter chill. Apple and Citi stood and watched. They both were detached and numb. The smell of a man burning didn't bother them one bit. Apple was ready to see more and torture him herself.

Cartier's eyes were so black toward Alexandro, it seemed like he was staring into a black hole. She had no revulsion or regret for his pain. She was ready to see him ignite…but bit by bit. She repeatedly held the scorching flames to his crotch, and Alexandro shook vehemently from the extreme heat charring his manhood. Cartier worked the flames everywhere on his body like an artist to a canvas. His skin began to melt, bubble, and alter into something disgusting. The smell of burning flesh was becoming intense.

"Aaaaaaaahhhh!! Aaaaaaaaahh!" he screamed like crazy.

"Tell me something, muthafucka!" Cartier screamed back.

Alexandro sat limp, leaning to his right. If it hadn't been for the restraints, he would have tumbled over. His skin was a charred black, like charcoal, and covered with blisters. The torture went on for nearly ten minutes, and the man was still stubborn as a mule. But he was fading. Cartier was ready to continue.

This time she neared the flame to his left eye. He tried to fight it, but Apple grabbed his head and held him steady to receive the pain. The flame was blinding, but before Cartier could burn his eye out, Alexandro weakened and uttered distraughtly, "It wasn't just me that wanted Hector dead, it was the fuckin' cartel, too."

"Which cartel?" she asked.

"The Gonzalez cartel. Hector was fuckin' up—they wanted him gone, too…and they promised me extra protection if I did the hit…and they would give me his throne. It…it wasn't just me involved. They want you, bitch, and they want you bad…and he pissed them off when he took you in," Alexandro said feebly.

Hearing that information made Cartier more furious. Citi intervened and shouted, "Who killed Marcus?"

Blood ejected from Alexandro's mouth, but he managed to chuckle at Citi's question. She was just too naïve to understand the game and realize the hit came from her own damn brother. He locked eyes with Citi and cursed, "Fuck you too, bitch."

Citi was ready to strike him, but it was useless—he was already falling apart. Cartier and Apple had done a serious number on him. Cartier was seething, though. The cartel and Alexandro murdered her man because he had taken her under his wing and protected her when they wanted her dead, and it was haunting her. She was the primary reason for his execution. But there were no more tears and no more feeling sorry for herself. Now it was time to do some execution of her own…starting with Alexandro.

She cut off the blowtorch and dropped it. Apple handed her a .9mm. Cartier gripped the gun in her hand and glared at Alexandro. The room knew what was going to transpire next. These bitches were gangster, hardcore, and as heartless as any gangbanger with a swinging dick—maybe even more heartless. They were women spawned from pain, rape, death, and betrayal. Each of them had nothing to lose and a strong point to prove. It was about to be a takeover.

Cartier stepped toward the tortured and beaten Alexandro. Her eyes fixed on the damage she had done to him. He was a mess. He was already a dead man. Cartier raised the .9mm to his head and said to him, "She couldn't kill you last night because she made me a promise. I wanted to kill you myself."

After those chilling words, she fired—point blank range between his eyes, and then again, again, again, and again until there was nothing left of his face to be recognizable. The trio stared at the dead man lying slumped and bent in the chair. This was their chilling life—there was no turning back now. They'd started something separately, but together, they would finish it.

Their operation became large-scale across the nation. The trio, who were now calling themselves the South Beach Cartel, were a ruthless group of women that the underworld wasn't ready for. They were smart, heartless, and cunning—and they were building an army of goons and killers, causing fear and intimidation not just in Miami, but on a national scale. Murder, extortion, prostitution, gambling, racketeering, and drugs became their forte.

Cartier was the brains, though. She came up with method of smuggling drugs—cocaine, meth, pills, molly, and weed—from state to state. With their wealth combined, the girls purchased half a dozen commercial trucks and two big rigs. To prepare the commercial trucks, they brought in a few brilliant artists to duplicate FedEx carriers. They ordered uniforms online, and the commercial trucks hit the roads and interstates in the guise of a legitimate company.

With the two tractor-trailers, concealing drugs in numerous hidden compartments was so much easier; many times, truck drivers trafficking drugs counted on the fact that most people don't know what is supposed to be on a truck and what isn't. Many types of custom-built canisters mounted on the outside of a tractor-trailer can be a potential hiding place for drugs. Sometimes these canisters will have fake lines and wires running from them into the truck, making them appear to be working pieces of machinery.

The numerous hidden compartments that Cartier had her drivers smuggle drugs in were the air filters/cleaners and lubrefiners, the air compressors, exhaust stacks, tubeless tires, fuel tanks, and the hydraulic system.

With this operation, their cartel was able to transport and distribute tons and tons of drugs across the States. But as business moved smoothly—money growing and flowing—they didn't forget about their main focus: revenge. They were plotting and at war with the Gonzalez cartel, and Apple was desperately trying to find her daughter and have her little girl in her life.

# CHAPTER 18

## *Manhunt*

The detectives shook their heads in shock and stared at the two bodies displayed in such a ghastly murder—they'd been thrown off the rooftop of a downtown high-rise from thirty stories high. The scene was so gruesome that a few people threw up at the sight of it. The bodies were almost liquefied and torn apart from the fall. Their faces and torsos had twisted violently from smashing into the concrete at a high and accelerating rate.

"Shit!" the detective uttered. "There are some heartless people in this city."

The two dead men were connected to the Gonzalez cartel. They were well-known contract killers with so much blood on their own hands. Finally, somebody had gotten the best of them—karma striking back. These were the fourth and fifth members of the Gonzalez cartel who had been brutally murdered in the past month. The cartel members were being hunted down like prey—slaughtered and gutted like pigs, their bodies displayed for a strong message. The South Beach Cartel's violent reputation was growing extremely quickly, and the fact that it was three women pulling the strings and getting the best of men infuriated so many people. But enough was enough.

The local Miami police force and the feds were putting together a joint task force to bring down everyone responsible for the gruesome murders and drugs. The South Beach Cartel and Gonzalez cartel were on top of their list.

The black Benz slowly pulled into the long driveway and disappeared into the two-car garage of the three-bedroom home in Hialeah, Florida. It was late in the evening and quiet in the sprawling suburbs. The passenger and the driver's doors opened simultaneously. Sin and Row were smiling and continuing their talk about the differences between New York and Miami. Row closed the garage door and once it was shut, Citi and Apple stepped into the garage.

"Did everything go okay?" Apple asked.

Row nodded.

He walked to the back of the car and popped open the trunk. Inside was someone bonded and gagged, squirming around in a large plastic covering. Their identity was not seen. Row and Sin snatched the person out of the trunk and carried them into the home. Citi and Apple followed behind them. It was the moment someone has been waiting for, for a very long time.

They carried the stranger into one of the empty bedrooms and dropped them on the floor like they were nothing—an inanimate object. But they squealed. The men stood over the person and waited for further instructions.

"Take that bitch out," said Citi with a frown.

They pulled away the plastic covering to reveal the identity of the captive. It was Ashanti. They had kidnapped her from one of her businesses and forced her into the trunk at gunpoint. When Ashanti turned to see who was scowling at her, she was shocked. She had no idea her daughter was still in Miami after all these months and had gained money, power, and respect on her own. She was definitely her mother's daughter.

"Citi, why are you doing this to me?" Ashanti cried out.

Citi was livid and unforgiving. She glared at her mother and felt her pussy dripping at having such a delicious opportunity in her hands. Finally, revenge was hers. Citi walked over and smacked her mother so hard, it echoed through the room and her hand began to sting.

"Shut the fuck up!" Citi shouted. "You ain't runnin' shit anymore, bitch!"

Ashanti looked up at her daughter in terror. Citi had morphed into a completely different woman.

"You think I was just goin' to go away, bitch? Wrong! Now look at you…look at you! I always hated you since you disrespected me, my father, and my brothers, and went to live a lavish life without ya fuckin' kids. You think I'm supposed to forgive that? Fuck you! You tried to embarrass me and put a hit out on me…." Citi couldn't even finish her statement. She smacked her mother repeatedly with tears leaking from her eyes, and blood showed on her mother's face.

"Citi, stop! Stop! Please stop!" Ashanti cried out in anguish.

"Fuck you! You know what I had to fuckin' go through when you kicked me out? DO YOU?!!"

Ashanti's eyes flooded with tears, the side her of her face showing blood from the blow.

"Do you, BITCH?!" Citi reiterated.

Ashanti had no words. She had been beaten and caught slipping; now her daughter was the one to boast and show her ass. With her fate in her daughter's hands, the tears fell like a waterfall from her eyes. Citi stared angrily at Ashanti. It was enough with the games. She wanted to see her mother hurt and cry out in so many ways. She looked at Sin and nodded. Sin beamed. As if on cue, the bedroom door opened and seven husky men walked inside, each smiling widely.

Citi looked at her mother and proclaimed, "I'm gonna leave now and let these niggas have some fun wit' you. And I mean, they are goin' to have some rough and dirty fun wit' you, Mother. They gonna take turns and rape you all fuckin' day until they get bored with you and then after that, they'll discard your body away like day-old trash. Fuck you!"

Ashanti was crushed and flooded with grief.

"Citi, don't do this to me…Citi, no!!" Ashanti cried out.

Citi made her way toward the door, and before she could make her exit the bedroom, the men started unzipping their jeans and pulling out their big dicks. Citi closed the door on her screaming mother as a multiple of hands started to tear away her clothing and reach for her goodies.

"Citi…noooo! Get them off me! No…no," she heard her mother frantically scream.

Citi exhaled. The sound of her mother's cries from the harsh rape and beating she was forcefully undergoing was like a symphony to her ears. She smiled and walked away. Revenge was so sweet that she damn near came on herself.

Cartier and Apple came to relieve their friend. This trio of terror had come a long way, and they planned on staying on top for a long time. They had outsmarted their rivals and survived the streets. They became a sisterhood—their pain, their loss of loved ones, and heartache was the foundation and fuel for their growth. Each one was wrestling with her demons and bringing her own vile and malicious ways into their budding cartel. Cartier was now that bitch in Miami—respected and feared, but there was always going to be a void in her life and a constant chill over her shoulders: her own family destroyed, her daughter murdered, and her past a haunting nightmare. But she'd come up roughly, learned a lot, and had history with the streets since her Brooklyn days, and the men under her respected her highly.

Apple was still at a loss. She continued searching for Peaches, and as each day went by, her anger and the violence she created became more extreme. Miami became her home, and her reputation for creating bloodshed and violence caught the attention of everyone, from the rival cartels she helped slaughter to the feds she had been eluding, and the task force—each organization had a bull's-eye on her. Apple was truly feared, and the streets were calling her the new Griselda Blanco—the godmother of Miami—because Apple was just as deadly and ruthless.

Citi got what she dreamed of: enough power, respect, and clout in the city, and finally killing her mother. She searched for Cane, but he was nowhere to be found. She started to fear the worst, knowing that a man like her brother had many enemies and anything could happen to him.

But despite their pasts, their troubles, and their rivals, they fought to keep in control of their new domain. The ladies became a strong team. They were the trio of terror—the South Beach Cartel with their reputation preceding them.

A new year was forthcoming in several days—2014 was approaching. The girls had a lot to celebrate. They'd survived another bumpy year. They'd lasted and had power and wealth at their beck and call. Cartier had a nice New Year's Eve event set up at the Park Place Regency cigar lounge in the downtown area. The ladies were ready to celebrate and enjoy the fruits of their hard labor.

# EPILOGUE

<hr/>

## DECEMBER 31, 2013

The blaring of multiple of fire trucks was heard screaming into the night. They raced toward the Park Place Regency cigar lounge in downtown Miami like a bat running out of hell. The Miami night had been calm on New Year's Eve, but the fire blazing across the Miami skyline was frightening. The smoke billowed out of the building, engulfing everything in its path. The firefighters desperately attempted to contain the flames, but the sprawling heat was just too strong. The upscale venue that only serviced very wealthy businessmen, where a lot of meetings and unions were formed—some legal and some illegal—started to look like rubble and shit. The blaze had spanned two blocks, swallowing up profitable real estate and businesses.

It took several hours for the firefighters to contain and then diminish the fire, slowly snuffing out the flickering, deadly flames. The new year had already begun in tragedy for so many people. It was only a half-hour until 2014, and already, families were homeless and businesses had been wiped out. It would sure be a night that people wouldn't forget. Bodies were scattered everywhere in the soot and ruins. Some bodies were charred beyond recognition.

It took weeks to identify the bodies caught in the fire—and then, several weeks later, the families of Cartier Timmons, Apple Evans, and

Cynthia "Citi" Byrne were all notified that their loved ones were in fact, not missing, but dead.

Fire investigators determined that the cause of the deadly blaze was arson. However, that's where the investigation's progress ended. Despite the massive nature of the crime and the resources that had been dedicated to solving it, authorities had no suspects.

# READING GROUP GUIDE
## SOUTH BEACH CARTEL
## NISA SANTIAGO

*About This Guide*

*The suggested questions are intended to enhance your group's reading of this book by Nisa Santiago.*

1. What do you think drives Apple to such destruction? Were you surprised at how things turned out with the lawyer?

2. Apple has always flipped on her female friends and run with a crew of male goons. Do you think that Apple is capable of co-existing in a cartel with two other headstrong females such as Cartier and Citi?

3. Cartier has been wanting to get out of the game for almost a decade, yet a series of events always seems to pull her back in. Out of the three females—Cartier, Apple, and Citi—who do you feel is most likely to get and stay out of the drug game?

4. Who do you think is really the baddest chick? Are you Team Apple or Team Kola, and why?

5. Growing up in a household full of men, Citi was doted upon and spoiled. Was her being drawn to her mother's husband, Marcus, the result of a spoiled child wanting to get her way? Or did it have everything to do with Citi wanting to hurt the very person who hurt her the most; her mother Ashanti?

6. Cartier had two men who were ready to lay down their lives for her: Head and Hector. Why do you think she ultimately remained loyal to Hector? If you were in Cartier's shoes would you have kept your promise and not left Head back in NY? With all that she's been through, do you think Cartier is capable of love?

7. Do you think growing up in the neighborhoods these women grew up in played a role in the decisions they made?

8. From the long list of characters, who do you identify most with? Who do you sympathize with?

9. The premise of this book is revenge. How important to you is getting back at those who wronged you? Do you believe in an eye for an eye? How often do you take matters into your own hands?

 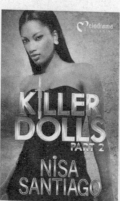 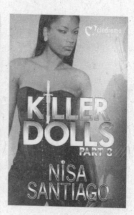

*Follow*

# MELODRAMA
# PUBLISHING

www.twitter.com/Team_Melodrama

www.facebook.com/MelodramaPublishing

# Order online at
bn.com, amazon.com, and
MelodramaPublishing.com

MIAMI, MEET BROOKLYN.

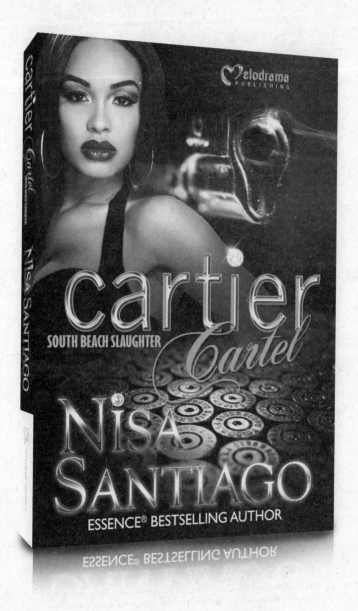

Connect with us online at
MelodramaPublishing.com